SCARRED

Damien Linnane

TENTH STREET PRESS

THIS EDITION

© Copyright 2019 Damien Linnane

Published by Tenth Street Press 2019
Cover design by Tenth Street Press

ISBN-10: 0-6484802-4-0
ISBN-13: 978-0-6484802-4-2

Also available as digital books
ISBN-10: 0-6484802-5-9
ISBN-13: 978-0-6484802-5-9

TENTH STREET PRESS
MELBOURNE SEATTLE LONDON
www.tenthstreetpress.com
Email: contact@tenthstreetpress.com

For every inmate who finds solace in the

prison library

Gefaehrlich das gebrannte kind.

(Translation: The burned child is dangerous.)

Lyric from "Feuer Frei" by Rammstein

Chapter 1

Jason Ennis smiled warmly as he filled the old man's Styrofoam bowl with soup, the rich smell of tomato stock and vegetables filling the air yet again before he replaced the lid on the giant simmering pot. The old man returned a large, mostly toothless grin. He looked very happy to have made it to the soup kitchen in Redfern, just a few kilometres from Sydney's Central Business District, in time to receive a free meal. Most nights the small soup kitchen and its crew of volunteers could not feed all of the hungry people waiting. It relied largely on donations and as often was the case when it came to charity, the demand outweighed the supply. Jason couldn't help everybody, but it gave him a warm feeling to think that some people, and particularly children, wouldn't be going hungry because of his actions. He was making a difference. A small difference, but a difference all the same. Somebody had to do something about the problem, and he was happy to take that responsibility upon himself. It was a frequently satisfying role, though unfortunately it did have its drawbacks. Most of the patrons were well-mannered and appreciative, but the drug-addicts and drunks that were inevitably attracted by free meals could sometimes be loud and unruly, occasionally even violent. Tonight, however, had gone without incident. More importantly, everyone in the line had been fed, and there was even food left over for the volunteers to take home if they wanted. As the old man took one of the empty seats at the kitchen, a feeling of pride and accomplishment came over Jason.

'Good job tonight as usual Jason,' said Margaret Pappas, a short stout woman with grey curly hair framing the radiant glow of her face. Margaret was always in such a good mood Jason wouldn't have been surprised if she was putting a fifth of rum in her coffee each night. Nobody else he knew was constantly in a good mood. Margaret was one of the other two volunteers at the kitchen tonight, and officially the manager, though she never flaunted this sliver of authority. Margaret was one of the few people who volunteered at the kitchen more than Jason did. She was retired, and had much more free time than Jason, who often stressed himself trying to make it there on time after coming from his lectures at the University of Sydney or his job at a warehouse in Marrickville, depending on which day it was. He hated running late all the time.

'Oh, it was nothing.' Jason shuffled awkwardly on his feet and held Margaret's gaze for a split second.

Jason liked working with Margaret. At least as much as he enjoyed working with anybody. He didn't have much in common with her, but Margaret was friendly, and more importantly, she was quiet. She rarely spoke just to fill the silence, or felt the need to gossip about the patrons or other volunteers. He was convinced some people volunteered purely because they couldn't find any other place that would tolerate their garrulous chatter.

'That reminds me, Max called me earlier to say he's going to a funeral this weekend, so I need someone else to cover the Saturday night shift now. Any chance you can do it Jason?' Margaret asked.

'Yeah sure, I mean, of course I can help you out,' he replied. He had actually been looking forward to his first Saturday night off in a long time, but Margaret needed help, and besides, he couldn't bear the thought of her being disappointed with him.

'Thanks, I knew I could count on you.' Margaret smiled and patted Jason on the back as she stepped past him to make herself a tea. Jason beamed. He took a single deep breath and allowed himself a few seconds to bask in what felt like the warmth of the morning sun.

'God, there's so much left over I won't have to buy food for a week!' said Caroline Barnett, the other volunteer working tonight, as she joined Jason and Margaret behind the counter. Caroline was studying at the University of Sydney as well, though she was a first-year arts student and he was final year psychology, meaning they rarely saw each other on campus. Jason also didn't mind working with Caroline. She was bright and bubbly and she talked more than he generally liked a person to, but she was attractive, and like most men, Jason had an enhanced tolerance for attractive women. He wasn't overly fond of her eyebrow piercing, which he thought looked unprofessional, and it annoyed him how she frequently dyed her shoulder length hair. *Just pick a colour and stick with it,* he often thought. For the last two weeks it had been a washy mauve colour, which

Jason thought looked rather gaudy, though it didn't detract from her smile which seemed to light up the otherwise dull evenings at work.

Jason frowned. 'I really don't think you'd get a week's worth,' he said, 'I'd say three days at most, oh, well, you're a bit smaller than me so maybe you could get four … out of …'

Jason's voice trailed off as Caroline started giggling. 'Geez Jason I was being sarcastic,' she said with a kind smile, 'why do you always take everything so literally?'

Jason blushed. It was the kind of question he'd been getting all his life. Through experience he was well aware that he had trouble reading between the lines, as the saying went. He could still remember the embarrassment when he was in year one, and the teacher had told him to 'pull his socks up' after he'd been late back into class from recess. Eager to make up for his tardiness, Jason had promptly reached down to his ankles and complied with the request, which had confusingly earned him a trip to the time-out area for being a smart alec. Trial and error had since taught him the actual meaning of commonly used idioms, though he had never managed to wrap his head around exaggeration or sarcasm. How everyone else seemed to understand it remained a mystery. Embarrassed, he decided to change the subject.

'Oh, right, so, when are you working next anyway?' He already knew the answer. The roster was printed and posted on the staff noticeboard and Jason had looked at it earlier in the week. People often commented on how good his memory was.

'Not till Sunday, but I've got a whole heap of essays to write this week. That should keep me busy.'

'Oh me too,' said Jason, reminded of his own unfinished essay at home. The deadline for submission was midnight tonight. He had hoped to finish it before he left for work that morning but he hadn't had enough time. If he hurried home after his shift he should be able to complete it. He was good at writing and it was nearly done.

'I'm really struggling with the one I'm working on at the moment, fundamentals of literature, uhh, give me a break,' she chuckled.

'I'm sure you'll do well. That last essay you wrote was great,' said Jason. His attempted compliment seemed to have gone well. Caroline blushed slightly and smiled. He had offered to proofread an essay of hers a couple weeks ago. It was decent, but more than anything he had hoped to make Caroline feel better.

'Thanks, and thanks again for helping me with it.' Jason could tell by the way she smiled with her eyes that she genuinely meant it. He usually struggled with recognising facial expressions, but a first-year psychology lecture he attended which had covered recognising genuine smiles, the 'Duchenne smile' as it was termed, had proved very informative.

'Anytime,' he replied.

Jason helped clean and tidy the kitchen as the last diners finished their meals. He was particularly thorough when it came to cleaning and organising things. Margaret observed that as usual he was putting in more effort than necessary. She considered him to be a quiet achiever, albeit an awkward and odd one. Even though he was busy cleaning, Jason took the time to wave, smile and nod at each person as they left.

'Did'ja get that jacket from Mad Max or somethin'?' asked the last patron as he walked past, a middle-aged man with a friendly smile.

Jason looked down at his jacket as if he'd never seen it before. People more frequently asked him if he rode a motorcycle when they asked about it, an assumption that wasn't helped by army style pants that were always tucked into combat boots. The jacket though, with reinforced padding seemingly placed everywhere it would fit and its unusual style had struck him as having a post-apocalyptic vibe when he found it online. He didn't mind the comment, but before he could think of a good reply the man was already out the door.

'Thanks for the help again,' said Margaret as Jason put the cleaning cloth and spray back under the counter.

Jason smiled, considering that to be a reply in itself to her thanks. 'See you Saturday Margaret, and I'll see you Sunday Caroline.'

Caroline looked up from her phone. 'Geez you're always here, I don't know how you fit it all in. I struggle with just one or two shifts here and uni.'

Jason shrugged. The truth was he constantly stressed himself keeping all the commitments he made, but he couldn't help himself. He was driven by a constant need to be productive. He attributed it, along with his teetotalism, to his alcoholic mother, who to the best of his knowledge hadn't accomplished a damn thing since giving birth to him. *We all rebel against our parents,* he thought. For him rebelling had meant getting a job, staying off drugs and going to university. After an awkward silence Jason smiled again, waved goodbye to Margaret and Caroline and went out the door. He put on his wrap-around sunglasses with the protective clear lenses and began walking home.

His apartment in Newtown was only a thirty-odd minute walk, and late at night was the best time to go walking, despite where he was. While the council had made an effort to improve Redfern's reputation as Sydney's ghetto in recent years, the process was far from perfect. The few people who knew about his volunteering were surprised to learn that Jason walked home alone at night through the area. He shrugged off their concern, knowing from experience that while the neighbourhood's reputation wasn't completely undeserved, it was grossly exaggerated.

Jason passed the familiar murals encompassing the entire sides of buildings. One, of a young

Indigenous girl staring out into the street with a sad expression, had always touched him. The one next to it changed every couple of months. Last week it had been a woman sleeping on a pile of bones, which he had quite liked. Now it was an odd series of technicolour swirls, which he did not think was an improvement on any level. He often wished his own art would reach as many people as these, though he was far too shy to even show it to anyone. Turning off the main road into a side street, the art became somewhat less professional. Undecipherable graffiti tags covered walls, doors, and even the footpath in some places. The vandalism was broken up every now and then by the tell-tale uneven dark grey squares of a paint roller. The cover up effort only highlighted how many decades old the original paintwork all around it was.

Jason noticed a syringe on the ground. He took a cursory look around, made sure nobody was watching him, before he carefully picked it up. He smashed the needle into a brick wall, snapping it clean off, before he placed it in the next garbage bin he walked past. It belonged in a proper sharps bin, of course, but now the needle part was broken Jason thought it was safe enough to dispose of in this way. Better than leaving it on the street where some child could step on it. Somebody had to do something about the problem, and he was happy to take that responsibility upon himself. As much as Jason liked making the neighbourhood safer, he liked keeping a low profile even more, and seldom did anything that he thought would draw the attention of strangers. Had anyone been watching, he would have left the syringe where it was.

He was in a particularly good mood tonight. His shift at the kitchen had gone without incident or stress, and more importantly, everyone had approved of him. He didn't notice his pace slow as he enjoyed his walk, all concerns about his essay falling from his thoughts. He was usually in such a hurry but tonight for a change, he felt relaxed. He looked up at the moon and smiled. The lights of the city made few stars visible, but the three-quarter moon seemed to be glowing particularly bright.

'Oi! Gimme all ya fuckin' money!' Snapped out of his fixation on the sky, Jason stopped and turned in the direction of the aggressive, slurred male voice. A skinny man wearing a tracksuit in dire need of washing and an old pair of sneakers was approaching him from a nearby alleyway. He had a small kitchen knife in his hand which was pointed in line with Jason's face. Jason stared expressionlessly at the man, considering him. How old was he? Mid-forties? It was hard to tell. The man had the worn-out look that only years of substance abuse could generate. The sunken look in his eyes reminded Jason of his father. His scruffy light brown hair looked like it hadn't been washed in weeks. His nose was running and the man seemed to be a little drunk, swaying as if he was a reed and there was a breeze.

From his experiences at the soup kitchen, and at most of his other jobs which somehow always seemed to attract the dregs of society, Jason concluded that the man couldn't be reasoned with. The man was a danger to society. That much was evident. Somebody had to do something about the problem, and he was happy to take that responsibility upon himself.

'Didn'ya hear me cunt? I said gimme ya fuckin' money!' The man was getting agitated. He'd done this many times before but a stoic and expressionless target wasn't the typical response.

'I'm gonna to count to–' The man stopped mid-sentence as Jason pulled out a pistol from behind him and aimed it at his forehead. Jason saw the man's eyes widen, and estimated he had about two-thirds of a second to realise he'd picked the wrong victim.

Jason's face remained expressionless as his finger squeezed around the trigger. The silencer removing all but the faintest noise. A small red circle appeared in the middle of the man's forehead and a spray of red mist and pinkish chunks blew rearward from the back of his skull. He fell to his knees and crumpled to his right side. The kitchen knife dropped from his hand to the street.

Jason squatted down and tilted his head to his left side, examining the fresh corpse. He liked how you couldn't predict exactly how a body would fall or how the blood would spray from an exit wound, or even where the exit wound would be in relation to the entry wound, if there was one at all. Bullets often ricocheted around tissue and bone and left the body somewhere unexpected. Tonight, while the bullet had entered the skull dead centre it had exited distinctly to the right at the back. Jason thought the entry wound looked comically small in comparison to the gaping hole at the back of the skull, which he could have easily stuck his fist in.

Jason felt like he'd made a difference, albeit a small one. One less criminal in the world. He had stepped on one cockroach in a city with thousands, but it was a difference all the same. He frowned at the kitchen knife. It was a poor choice of weapon; a cheap thing that only would have cost a few dollars. He picked it up with his left hand then stood, looking around to make sure there were no witnesses. He wasn't sure what he would have done if there had of been an innocent witness, and was relieved to find the street deserted. He holstered his pistol and recommenced walking home. He threw the small knife down a drain a couple blocks away. He had no use for it, and knives shouldn't be left lying in the street where children could find them. Jason looked back up at the moon as he walked. Was it just his imagination, or did it seem brighter now than it had before? He suddenly remembered about his essay due tonight and cursed himself. He had dawdled on his way home and now this unexpected incident had delayed him even more. He picked up the pace, worried now that he wouldn't be able to submit his essay before the deadline. He hated running late all the time.

Chapter 2

A few seconds after she regained consciousness, Kelly Steiner wished she hadn't. The first time she had woken up with him on top of her it had taken half a minute for her to fully understand her situation. This time it had only taken a brief moment. He ran his tongue up her cheek as he pulsed forward again, his foul-smelling breath rolling all over her face. Kelly turned her head to one side in a fruitless attempt to get away from him. Her vision half obscured by her long black hair, she could still see the bruising around her right wrist. It had spread a couple inches up her forearm since yesterday and the cut from the cable tie securing her to the black iron of the bed frame looked infected. The only other thing she could stare at on this side of the room was the mould which seemed to be on a slow journey from the ground to the ceiling, currently about one third of the way up the bleak concrete wall. The view on the other side, only slightly more scenic, consisted of several cardboard boxes and some dusty wooden furniture. Kelly didn't see any point in looking at her other wrist, it felt as bad as her right looked. Her ankles didn't feel quite as bad. For some reason he had tied them with rope instead. Unlike her wrists, which ached constantly, her ankle restraints only hurt when she struggled, and she'd stopped doing that some time ago.

How long had she been here? There was no way to tell. The single globe hanging from the ceiling of the basement was always on, making it impossible to tell day from night. She was drifting in and out of consciousness as the dehydration took its toll on her small frame. Had it been two or three days? It felt like a lifetime. The last thing she remembered before waking up was walking back to her student accommodation block alone. It was 2 AM and the bar on King St, the main road of Newtown, was closing. Her girlfriend Sally was supposed to be giving her a ride home, even though she was almost certainly over the legal blood alcohol limit to drive – not that it had ever stopped her before – but she had disappeared. Kelly declined the advances of the two young men who, unsuccessful in their efforts to pick up inside the club, were now making a desperate last attempt to woo the drunken female patrons who were leaving. She wasn't anywhere near drunk enough to even consider them. Her buzz had almost completely worn off from the frustration of searching for Sally, who was the only reason she had come out in the first place. Not having the money for her own taxi in this week's budget, she would have to walk home. It was only a few blocks away, and she thought the walk would probably wear off the last of the alcohol anyway. Still, she wasn't going to let Sally hear the end of this tomorrow. As she began her walk she tried calling her missing friend one last time. A few kilometres away a chirpy ringtone calling out from a jeans pocket on the floor remained unheard by either Sally or the guy she had taken home forty minutes ago.

Sally had woken up with a severe hangover and regret for her choice in men. Kelly had woken up with something far worse. Folding her arms against the light chill, she was about half way home when she really started wishing she had of brought a jacket with her. The black miniskirt and pink tank top had been a good choice for the dance floor, but they weren't doing much to protect her from the elements. She had just slipped off her high heels, so as not to torture her aching feet for the rest of the walk, when she heard something behind her. Kelly remembered wanting to look to see what it was, but she couldn't recall if she had. Everything had turned grey before she knew what was happening. From the ache she felt at the back her skull when she woke up, Kelly assumed she had been hit from behind. Her first thought was why her head hurt so much, her next was trying to figure out what was on top of her. Once she had realised, she let out a scream that was cut short by a fist to her jaw. When he was done with her he taped her mouth shut, and it had been like that ever since. Sometimes, strangely, that felt like the worst part. Not even being able to scream, robbed of the last visceral freedom of a trapped creature. When you couldn't even cry out for help, what possible hope did you have left?

How many times had he come down to use her body since then? Four or five maybe. He came and did what he wanted, whether she was awake or not. Any attempt to struggle only resulted in beatings. The last time she hadn't resisted at all. She had no way of guessing that her lack of resistance would quicken the inevitable. She wondered how long she could survive this. He hadn't given her anything to eat or drink. How long could the human body survive without water? A faint recollection of one of her nursing degree lectures earlier this year told her it was three or four days, but she wasn't sure if that was right. She wasn't sure of anything anymore. Her thoughts were clouded, painful, everything was painful when she drifted out of the dreams in her sleep and into the nightmare of her reality. *Why can't I just pass out again?* He hadn't untied her at all, giving her no choice but to urinate on the mattress. It surprised her that he didn't seem to notice.

He finished only a couple minutes after he started. She was glad it never took him long. He would go away now. After the first time he had spent what seemed like an age just staring at her. Kelly found it disturbing that he never spoke, but perhaps that was best. She could only imagine what a sick man like this would have to say. But the next time after he finished he had left straight away, and each time after that.

Now he was staring at her again. Still on top of her. A bead of sweat dripped off the end of his nose and landed above her eye, repulsing her even more than when he came inside her. She met his gaze. He was an ugly man. Sunken eyes, broken nose. Brown hair, unkempt, receding at the front and flaked with dandruff. He stank, even over the smell of her urine. As she looked into his eyes, she tried to guess what he could possibly be feeling.

* * *

Boredom. Howard Silverman was feeling bored.

Seeing her walking as he drove home from his regular Friday night curb crawling at Kings Cross, he had felt exhilarated, deciding without much thought to play out a fantasy he had been thinking about as long as he could remember. He'd already had some fun tonight, but it had cost him $60. Fifty for the sex, and the whore had actually charged him another $10 for open-mouth kissing. Still, some of the whores wouldn't do that at all, and it was the best part, certainly more fun than the paltry squirt that brought an end to it all. The intimacy, feeling like they actually wanted him, even if he knew deep down that it was bullshit. This fun, however, wasn't going to cost him a damn thing. Parking ahead of her and waiting in the trees, he had hit her with his tyre iron. Then it had been a matter of dragging her into his van, and then from his van to his basement. He could hardly believe it. He had gotten away with it. It had been so easy, he wished he had done something like it years ago. The thrill of tying her up in his basement had given him an erection, and he had taken her for the first time there and then. Her shock, the smell of her fear as she had woken up and realised what was happening to her had only served to excite him further. Seeing how afraid she was just as he walked down the stairs the next three times had made him hard before he even forced himself on her. As it turned out, real fear was even better than faked intimacy. However, the next time, the last time before now, she hadn't looked afraid at all. She still looked like she was in pain, which was something at least, but she hadn't even fought back. It was as if she had accepted that this was her new life. She was beyond fear. This was the way things were now. And this time it had been even worse. She hadn't even looked at him until he was done.

Hoping to reignite the thrill, he waited until she was unconscious again this time, creeping down the stairs as quietly as possible. Nothing. No reaction at all. It reminded him of the toy pinball machine he had been given on his seventh birthday by his grandmother. Only a few days after he had gotten it, the spring mechanism that launched the pinball had broken. His shiny toy looked so fresh and new, but it just didn't work anymore, and no amount of crying or yelling would make it better. He couldn't even ask his grandmother for a new one. She'd died not long after, leaving just Howard and his father.

Howard looked at Kelly. This wasn't much fun anymore. The sex was worse than with the cheapest, drugged up hookers he paid for. He wanted her to look alive again. To feel alive. But he didn't know how. Desperate and petulant, he tried punching her in the face for good measure, but all he got in response was a whimper. She wasn't even crying. Howard frowned. What could he do now? He wrapped his hands around her throat and her eyes widened. For a moment it just looked like confusion then her look changed to sheer terror. *Here we go.* She sure looked alive now. Her struggle to hold onto her life was so pathetic it was beautiful. He squeezed even harder. Now she was really panicking. Faint croaks escaped her mouth as her body convulsed. He was straddling her abdomen with the full weight of his 95kg frame, but she fought so fiercely she almost threw him off her. Twice.

The affair was as short as it was brilliant. Just when Howard thought her spasms couldn't get any stronger she gave one final push against his body and collapsed. Howard kept the pressure on the neck of his now limp victim. As exciting as this had been he knew he would never get the same response from her again. This one was all used up. He needed another.

Howard looked down at his naked body atop hers. The thrill of watching the life drain out of her had given him another erection. He figured the sex would be even blander now, but he may as well make use of her body one last time before he marked her to let the world know that she had been his. He had planned that from the beginning, it went without saying, but he still didn't know how. As he pulsed back and forth on top of her, he wondered how he would do it. And where he would leave the body.

Chapter 3

Jason entered his apartment complex, his boots crunching on a collection of dead leaves and old newspapers in the downstairs foyer. Once upon a time he'd made an effort to keep the area clean himself, even though it was the responsibility of the landlord, but he'd given up bothering years ago. He climbed the two flights of grimy stairs to his top floor apartment. The building wasn't much to speak of, but because of its proximity to the city it still cost him almost half of what he earned a week at the warehouse. Not that it bothered him. Apart from food and textbooks the only thing he spent money on was the contents of his footlocker, and that collection was mostly complete. Reaching his door he slid in his key. Apartment number six of six. He was polite to his neighbours, smiling and saying hello to them on the stairs, but he never bothered to get to know the frequently rotating group of people in the block. He had moved there eight years ago and now was the longest standing tenant. The Spartan accommodation held an interesting rotation of university students, misfits, backpackers and the recently single, all of whom usually moved on to bigger and better places, but Jason was perfectly content with his living arrangements. The lock latched as the front door closed behind him, and he took the time to fasten the additional two locks he had installed on it himself. The apartment was tiny, a combined living and kitchen area with an adjoining room featuring a shower and toilet. Nevertheless, it looked deceivingly large as it was almost empty. It had come unfurnished, and the only things Jason had bought for it were a cheap desk and chair from the nearest opportunity shop, a frypan, kettle, and just enough cutlery and utensils for one person. He had realised years ago that if he only bought enough food to eat for a day at a time it eliminated the need to own a fridge. Every day was the same routine. Cooking eggs for breakfast, making peanut-butter sandwiches for lunch, and purchasing exactly enough ingredients on his way home to cook a simple dinner.

Spinning the dials on the combination lock, Jason unlocked the large military style footlocker that contained all his worldly possessions except his clothes, which were in the duffel bag next to the locker. His single blow-up mattress and sleeping bag lay next to the duffel bag. Years of having to move from one foster home to the next had left him with the need to be able to pack up his things and be ready to move as quickly as possible, but even he thought it wasn't worth the extra effort to pack up the mattress and sleeping bag every morning. Still, a few times a year he would deflate the mattress and roll up the sleeping bag just to make sure he'd left enough room in his locker to fit them in with all his other stuff. On the one occasion he hadn't, he'd immediately gone into panic mode, first spending a couple hours playing Tetris with his belongings as he tried to find a more efficient way to fit them all in together. After realising it was a lost cause he had laid his possessions out and spent the remainder of the night deciding which one he needed the least before listing it on eBay. He didn't worry about trying to fit the household items like the kettle in the locker. If he ever moved again, he intended to leave all the stuff he had bought for the apartment here. It would help out the next tenant and free him of the burden of taking them at the same time.

He opened the lid of the locker and a thin smile

came across his face as he admired his belongings. Surveying its contents, he saw his small collection of tools at one end. Jason took pride in his ability to repair almost anything himself. You couldn't really rely on anyone except yourself; he had learnt that a long time ago. Next to his tools were his assorted weapons and armour, with several noticeable gaps for what he was currently carrying. Finally, there were a series of small boxes at the other end containing disparate collections of items. One held his boot cleaning kit. One all his various electronic gadgets. There was an outdoor survival kit, not that he had ever really been 'outdoors', and a first aid kit. Underneath those were all his sketchbooks. There were six now, five of them completely filled. Jason thought it was important to have a hobby.

Tonight he removed the box containing his pistol cleaning equipment and placed it aside, knowing he would be using it later. He took off his bulky jacket and placed it over the back of his chair. Feelings of vulnerability began to creep up the second it was off, and Jason instinctively checked to make sure his door was locked again before he allowed himself to relax and unzip the front of his military style black vest. He liked the look of the thin vest, but its only purpose was to conceal his armour when it was too hot to wear his jacket, or if he had to remove the jacket for some reason. Jason wore it even when it was uncomfortable to do so, lamenting when he simply had to remove it during the heat of summer. Winter was his favourite season, as he never had to remove his jacket and lose the added protection its slash resistant Kevlar lining gave him.

He had spent a lot of time trying to find the best protection. He had started with motorcycle and sports armour, before finding there was an entire industry of tactical and security clothing. He eventually settled on what others now pejoratively called his 'uniform'. He tried out four different sets of combat boots before he found the ones he thought were best. The military pants came with built in kneepads and pockets to conceal all kinds of gear. He had three pairs of them. He complimented the khaki pants with the black jacket. He would have preferred to have worn all black, but he found that drew too many stares. He didn't mind looking odd, but he didn't want to look so strange that people stopped, stared, and pointed him out to their friends. It was important to find the right balance between protection and keeping a low profile.

Jason removed the fabric vest, revealing the bullet-resistant one underneath. He had wanted one since he was a child and recalled how happy he had been when it had come in the mail from America. He took it off and placed it back in his locker. He then removed his brown undershirt, which as always had a deep patch of sweat at the back and front. Body armour didn't exactly breathe well, but over the years, Jason had learned to live with the excessive sweating the vest caused. The comfort the vest provided far outweighed the sticky, sweaty feeling that was one of its few drawbacks. He folded the undershirt and placed it in his dirty clothes pile in the corner, making a mental note that there were now enough clothes to warrant a trip to the laundromat. Unfastening his tactical belt, he pulled it through the loops of his pants with one hand as he placed the other against the pistol holster which the belt supported. He put the pistol and holster on top of the cleaning kit, taking some extra time to admire its sleek design. It had been a lucky find. Jason had known his father was a criminal long before the police had come and finally taken him away. He had still been surprised to find the gun amongst his father's possessions following his fatal drug overdose. Almost as surprised as the discovery his father still listed him as his next of kin, even though they hadn't seen each other for over a decade. Jason associated his father with the most heinous forms of cruelty and petty crime, but a pistol just didn't seem to fit in with the kind of criminal he was. He wouldn't have been surprised at all if he had of learnt his father had simply been told to hold on to it by one of his criminal associates who had had his bail revoked. Jason hadn't even known his father had been released from prison. They'd denied him parole due to his frequent drug abuse and violence inside, and he'd served the entire ten-year sentence he'd gotten for possession, distribution, conspiracy to import a commercial quantity of a prohibited substance and a dozen odd other charges that typically went hand-in-hand with those. Two months out, he was already breaking the law again by taking drugs. Jason had been disappointed to learn about his father's death, but not surprised. He had spent whole nights thinking about tying down his father, soaking him in petrol and giving him some scars of his own. But he supposed his father had done him a favour by effectively assassinating himself. Jason wouldn't have to waste the energy now. At least that's what he tried to tell himself. He couldn't help but think it was one of those things you had to do yourself, but there was nothing he could do about it now.

The pistol had been in a small wooden container when he found it, along with a box of fifty rounds and the unattached silencer. Late one night at the local park he tested the pistol once with and without the silencer. The lack of noise with it fitted had seemed comical juxtaposed with its original thundering report, and the decision was made to keep it attached. Jason didn't know what he was going to do when the bullets ran out though. Now that his father was dead he didn't know any criminals. Still, that problem was a while away. Including the two fired at the park, Jason had only used ten bullets in over five years.

The pistol soon became part of Jason's everyday carry, along with his armour, knife, mini med-kit, phone, notebook and pen. Tucking it into his belt was uncomfortable, and left him with a nagging worry that it may come loose and fall out. He decided to keep it in a small, inconspicuous carry satchel by his side in summer, and bought a holster that allowed him to draw the weapon smoothly when it was concealed under his jacket. The night he spotted the drug dealer sitting at one of the tables in the soup kitchen three years later was the first time he drew it in anger. Jason had never even thought about buying drugs, lowering himself to the level of his father and the scum he had associated with. But he didn't need experience in buying them to realise what was going on from the quick exchanges of cash for small bags under the table. The dealer was only making a perfunctory effort to conceal what he was doing and Jason had a clear view. Jason wondered if that was more a reflection of the dealer's lack of intelligence or of just how much this neighbourhood had deteriorated – it was like nobody cared anymore. But Jason cared. Somebody had to protect society from this poison. Jason knew all too well what it felt like to not be protected, the scars on his torso were a constant reminder.

Jason watched the dealer leave the soup

kitchen as it closed. He was about the same age as he was at the time – early-twenties – and judging from how pale his skin looked, his jet-black hair colour had to have been dyed rather than natural. The man walked across the road, then leant against the wall a couple shops down, pulled out his phone and appeared to take a keen interest it. Jason hoped he would still be there when he finished work and rushed to get the place cleaned.

'What's the big hurry?' Margaret had asked.

Jason froze. 'Uh, just keen to get home, I'm competing in a video game tournament tonight,' he lied before flashing the best smile he could manage.

Margaret smiled and shook her head.

Five minutes later he waved goodbye to Margaret and the other volunteer, and started off in the direction he always took leaving the soup kitchen. He crouched behind a parked van and waited, anxious that the man might leave any second now, but conscious of the fact his shooting would attract the police. Jason needed the murder to occur after he was seen leaving the area. Fifteen minutes later, he crossed the road and headed back in the direction of the man, his hands in his jacket pockets to hide the latex gloves he had taken out of his mini med-kit. Why was the man still there? His low-life customers had long since left. Probably just waiting for a lift, Jason told himself, as he undid the strap on his holster and wrapped his hand around the pistol. His heart was beating fast. He'd never shot someone before.

The dealer flashed Jason a curious glance as he heard him approach. Recognising him from the kitchen, but not considering him to be a potential customer, he went back to looking at his phone. As Jason passed the man, a metre and a half to his left, he stopped in front of him, pivoted, and pulled out the gun. Taking little time to aim, he pointed the gun at the man's centre mass and fired. The shooting was sloppy, but it didn't matter, it was impossible to miss at this distance. The bullet caught the man in the stomach. He gave a sharp cry, dropping his phone as his hands rushed to his wound. The man was doubling forward when the pistol fired a second time, catching him in the right shoulder. Jason observed how, unlike the last bullet, this one ripped right through the flesh, painting a vivid spray of red on the brick wall behind him.

'Jesus! The fuck?'

His left hand against his right shoulder, his right hand against his stomach, and neither staving off the flow of blood, the man fell backwards against the brick wall and slumped to the ground. He looked up at Jason, a mixture of pain, confusion and hate filled his eyes. Jason's only response was to aim the pistol at the man's head.

'Why? Wait! I have money!'

Yes. I bet you have plenty of money you filthy fucking predator.

Jason pulled the trigger and the third bullet, muffled again by the silencer, hit the man below his right eye. Oddly it seemed to come out his jaw on the same side. Jason had been puzzled enough to search the internet later about how bullets ricochet off bone and tissue. The man slumped onto his back, all comprehension and life had gone from his open eyes. Jason didn't like the gargling sound that was coming from the man's mouth, nor the muscle twitches in his head and neck. The shot to the head should have rendered the man completely lifeless. Without thinking too much about it, he fired a fourth round directly into the man's chest. A fresh red patch blossomed, though the gurgling sound and twitching remained, seemingly indifferent to the new wound. Satisfied the man would die, Jason holstered his pistol and searched him. He fished an uneven pile of bills out of the man's jacket pocket. Another pocket contained a couple dozen of the small zip lock bags. Each contained a cloudy amorphous crystal substance, about the size of a fingernail. Not knowing exactly what it was, but repulsed by it all the same, Jason's first thought was to throw it down the drain. To purge it from his neighbourhood. He clenched a fist around several of them before he reconsidered. *No. I want everyone to know why this man was killed.* The evidence would speak for itself. Drug dealer punished. Jason smiled. He pocketed the money and hurried home. When the police approached him and the other volunteers and patrons at the soup kitchen the following night, Jason said he had walked home as soon as it had closed. His statement was confirmed by Margaret then and there. The officer seemed to believe him. It was the first time Jason had spoken to an officer since they had taken him from his mother. He had been disappointed when the newspapers hadn't realised the dealer was being punished. They called it a gangland slaying, but at least they'd understood he was a drug dealer. Even though Jason thought he was in the clear, he supposed it was best not to tempt fate. He decided against looking for trouble again in the immediate area for at least a month. The surge of power following the shooting led him into a fruitless search to find another dealer. Jason wondered how people went about buying narcotics. It soon became clear to him that it wasn't by hanging around on the sidewalk or in shady back alleys.

Eight months later Jason was only a few minutes into his hour long walk home from his then night job at the bar in the CBD. He heard the commotion before he saw it. It sounded like every argument he remembered his parents having when he was scarcely more than a toddler. He turned and looked at the couple just in time to see the man shove his female companion into an alleyway. Jason stopped. Watched. As the man's shoves grew more and more forceful Jason felt the blood rush to his wrists. He puffed forward his chest without realising it. The man had short dark cropped hair. He was wearing a polo shirt and jeans. He looked nothing like Jason's father, yet in a sudden flash all Jason could see was his father beating his mother. Remembering the way it had made him feel. So helpless. Too small to do anything about it.

That was a long time ago.

He stormed towards the man and reached for his pistol when the man jabbed the woman in the stomach. She fell to her knees, the wind knocked out of her. Seeing Jason approach out of the corner of his eye, the man turned to face him head on just as Jason raised his gun, inadvertently making himself a perfect front-on target. The man had a brief second to notice the weapon, but Jason saw no change of expression in his rage filled eyes. The two rounds fired off in quick succession took the man in the upper chest and he fell backwards. Jason cautiously approached with the pistol still pointing at him. He was stone dead. Satisfied the problem was solved permanently, he holstered his weapon and approached the woman.

'He can't hurt us anymore,' he said. To Jason's confusion, the woman looked horrified, more afraid of him than she had been of her abusive partner. As he approached her she slid her body backwards away from him, still on the ground, still winded. Jason paused, unsure of what to do. He had put his gun away, so he didn't understand the woman's fear. He had made it very clear that he wasn't going to shoot her. He tried smiling and recommenced his approach. She kicked out one of her fishnet coated legs at him, the base of her high heel struck him on the bone just above his combat boot. Jason cried out in pain and gave the woman a look which conveyed he was more emotionally than physically hurt from her attack. He looked at the woman's odd clothes. She clearly didn't mind looking different either. The high heels were clear, the miniskirt vinyl, the waistcoat with its top two buttons undone revealed almost all of her breasts. Jason, however, looked at her without lust. He had saved her from her abusive partner, now he just wanted to comfort her. The woman tried to speak as her breath returned.

'My John! What the fuck do you think you're doing you fucking psycho?'

'Uh, I was just …'

'Get the fuck away from me!' the woman cut him off, then repeated the command more forcefully.

Confused, Jason backed up two steps. When

she screamed at him again he turned and ran. He didn't understand and it was only a matter of time before her screams drew attention.

Jason scoured the news websites over the next week, afraid there would be a description or police sketch of him in connection with the shooting. But the woman hadn't come forward. Jason assumed she must have come to her senses and realised he had saved her. She had clearly been confused that night. She had called the man John, when the papers said his name was Gary. Jason was bitterly upset to read the newspaper describing Gary as an upstanding citizen. If only they'd known what he was really like. Jason wished he had some way of clearing up the confusion. He also wished he had some way of contacting the woman now that she had realised he was a good guy. He never would have imagined she was too busy trying to erase what she had seen working that night with a syringe to know what day it was, let alone contact the police.

The ninth time Jason fired the pistol was the only time during the day. It was over a year later, and he had been enjoying his lunch break in The Domain, sitting on the ground at the base of a

Moreton bay fig tree, snuggly nestled between two of its gargantuan roots. The Domain was his favourite park in the city, but that day it only offered limited relief at the halfway point of a painful shift at his then job at a café. Someone had called in sick and the orders were coming out slow. Jason, being the front of house was on the receiving end of all the complaints as if it was his fault. He only had twenty minutes to enjoy the silence before he had to return to the nightmare.

As he considered this, Jason noticed a rotund middle-aged man in office attire chuck his empty chip packet at the base of a tree. Taken back, Jason searched his memory. It occurred to him that he'd never seen someone deliberately litter before. He couldn't understand the sheer laziness. There were plenty of bins in the park. There were no bins at the train station, or on the trains Jason caught to work. More than once Jason had left some rubbish as neat as he could on his train seat. He figured if the government wanted litter disposed of properly they would provide bins. But this was completely different. He watched the man finish his can of soft drink and throw it under a park bench. Jason was furious. The Domain was one of the few tranquil places in the bustling city. Why would somebody do such a thing? Jason was about to close his eyes in resigned frustration and anger when he saw the skinny young woman decked out in active wear running up from the opposite direction. As she neared the man he casually stuck out his hand, reaching towards her chest. The woman jerked out of the way instinctively, the tips of the man's fingers just catching the side of her body.

'You fucking creep!' The woman's dark brown ponytail swished violently as she turned to yell, never slowing her run. The man turned his head and only gave her a lecherous smile in return as he continued his walk.

The audacity. As if the littering hadn't been enough. Jason had been hidden from the man's view, and there was no-one else in sight. But still, if that was what the man did in broad daylight, Jason could only imagine what he was really capable of. That couldn't have been the first time he'd tried to pull something like that. Jason got up and followed him. He slowly closed the distance between them as he rounded the corner at the edge of the park. The sandstone walls of the State Library on his left, a busy street on his right. A block later the gap was almost closed when the man turned into an underground car park. Jason looked for security cameras, and other people. Satisfied to find neither, he reached into his satchel bag, pushing his water bottle out of the way with his knuckles as he took hold of the pistol. He shot the man in the back of the head. The man never saw, or heard, a thing. Jason accepted the berating he got from his manager for being several minutes late back to work.

* * *

Jason sat down at his desk in front of its sole occupant, his laptop. Having always considered TV to be the opiate of the masses, the laptop was the only way he interacted with the world at home, reading the news or playing the occasional video game, but mostly he used it for university work. As he prepared to finish his essay he reflected on everybody he had killed. Over the years a handful had gotten away, of course, usually as there were too many potential witnesses for him to make a move. But he was proud of the ones he had managed to kill. Adding tonight's kill to his tally, there were five now. The mugger, the sex offender, the wife-beater, the drug-dealer. And of course, Peter. Jason hadn't needed a gun to kill Peter.

Chapter 4

Jason leaned back in his chair and breathed a sigh of relief. He had proofread his essay and, content he couldn't improve it further, submitted it with nearly half an hour to spare. It was always a relief to get another assessment completed. One step closer to finishing the degree, but he wasn't any closer to knowing what he really wanted to do with his life. Since scraping through high-school there'd been a series of failed and dead-end jobs. Supermarket shelving, where he had assumed the job wouldn't involve him having to talk to anyone, but every few minutes people came and asked him if he knew where any imaginable item was located in the store. His shifts had gradually been cut back to only one a week without explanation, forcing him to find a better job. He'd been let go from his stint as an electronics salesman for below average sales. Fired from his job as a barista for arguing with a customer. A woman had gotten aggressive with him because the store had run out of soy milk. Jason hadn't been in charge of ordering stock, so it wasn't his fault, and he couldn't let her get away with treating him like it was. His next job as a bartender only served to remind him how much he hated people who drank. It was the only job he had ever walked out of. He had refused service to a drunken man who had responded by threatening to 'bash his head in'. Jason considered the only two appropriate responses to such a threat, destroying the source permanently to protect himself and everyone else or walking away. The high number of witnesses removed the option of the former, though in retrospect he supposed it was the excuse to quit that he had been looking for. A brief and extremely painful stint as a street fundraiser had convinced him that he needed a job that didn't involve interacting with the general public. His last job before his current one, working for a small afterhours cleaning company, had gone surprisingly well for several months. Jason stayed up late at night anyway and there was no-one to bother him while he worked. Then the company had changed hands and the new owners had brought in their own staff. Jason hadn't been fired, but as he and all the other workers were casuals they simply hadn't been given any more shifts. Jason had never had a permanent job before, though not for a lack of applying for them. Once a manager had actually emailed him some feedback following a failed job interview, telling him that while his resume was all well and good, he should work on his interpersonal skills to make a better impression at interviews in the future. While he'd appreciated the feedback, Jason had found the concept confusing. The job was for a position painting houses, something he'd specifically applied for because he thought it wouldn't need social skills. Why did he need to impress someone during an interview with a skill that the job he was applying for didn't actually require? He filed the information away onto his always expanding list of things that just didn't make any sense.

After several years of disappointing jobs, and limited satisfaction from volunteering at everything from charity shops to the community garden, Jason had decided to go to university for no other reason than he had nothing better to do. He had hoped it might also give him some direction in his life. It hadn't. Jason had thought nursing would be a practical choice of career. He was interested in wounds and anatomy, and he thought the medical training would be an excellent survival skill. Studying to be a doctor or a paramedic would have been more desirable, but he hadn't scored well enough on the entrance exam to study medicine, and the closest university that offered paramedical science at the time was in Bathurst. Simply starting at university itself was a big enough change as far as he was concerned. He didn't think he would handle relocating to a country town at the same time. Jason quickly discovered he had neither the patience nor the social skills to be a nurse. He was on his first practical placement, only a couple months into the degree. He had been excited about it, expecting to see stab wounds, amputated limbs, even a severe beating would have been sufficient. Jason wasn't at all squeamish. He imagined he would be very calm and practical dealing with a traumatic event that others would have struggled with. What he had gotten in the medical ward at the local hospital, however, was a sea of needy elderly people. Cancer, broken hips, heart problems, skin conditions. Some weren't that sick, they were just craving attention. Others were just waiting to die. He had realised he'd made the wrong choice in degree by the time he was first told to clean up a urine spill.

Once the practical placement had finished Jason had immediately transferred to biomedical science. He liked the idea of working in a lab. It was a respectable career, and in a lab he would be away from the general public. For a year he went ok. The second year, however, was difficult. Many nights were spent staring at his organic chemistry textbook, wondering how anyone was able to excel at this subject. His grades dropped significantly, barely managing a pass. Certain he wouldn't be able to pass the second half of the year, let alone the third year, he realised he had the choice of either dropping out or changing degrees again. The thought of being typecast as a university dropout did not sit well with him.

Jason decided to transfer to psychology. He had taken a psychology unit as his first-year elective, and it had been the only unit where he had gotten a High-Distinction. Psychology hadn't required equations, nor had it required a practical placement that involved social skills. The unit had only required two essays, and he was good at writing. Reading had been his only form of escape as a child, and it had left him with excellent comprehension and a vast vocabulary. It often wasn't until he used a word in conversation for the first time that he realised he'd been pronouncing it wrong in his head for several years.

Psychology was interesting enough, and several of the things he had learnt had made the world a slightly less confusing place. Learning about phenomena like the self-serving bias helped explain why people continued to smoke and take drugs, despite the overwhelming evidence showing the dangers of it. The so-called bystander effect at least explained why other people weren't willing to step in and help when something that was undeniably wrong was happening. Still, he found it far easier to write about social issues than interact with any actual people. His ability to write resulted in consistently good grades across his subjects, with the exception of the loathsome statistics units which he struggled with, but he didn't see the degree leading to any career opportunities. All career outcomes for the degree – psychologist, social worker, youth liaison, counsellor – seemed to involve a considerable amount of human interaction. That was the problem with most degrees, and just most jobs in general he thought. He'd considered several options, but there seemed to be an issue with everything. Working with computers would have been appealing, if he'd had a mind for coding. Being a night-watchman would have been great, up until the point where he'd actually have to deal with an unruly person in a manner that didn't involve blowing their brains out. The only conclusion about his life he'd reached after five and a half years at university was that he didn't want to study anymore. He had no idea what he was going to do when he finally graduated in a few months. Probably just take on more shifts at the warehouse.

Jason closed his laptop and stood up. He took off his pants, folded them and set them down on his trunk. They would still be clean enough to wear tomorrow. He threw his underwear on top of his neat laundry pile and stepped into the shower. When he got out a couple minutes later he looked at himself in the mirror. He was as happy with his body image as he was with the clothes he had carefully selected. His sandy blonde hair was neat and cropped short, his face still clean shaven from this morning. He did think it was unfortunate his smooth complexion made him look even younger than he was, but he just couldn't stand the feel of even stubble on his face. Growing a beard to look older was out of the question. He met the gaze of his light-brown eyes and looked down to his body. His chest and arm muscles looked as good as they always did, though he wished there was just a little more definition in his six-pack. The tribal tattoo, which he had designed himself, stretched across his chest and the front of his shoulders, and continued about one third of the way down his arm. He had designed it so that it wouldn't be visible underneath a short-sleeved t-shirt. He didn't want any extra attention, and more importantly, he didn't want anything for witnesses to identify him with.

Jason peered closer at the mirror. He could still see the scars underneath his tattoos, but they were almost completely obscured in most parts. Unnoticeable from a distance. The tattoo did a good job in covering them up, as had been its intention. Only the people in the tattoo parlour and his ex-girlfriend Lisa had ever seen Jason without a shirt on since he was a child, but that wasn't the point. The point was he had made the most of the terrible hand he had been dealt. He had turned something disfiguring into a work of art. And he was taking control of what had happened to him. As the work progressed over a few months as he could afford it, his chest gradually stopped being a daily reminder of what his father had done. Jason considered himself to be good at making the most of what he had been given. He was in control of his body now. The next person who tried to burn or cut him was going to have a hell of a time trying to break through his armour. Not to mention he was more than capable of fighting back now.

He finished drying himself and put a clean shirt and underwear on. The clean clothes looked identical to the ones he had taken off. All his clothes were identical. 'I find something I like and I stick with it,' he would say if anybody ever questioned his never changing wardrobe. Most people didn't seem satisfied with the answer, but that was their problem, he thought. *Everyone should be as practical as I am when it comes to clothing. It would make life so much simpler.*

Jason disassembled his pistol, meticulously cleaned each piece, then reassembled it. Satisfied everything was in order, he unrolled his sleeping bag, climbed inside and tried to go to sleep. As usual he would be getting up at 6 AM to go to the gym. As usual, he was also having a hard time getting to sleep. He usually found something to obsess over once he went to bed. Tonight, he was thinking he should have checked to see if the man he had shot had any money or anything else on him worth taking. He hadn't been able to check the last two bodies due to the possibility of witnesses, but there was no excuse this time. He had found over $2,600 on the drug dealer, which had paid for the laptop he was still using, and for the bullet-resistant helmet he had always wanted. It was unlikely the man had anything decent on him. He hadn't enough money for himself, hence the attempted mugging, and Jason thought if the man had a better weapon on him he would no doubt have used that instead of the kitchen knife. Nevertheless, as he tossed and turned he still couldn't shake the thought that he should have at least checked the corpse.

Chapter 5

Detective Brendan Ames furrowed his brow at the ballistics report, still warm from the printer at Glebe Police Station. It had come via email, but Ames had always found it easier to read anything of importance when it was on paper and in his hand. Not to mention he usually took any chance he could to get out of his cubicle for a minute. *Their cubicle,* he reminded himself bitterly, his partner occupying the other half of their side of the moveable partition that was supposed to give adequate privacy to the four detectives at work in the centre of the room. He supposed it was better than nothing. His partner, Michael White, was seated behind him and faced a desk in the opposite direction, and the divider meant he had to stand if he wanted to see detectives Brooks or Oaten working on the other side. But still, hardly what he thought suitable for the lead homicide detective for the Sydney Central Business District, even if that job title sounded a lot more impressive than it actually was. Despite the population density, there weren't actually that many murders in or around the CBD, meaning a lot of the time he was either working cold cases, assisting in someone else's investigation, or even being assigned cases in the surrounding suburbs. He'd caught the beginning of some bullshit American cop show a few weeks ago, and laughed scornfully when they showed the lead detective's spacious office with picturesque harbourside views. Maybe things were different in America, or maybe that was just how some overpaid and underinformed writer imagined it being. Ames didn't have a view of the harbour, he had a view of the hallway that led to reception, where sometimes, over the sounds of constant typing, phones ringing and chatter that otherwise surrounded him, he could listen in to the ridiculous complaints of some lowlife harassing whichever constable had been unlucky enough to get the front counter shift.

Standing at the far end of the room next to the printer, Ames sighed. He hadn't expected this when forensics dug the slug out of the brick wall behind the body. Of course, he could never begin to predict when this particular firearm would make another appearance in one of his reports. That was the confusing part. Confusing, but not surprising

DAMIEN LINNANE

anymore. Ames was rarely surprised these days. Nineteen years on the force had taken care of that. After six years pounding the pavement on general duties he had considered his promotion to detective, and his next to lead homicide detective two years ago to be steps up in the world, and he still supposed they were. He liked the status, not to mention the extra pay. He lamented that the pay rises had been accompanied by a slow yet steady increase in his girth and the number of grey hairs interspersed in his dark brown side-part haircut. Ames had wrongly guessed that getting off the beat would reduce his stress levels. No more callouts to teenage vandals, drunk and disorderly morons, and his least favourite of all, domestic violence, which was more often than not combined with drunk and disorderly. After a few months of regular detective work, he secretly wished he could have traded his new job buried in paperwork for his old one. At least going to arrest punks got him out of the office more, and it beat looking at the grisly remains of corpses and half the time being unable to get any justice for them. Still, he liked to kid himself investigating murders wasn't dramatically increasing his chance of an early heart attack. 'You get used to seeing dead bodies all the time,' he told his friends. But the truth was, he never got used to death. Like his fear of heights, it was always there, just forgotten about until the next time he had to be on a plane or on the top floor of a building for some reason. When he had stared into the blank eyes and almost perfectly circular hole in the middle of the forehead of the city's latest murder victim, Ames remembered how much he hated this shit.

It had been a while. There hadn't been a murder in his jurisdiction for over two months. Now there had been two in four days. Ames still wasn't over the girl, Kelly Steiner, they found at Centennial Park on Tuesday morning. An early morning jogger had called it in, and Ames had made the mistake of joking to one of the GDs, the general duties officers who had cornered off the area, that not finding dead bodies was a good a reason as any to not take up jogging. The lack of stripes on her blue shoulder epaulets indicated that she was a probationary constable, first year on the job. As he stared at her cold response to his macabre humour, Ames had hoped that if she hadn't developed the right attitude to cope with the job yet, her months of experience had at least taught her not to put in a fucking complaint about a senior officer. Thankfully it appeared she hadn't.

The victim was a fucking mess, her body dumped unceremoniously, face down in long grass at the edge of the duck pond, scrapes in the dirt indicated she'd been dragged from the road about fifteen metres away. It didn't take a detective to figure out she'd been killed elsewhere and dumped here. There were obvious signs of being restrained. Strangled. And raped. The ID came quickly, she was clothed and her purse was under her shoulder, still containing her driver's license, phone, makeup and other paraphernalia, including the ace of hearts. Something about that last item was eating at Ames. Her family hadn't known anything about it. Was it something she had picked up at the club the night before she had been reported missing? A recently acquired good luck charm? Ames didn't know. Maybe he was just over analysing. It happened in his line of work. Not everything was a clue. Maybe she'd just been playing cards and the top card had slipped out of the deck she was carrying.

The new murder scene had been a step up from the last one, not that that was saying much in itself. But a slob of a man with a couple holes in his head was a hell of a lot easier to deal with than the brutalised remains of a young woman. Ames was self-conscious of how much he had aged in the last few years, but felt mildly better after noting how much older Vickery looked although they were both thirty-nine. He had recognised Scott Vickery immediately. Ames had arrested him for possession of heroin seven years ago. Vickery was a serial offender. A good behaviour bond from when Ames' arrested him, then three and six months in prison for two subsequent drug offences. Only one month after getting out of prison the second time, he had gone back in for three years. Armed robbery. Three years for netting $96 and two packets of cigarettes from robbing a convenience store with a screwdriver. After getting out of prison over a year ago, all Vickery seemed to have done was drop out of a voluntary drug rehab program and collect unemployment benefits.

After a comprehensive check of Vickery's background and the limited evidence at the crime scene, there was no apparent pattern to why he had been this pistol's fourth and latest victim. The only common ground was with the pistol's first victim, Corey Campbell. Both had drug convictions. The similarities ended there. There was no evidence to suggest the two had known each other, although it was possible. Ames remembered the Campbell case well. It had only been his third homicide since making lead detective, but the first by shooting. He had lost count of how many he had worked on since then. It would have been easy enough to figure out, surely no more than twenty he thought, but he had no interest in keeping score. Campbell was a twenty-two-year-old high-school dropout. He had three convictions, two for possession and one for distribution. All small time. His corpse had revealed that he had moved slightly up the food chain of the criminal world. There was $1500 worth of methamphetamines on his person when his body was found, though no cash. That had bothered Ames. Someone had taken whatever money Corey had on his person – you don't have that many drugs on you and no cash – but they had left the drugs. If Corey wasn't a known dealer, Ames would have considered the possibility that the drugs had been planted. Still, it made no sense why the drugs had been left there. Ballistics had confirmed the shooting had been from close range – definitely not a drive-by. A turf issue? Unlikely. Unsurprisingly none of the known dealers in town had given him any decent information on the case – you didn't make a good reputation for yourself as a drug dealer by co-operating with the police – but Ames had gotten the distinct impression they were all as baffled as he was. Corey hadn't been a saint, but he frankly hadn't struck Ames as being important enough for anybody to want to gun down. Drug debts? Then why hadn't the killer recovered the drugs to recoup their losses? The presence of the drugs also ruled out the possibility it was a disgruntled customer. Meth users weren't known for their rational behaviour, but expecting an addict to leave a pile of drugs intact was like expecting your pet dog to ignore an unguarded pile of meat. Being his first shooting, Ames had put more effort into investigating the murder than he would now, but he hadn't exactly lost any sleep over the case being unresolved. None of the cops in this city would lose any sleep over a dead meth dealer.

The gun's next target had been far more puzzling. Gary Meredith. Twenty-seven-year-old construction worker. No criminal record. One of the boys according to everyone at his workplace. Loved by his family and girlfriend. No-one could give him a single reason why they thought someone would want him killed. Still that didn't explain why his blood alcohol rating was so high. Or what he was doing at the outskirts of the Kings Cross red-light district in the early hours of the morning. Or why they'd found a used condom with his semen in it in a back-alley nearby. Two gunshot wounds to the chest fired from five to ten metres away. One round still inside him, the other had exited out his shoulder blade and was never recovered, but one bullet was all forensics needed. Ames had lost plenty of sleep over that one. He assumed the gun had changed hands. Guns were sold and traded all the time. It had been eight months and the shootings seemed completely unrelated. Besides the murder weapon all they had in common as far as he could tell was that they both occurred at night and in the same city. For that reason, Ames hadn't even bothered to update the media when the ballistics report had come back linking the two murders.

He did mention it after the next murder. Alex Bryant, fifty-two-year-old IT consultant. Several misdemeanours in his youth, but no legal trouble in the last half of his life except for a plethora of parking tickets and a few more speeding fines than the average person. One shot, point blank from behind. The rear half of his skull was non-existent; the bullet was buried in the one remaining lobe of his brain. Broad daylight, but no witnesses. There were never any goddamn witnesses with this pistol. He couldn't find a single factor connecting Bryant to either Campbell or Meredith, and couldn't find a solid motive for anyone to want to kill him. He hadn't exactly been employee of the month at his workplace. By all reports his work ethic, general attitude and even hygiene were poor. Ames had thought Gary's workspace in the IT department was filthy, until he saw his house. The smell hit him immediately after opening the door. Like an entire wheel of cheese had gone bad, but that wasn't it. There was no spoilt food to be found, just general filth. How someone could stand to live in that smell, Ames would never understand. Never married,

Gary's only living family had been a sister in Tweed Heads, who had been remarkably indifferent to the news of her brother's death. That had made her the only suspect for a very short time, until they had found undeniable proof she hadn't left her town several hundred kilometres away on the day of the murder. The autopsy ruled the only drugs in his system were traces of alcohol and paracetamol, so that ruled out drug addiction and drug debts. Bryant did have a decent amount of credit card debt though. Ames had scoured through his financial records thinking he might have other debts to less reputable institutions than the major banks. But several years of records hadn't shown any major amount of money coming in or going out, just some poor spending habits. Despite his best efforts, he wasn't a single step closer to figuring out why Bryant had been killed, or why three people had been killed with the same pistol. Out of frustration he'd circled the case around to other detectives for second and third opinions, but with no new evidence, this had just been a waste of time.

The theory of the gun being sold after each murder seemed the most probable explanation.

Ames could only think of two other possibilities. The first was it was the work of a contract killer. That seemed remarkably unlikely. Even Campbell, a drug dealer, didn't seem to warrant the kind of cost an assassin would attract; Meredith was, at least on paper, an upstanding citizen, and as far as he could tell Bryant was just a garden variety asshole. Who would pay money to have them killed? That left just one other possibility.

'You reckon we got a serial killer Brendo?' said detective White as he read the latest report over Ames' shoulder. Ames thought White was a good kid, eager, full of potential. He still believed he was making a difference in the world. Ames remembered feeling like that when he was White's age, twenty-seven. White would get over it in time, as he replaced his athletic physique and serenity with a couple of pay rises and a troubled marriage. Ames thought the kid's jarhead haircut, an inch high on top and a zero at the sides, made him look several shades dumber than he actually was. Why someone would pay money for such a bad haircut, Ames would never understand. The last vestiges of his four years in the military straight after high school he supposed. That and the tattoo. 'Ich Dien', proudly displayed on one of his muscular forearms, the business shirt rolled up to the elbows as always. Having never really understood tattoos, he had asked about it on White's first day. His army unit's motto, apparently. 'I Serve'. Don't we all, thought Ames, though he did often wonder to what purpose. His career had been decidedly less rewarding than he had imagined it being when he was still at the academy.

'Yeah I can see why you'd think that, but I doubt it. There's no pattern. Serial killers have a type. At least that's what they tell us,' Ames said, passing the report to White.

'Who's they?'

Ames paused, then shrugged in response to his partner. Come to think of it, he didn't really know. He hadn't exactly had any experience with serial killers. The only thing connecting the crimes was the pistol, and even the media hadn't shown much interest in its connection, beyond a passing mention in a follow-up article on Bryant's murder. Still, considering the alternative possibilities, a serial killer did seem a likely explanation. Ames was morbidly curious to see who, if anybody, would be murdered with the pistol next, and whether it would shed any light on his investigation.

Vickery's corpse wasn't shedding any light at all. He had only lived a few blocks from where he was found. He could have been heading home, but from where? Ames hadn't been able to establish anything about his movements since he had reported to the unemployment office three days earlier. The two other addicts he lived with weren't exactly the reliable or helpful type. They had seemed less concerned that their flatmate had been killed and more concerned that Ames might have had a search warrant for their residence, which he didn't. There would have been drugs and drug paraphernalia there, but that wasn't his job. Vickery had been shot point blank directly from the front. Nothing on his person had been found except a set of keys and some loose change. Judging from the ballistics report, it seemed possible someone had casually shot him in the head as he walked past. That certainly fit in with the serial killer theory. But it was also possible that Vickery had been up to no good. The ballistics report had come back just after the toxicology one. Vickery had still been using heroin, but Ames had already known that from the pincushion that was the man's upper forearm. The toxicology report showed that he hadn't scored in over twenty-four hours. An addict of his level would have been hanging out by then. Until the ballistics report came back, Ames had considered that Vickery might have been in a fight with a bigger or at least better armed fish. It didn't bring any explanation, however, as to what the previous two victims had done to deserve their fate.

Ames had a bad feeling he was going to have to wait for another ballistics report that matched this gun before he solved the mystery. He left White at the printer and went to the kitchen to pour himself another cup of coffee. Stepping out the front of the station he lent against the pillar advertising the station's name to the tree-lined side street, balancing his fourth cigarette for the day in one hand with his third cup of coffee in the other. As he stood there and watched traffic, he did a reasonably good job of convincing himself that there was nothing unusual about hating your job in this day and age. *Lots of people don't like what they do for a living, but that's just life*. He had a mortgage to pay off, a wife to keep happy and a daughter who was entering the joys of puberty. He told himself it was worth the money as he flicked the remains of his cigarette in the direction of the small bin out the front of the station. It bounced off the top and disappeared behind, out of sight. 'Fuck it, close enough,' Ames said to himself as he stepped back inside.

Chapter 6

Jason left his apartment and started his walk towards the University of Sydney, a twenty-minute journey on foot along the Princes Highway, then another several minutes to get to the lecture hall once he'd reached the university grounds. Newtown was central for pretty much everything he had going on. While they were all in different directions, his work, volunteering and studies could all be reached within half an hour on foot.

Spread over both sides of the busy highway, the university loomed into view as he walked, Sydney Tower poking its head over the green-tinted glass lining an overhead walkway for students. Jason reached the set of traffic lights he needed to cross and waited with about a dozen other people. Crossing the busy street, a young Asian man was directly in his path coming the other way. Jason stepped to his left to get out of the way. At the exact same time the man stepped to his right to do the same. Jason frowned. Still head on, Jason now stepped to his right. The man had had the same thought. Jason grimaced and tilted his head to one side. Scarcely a metre away from each other now, the man met Jason's eyes and gave him an awkward shrug and chuckle, seeming to ask what was going to happen now. Half panicking, Jason lunged to the left, taking far more space than he needed to in order to break free from the painful situation he found himself stuck in. He inadvertently scraped past the shoulder of a woman to his side in the process. He picked up his pace to a half jog in the hopes she wouldn't say anything to him about it. Reaching the other side, he breathed a sigh of relief. The ordeal was over. He shook his head, wondering why people just couldn't understand how he preferred to walk at night when there was less foot traffic about.

Jason followed a path choked with students coming to and fro and stayed as far to one side as he could in the hope of getting what little space he could from them all. Passing a series of three-sided outdoor noticeboards, Jason took note of what posters and flyers were currently on display. Several gigs were advertised, along with a rally against proposed funding cuts for student services, something written completely in Chinese, and flyers for an activist gathering on climate change that had occurred two days ago. He was tempted to take the flyers down on principle now the event was over, but he just didn't have the time. The last billboard in the row was covered with half a dozen green A3 flyers, bearing in striking white text 'Jesus Loves You', along with the Bible society's logo in the top corner. Some smart ass had written 'But everyone else thinks you're a jackass' in thick black marker underneath one. Jason managed a small smile as he rounded the corner towards the faculty of science.

Following a stream of students into the lecture hall, Jason climbed the steps towards the rear of the auditorium and took a seat at the left side of one of the back rows. Today's lecture was his integrated physiology class, one of the two remaining units of his degree, and his last remaining elective. As the lecturer's PowerPoint presentation came into view on the giant screen down the front, the chatter in the half-filled room gradually came to a stop as if someone was turning down the room's volume knob slowly but steadily. The lecturer, a well-dressed middle-aged woman, stood over her laptop at the podium as she spoke into the podium's microphone.

'Continuing from last week's lecture on the effects of alcohol on the body, today's lecture will focus on how chronic alcoholism leads to malnutrition.' She clicked her mouse and the first slide, which only showed the name of the class and the topic, gave way to the second, displaying an overview of the key learning points. The lecturer spoke again, and Jason was grateful she wasn't the kind who just read out paragraph after paragraph verbatim from her slides. She knew how to speak in front of a class without boring them to death. A lot of the students were typing away on their laptops, but while Jason's laptop was one of his most prised possessions, he found it easier to take notes the old-fashioned way. He summarised what was being spoken on his notepad in front of him. Alcohol and its direct impairment on the intake of nutrients, how chronic alcohol use inhibits the body's ability to absorb the nutrients the body does manage to intake. His hand wrote furiously trying to keep up with the speed of the lecture, only half hearing what was being said, but feeling smug that he never drank alcohol, and accordingly, didn't have to worry about any of these things happening to him.

The lecturer continued: 'A lot of the nutrient impairment associated with alcoholism, however, does not come from the actual alcohol itself. Lifestyle factors typically associated with substance dependence, such as irregularity of meals and disruption of social lives, play a major role. These factors tend to compound each other. For example, meal times will be more irregular the more that social lives are negatively affected, and social lives will be more negatively affected with higher alcohol consumption. Chronic alcoholism also often leads to a poor financial situation, which leads to an inability to purchase good quality foods.'

An inability to purchase good quality foods. *More like an inability to purchase any fucking food at all,* Jason thought. He suddenly found himself scowling about how many times his first primary school had to give him one of the 'emergency lunches' provided for any child who, for whatever reason, hadn't brought their own lunch to school. He remembered going many nights without dinner. He remembered trying to rouse his mother one morning because he was hungry. She had slept on the couch again, and in her semiconscious state she had slurred a tirade of objections when he had shaken her shoulder. By lunchtime she had still not woken, and he had taken himself to the corner store. It wasn't far, though easily twice the distance to his school, the furthest he had been out on his own. When the young shopkeeper had caught his clumsy attempt to steal the brand of bread that his mother sometimes bought, she had, to Jason's surprise, let him go. He recognised the gesture for what it was, charity, though he had never gone back to the store again on his own, deciding he preferred the feeling of an empty stomach to the feeling of shame. He would have been five.

The more he thought about it, the more his mother's alcoholism seemed to be the root of a lot of his problems. Or maybe it was his father running out on her. Her drinking had gotten a lot worse after that. At least his mother realised in her rare moments of sobriety that she had a problem. When Peter, the man in the flat next door, offered to watch and feed Jason whenever she wanted, she had jumped at the opportunity. Jason couldn't remember anything distinct about Peter. He was average looking. Dressed normally. There was nothing unusual about his apartment. No warning signs at all. Everything about him was painfully ordinary on the outside, which was perhaps why his mother had been so trusting. Or maybe she just hadn't put any thought into it.

Peter watched Jason the first several times without incident. It wasn't until he spent the first night there that it had happened. Jason couldn't remember exactly why he had spent the night there, though he guessed it had something to do with his mother's drinking. He had known Peter for several weeks at this stage, by which time he'd been making an effort to be sitting out the front of the apartment block when he came home from work in the evenings. Sometimes there'd be chocolates from Peter's lunchbox, and Peter would take the time to chat with him. At worst he'd get a smile and a friendly 'How's your day been kiddo' as he walked past, which was still more warmth than he'd ever gotten from his own father. When Peter had suggested they share the fold-out sofa to sleep on together as they watched TV, Jason had thought nothing of it. If anything, he had looked forward to it. His mother never watched TV with him at night, or at all for that matter. She was considerate enough to rent him video tapes from time to time. He would stay up late at night and watch cartoons over and over. It was lonely, but as long as he had food in his stomach, he would be content.

Peter made his moves so casually and spoke so friendly that Jason had felt confused about what occurred next, even though he knew something wasn't right about it. Peter spoke soft, reassuring words as he undressed the two of them. He touched Jason and instructed Jason to touch him. Afterwards he told Jason it was their secret, and if he told his mother or anybody about it they would both get in big trouble. Jason wouldn't have told anybody even if he did have someone to talk to. He was ashamed and confused and just wanted to be left alone. He was already a quiet and reserved boy and his mother didn't even notice when he retreated that little bit further. Evidently someone had noticed something. A couple months later the school receptionist had come and taken Jason from his classroom. The receptionist took him to an office where a policeman and a woman, someone from a child protection agency Jason would later realise, had spoken to him.

He had initially been worried he was in the big trouble that Peter had warned him about, even though he had told nobody. On the contrary, he was told that he had done nothing wrong, but that he wouldn't be allowed to live with his mother anymore. Jason cried. He had still loved his mother at the time. They tracked down Jason's father and sent him to live with him. As an adult, Jason wondered why his father had agreed to care for him. Care being a very loose term. To this day he still couldn't look at a cigarette without shuddering and feeling a sharp burning pain in his chest from underneath the scars. At least he'd managed to conquer his fear of knives. Between all the lessons his father frequently administered, Jason learnt quickly to stay in his room. It was important to not be in the way. It was important not to ask questions about the people who frequently came to his father's house and left two or three minutes later. It was important not to touch the small packages his father hid under the lining of the garbage bin in the kitchen. In the stuffing of the split cushion on the lounge. Taped underneath the laundry sink.

Jason didn't mind hiding in his room so much.

His room had a shelf of old books in it, the kind that gathered an exchange rate of about two dollars per metric tonne if you sold them to your local second-hand book shop. He had no idea why they were in his father's house, but he didn't dare ask, and in any case, he wasn't complaining. Friends that were described with all the gripping excitement that one would expect from a VCR instruction manual were better than none at all, but sometimes he'd find hidden gems in the dusty, weather worn pages. Once he finished all the books at home he started heading to the public library after school. There he basked under the soft glow of the lamps in the kids' reading section, and the approving but sad smile from the librarian as she watched the polite young child with his scruffy shoulder-length hair and school uniform that seemed to be washed as frequently as the change in seasons. There Jason escaped to faraway worlds. Distant islands with his friend Jim Hawkins, distant planets with his friend Ender Wiggen. He'd hope his father would be passed out from indulging in too much of his own wares or too busy to notice him when he slunk back into the house at night, and most of the time he was. Most of the time.

His father only did it a dozen times or so over the few years they lived together, maybe less, but it was the last time Jason remembered the most. He'd heard the men arguing from two houses down as he approached his home. Jason decided to avoid the heat and come in through the back, easing the creaky screen door as if it were wired with explosives that would detonate if the rusty aluminium hinges emitted even the slightest of sounds. He needn't have bothered. The growing argument inside could have drowned out a yodelling contest in the middle of a construction site.

'Don't fuckin' lie to us Vince, where's our money?' said a man Jason had heard several times but never actually taken a good look at.

'You know what happened to the last person who got caught skimpin' off the butcher's take?' said a deep voice Jason thought could easily belong to the giant from Jack and the Beanstalk.

'You know why they call him the butcher, don't ya Vince?' came the first voice again.

'I ain't been fuckin' stealin' from no cunt,' said Jason's father in his thick Welsh accent, 'I swear on me ma's life.'

'On me ma's life,' repeated the first man sardonically in a poor imitation of the accent. 'You know you're a lucky man Vince, ya family all safe shaggin' sheep back where ya came from, ain't nobody over here we can threaten, 'cept that boy of course, and somethin' tells me if we took a Black n' Decker to his kneecaps you'd be fightin' to do it yourself, you sick little fucker wouldn't ya? Saw him in the backyard without a shirt on one day when I came to collect. Swear if that kid had any more bruises he could've passed for a fuckin' nigger.'

The giant laughed.

'Look, that's all the money I got, I just gave it to you, every cent!' Vincent pleaded.

'Then where's the fuckin' product Vince? You expect me to believe ya sold a whole ounce and this is what you got for it? This! What the fuck is this? Did you raid your fuckin' kid's money box or something? Did ya roll a fuckin' hobo for his paper cup?'

'Times been tough man, I ain't even ...'

A dull thud followed by the sound of something big hitting the floor cut off the sounds of Vincent's weak protests. Jason pictured his father lying on the ground, nursing a broken nose or jaw.

'No more excuses Vince. The money. By the end of the week. Last chance. Don't fuckin' make me come back here. And here's some more incentive, 'case you forget.'

Jason listened to the sound of the two men doing their crass but not unimpressive interpretation of *Riverdance* into his father's body. He might have enjoyed the sounds, but he knew what would probably come later as a result. Shit rolled downhill, as he had once heard a character in a film his father was watching say. He had asked the librarian what that meant the next day, though had chosen to substitute the word 'poop' for shit so as to not get in trouble. The librarian had laughed so hard he had nearly cried, before taking off his glasses and doing the best job possible of explaining such a saying to a seven-year-old.

He woke in the middle of the night, his father's knee in his chest felt like an anvil had been dropped on him. The sting of being slapped in the face brought him fully back into the land of the living.

'Bet you enjoyed hearing your old man getting beaten' up,' Vincent said as the smells of tobacco, blood and gingivitis rolled into Jason's face. Jason could tell from his father's slurred speech that his jaw had been given a good working over. He said nothing to the dark figure above him on the bed. No amount of begging, bargaining, crying or reasoning would stop his father. He'd learnt that a long time ago. His father took a drag on his cigarette. The mild red embers burned bright, bathing his father in a soft orange glow. For just a second Jason could see exactly how badly his father's face had been remodelled. That meant Jason would be getting an exceptionally brutal punishment tonight, but at least his own face would be ok. His father never left a mark on his face. Jason knew his father wasn't a smart man, but he wasn't dumb enough to put his sick little hobby on display, have some do-gooder call child services like they had on his mother. No. Jason's scars were all where the public weren't liable to see them.

His father ripped open Jason's pyjama top. Buttons popped off like a poker machine had just struck a small combo and was paying out a few measly coins. Jason would sew them back on tomorrow. He had taught himself to fix pretty much everything. His father didn't bother tying up Jason's arms. He hadn't for the last few times. Vincent knew his son was a smart one. He'd already learned that fighting back was only going to make things worse. Jason steeled himself, bracing for the pain.

'How many you reckon' you can take before you start screamin' tonight boy?' Vincent asked, with all the tone one would expect if he'd asked his son what he wanted for dinner. Jason said nothing. There was nothing to say. His father chuckled.

'Well let's stop fuckin' around and just get started, shall we?' Jason had guessed it was going to be burning tonight, but you never could tell until it started. Sometimes his father smoked while he used the knife. Jason preferred the knife. The wounds healed quicker. His father took one last drag on the cigarette and brought the burning tip into Jason's chest. Jason didn't start screaming until the fourth burn. His father stopped after eleven.

Jason supposed his father must have paid his debt, for he was still alive when the police raided their home a month later. The police asked Jason a lot of questions, but Jason didn't have much to say to them. He didn't show them the scars. He was too ashamed, and anyway, he'd already decided he wanted to take care of that in his own way. He was good at fixing things. Jason had assumed they would move him back to his mother. The foster parents, however, had proved much less painful to live with. There were many. Some were pleasant. Others were clearly only in it for the government funding, though Jason didn't mind their indifference. In fact, he preferred it when people left him alone now. His mother made infrequent attempts to get in contact with him. He had been eager to see her at first. The older he got, the more he came to despise her lifestyle. She looked worse every time he saw her. He lost interest. One day it occurred to him that his mother hadn't attempted to contact him for over a year. It had been over ten years now.

His father had been safe in jail where Jason couldn't get a hold of him at the time, so he seldom thought about him. But he thought a lot about Peter. Jason couldn't pinpoint exactly when he started making plans to kill him, but it was in his final year of school. By that time, he had long been old enough to understand exactly how heinous Peter's crime was. He never found anyone he was comfortable enough with to confide in. His parents were out of the equation. Jason was vaguely aware of an uncle and some cousins on his mother's side. His father had immigrated from Wales, but if he had any family back in the old country Jason wasn't aware of it. Jason had only ever managed to have a couple casual friends at school. By year twelve most of the other children had formed strong bonds over more than a decade. He, on the other hand, had changed schools seven times as he moved between parents and foster homes. Once at an inter-school sports event, Jason had recognised a girl he had shared a couple classes with four years and two schools ago. He had tried to talk to her about it, and she seemed genuinely apologetic after seeing the hurt expression on his face when she said she didn't remember him. Staying up late at night, and even during school, Jason would be distracted by fantasies of killing Peter. Sometimes in his mind he would slit Peter's throat and just get it over with quickly. Sometimes he would give him a hundred small cuts and watch him bleed to death for hours. Other times he would cut out his eyes and piss in the wounds. Sometimes he just wanted to strangle that fucking piece of shit like there was no tomorrow, grab him by the neck and just choke the god-damn fucking li–

* * *

'Don't forget the major assessment is due in next Friday,' said the lecturer as she closed down her laptop. The PowerPoint slide on display to the room was suddenly replaced by a blue screen as the connection was cut.

Jason looked down at his notepad. *Shit.* He couldn't even remember at what point he'd tuned out. Luckily all the lectures were recorded and posted online, but he'd just created an extra hour of work for himself at home by daydreaming again. He'd lost count of how many times this had happened, but at least it would be over soon. Another few more weeks of this pointless degree to go and then he'd have more time to, well he didn't know, but he was sure he'd fill it with something. He always found a way to overburden himself. Jason stood up and followed the crowd out the door. If he hurried he wouldn't be late to his lunch-time shift at the soup kitchen. As long as the kitchen kept running, at least a handful of kids wouldn't be going hungry today.

Chapter 7

Howard sat in his van in the car park behind his favourite liquor store, only a few blocks from his house. One hand rested on the steering wheel, the other firmly grasped the tyre iron in his lap. The girl who worked in the store here on Wednesday nights wouldn't finish work for another twenty minutes, but he was already feeling the rush. The same rush he had felt when he had decided to take Kelly, but this time he had put a lot of planning into his work. His real work. Not that horrid day job he had cleaning carpets for the old prick. Howard hated his job, but he was loving his work. At least his job had given him access to the company van. It had come in handy last time, and it was going to come in handy again. Howard chuckled. He wondered what the old prick would think if he knew what Howard was doing with the company van after hours.

The deck of cards rested on the dashboard. He wouldn't take another card from it until the new girl was finished with, but he felt like carrying it with him wherever he went anyway. It reminded him of his accomplishment. He looked forward to the day when the deck was empty, and he had made fifty-two sluts 'his'. He wondered how he would start marking the girls when that day came, but at least he'd have plenty of time to think about it.

Reading the newspaper about the last girl, Howard had been disappointed the mark he had left on her hadn't been mentioned. Had it slipped out of her purse somehow? He hoped not. How else would they know she had been his? Maybe they just hadn't made the connection yet. Well no matter. He had a plan to really get their attention with the next card he left. It had been five months since he had dumped Kelly's body, but he still thought about it every day. It was usually what he thought about while he masturbated. His collection of pornographic rape films had gone unwatched for over a month. Memories of the real thing left an impression far greater than anything the lifeless monitor of his computer could emit. Besides, Howard suspected the film scenes were staged. Scripted. The girls not really being raped at all. There was no power in that. Howard remembered the power more than anything. Being able to take her whenever he felt like it.

Deciding exactly when, and exactly how she would die. He hadn't felt power like that since his mouse. Eleven years old and he had grown tired of the pet he had begged for only a year earlier. First, he had kept poking it with a stick. Then he burnt it with matches when that had grown tiresome. He still remembered exactly how it had all ended. He had taken the lid off the cage and tried to grab the filthy little thing, which by this stage would run around frantically in circles whenever Howard came near. Howard wondered if it knew it was just wasting its time and energy. It was in a fucking cage for Christ sake, he would get his hands around it eventually. Well as always on this day he had, his hands tightening around its ribcage as it squirmed against his fingers, tiny pricks of pain in his palm as its feet tried to find enough purchase to break free. He'd left the head poking out through the top of his fist so he could see the fear in his eyes, except this time he was holding the thing too far down. It craned forward and had bit his knuckle. Had drawn fucking blood and everything. After a fit of crying Howard had taken it straight over to his father's workbench and had sawn the thing's head off with a hacksaw. The emotion came in two waves. The exhilaration was as quick and intense as giving himself an orgasm, a hobby Howard had only recently discovered at the time, but then the fear of being caught crept up from behind and engulfed him. He had panicked, and quickly buried the mouse in a shallow grave in the backyard. He buried the cage behind the junk in his father's tool-shed. He had hoped his father wouldn't notice his pet's disappearance. He hadn't. Or if he had, he hadn't given a shit. Howard's father hadn't given a shit about much at all. His car. His beer. And discipline. Those seemed to be Patrick Silverman's three passions in life. Howard had felt unloved as a child, but now he could finally understand why his father had beaten him so much. It felt so good to be on the other side. Killing Kelly, Howard had seen things from his father's side, making him feel close to his father for the first time since his death. The old man had succumbed to a heart attack when Howard was eighteen. Nineteen years ago. Howard had inherited everything. The house, the car, the furniture. He was yet to replace anything substantial other than the TV. He enjoyed sitting in his old man's recliner and having a beer when he came home, just like his father had. And now he understood the beatings. His father had taught him an important thing in life, Howard realised now. The power. The pleasure. You could get it from others. Take it right out of them. Howard had held his abuse against his father from his childhood all the way through his adult life, but he couldn't hold it against the old man now. Now that he understood.

He didn't know the name of the girl who worked in the liquor store, but she worked here every Wednesday night. Howard saw her around on other nights from time to time, but she was always here Wednesdays. He'd been coming here long enough to know that. She was practically begging to be taken. The way she left the top two buttons at the front of her work shirt undone, inviting him to look at her chest. The heavy mascara and dark crimson lipstick she always wore just to tease him. They were all teasing him. They'd been doing it for as long as Howard could remember. Howard remembered how they'd teased him at school. Snickering and laughing at the chubby boy who finally summed up the courage to ask out the girl he liked. She'd been even fatter than he was. Howard had known he'd have no chance with the pretty girls, so he'd set his sights lower. Having seen the way she looked at him, he thought he'd definitely have a chance. But she'd still rejected him. Laughed awkwardly and shook her head when he'd asked her in front of her friends. Sarah. Sarah Herring. Nearly thirty years ago and Howard could still remember that first teasing slut's name.

Howard wished he knew this girl's name, but he was sure she would tell him soon enough. She wore a name badge that started with an R, but it didn't look like any name starting with R that he had seen before. Howard had shown some promise reading in his first year of school, but his father, and his father's belt, had quickly put an end to that.

'I got through life without no readin' skills and I turned out damn good. Ain't no point learnin' to read boy. You think yer better than yer old man or somethin'?'

No. Howard had not thought he was better than his old man.

The girl turned the store lights off. 11:30 PM. Just like the sign on the door had said. A minute later she exited the front door and locked it behind her,

her blond bob bounced as she walked to her car. Howard knew it was her car. It had to be. It was the only other one in the car park. Deliberately parking between it and the shop entrance had been a smart choice. She would come right past him. Howard stepped out of his van, his knuckles turned white as he gripped the notched steel on the tyre iron. Just like the last one, she never saw a thing.

Chapter 8

The forklift beeped out its steady cadence as Jason put it in reverse. He looked over his shoulder as he backed away from the shelf he had just placed a crate of canned beans onto, and headed back to the delivery truck for another. He'd been working at the warehouse in Marrickville for about eight months now. Jason wouldn't have gone as far as to say he enjoyed working for the wholesale food company, but at least he didn't hate it like he had hated most of his jobs. At least it didn't involve interaction with the general public.

It had been five months since he had shot the attempted mugger, and two months since he had finished university. While he was relieved to have finished his degree after such a long time studying, there had been no great change in his life. Finishing university had simply left him with a larger void. He put his name down for more shifts on the casual roster at work. Surprisingly though his shifts had decreased slightly in the last month. He still had steady work at the soup kitchen, although volunteering there had felt particularly unrewarding as of late. Two weeks ago, a disgruntled patron had come back and thrown a Styrofoam cup full of urine at Caroline, after she had refused him a second helping when he had pushed back into the line. Jason had wanted to punish the man, but he wasn't stupid enough to do it with witnesses around, and he didn't know where to find him. The frustration of being unable to get any justice for Caroline, the fact that this violent sadistic prick of a man had gone unpunished for his crime. Jason had been sleeping even less well than usual ever since. Being unable to get any justice for what his father had done to him was one thing, but the fact that someone had hurt a woman he liked was a whole other ball game. Jason seethed day after day, his teeth clenched as he thought about how many other victims that piece of shit had already created, about how someone needed to make him disappear before he hurt anybody else. The feelings would die off in time, Jason knew. His rage always did, even if it often took a few weeks.

Six weeks ago, on his way home work he'd seen a loud mouth drunk walking in front of traffic, cutting off cars and randomly screaming profanities at the drivers. Jason followed the man for several blocks, hoping to catch him alone, though the man had met up with several other people, clearly his friends, on a street corner. Jason crossed the road and gave up. He couldn't kill the abusive man with so many witnesses, plus there were other problems to consider. Pistols were a lot less accurate than films and TV led you to believe, and they were even less accurate with a silencer fitted. Jason knew he had to get well within ten metres for a clean kill, and at that distance he couldn't gun down the other four scumbags if they all rushed him at once. He had spent a lot of time studying close combat, and knew from reading a military shooting handbook he had found online that if someone was within four metres of him they could easily tackle him to the ground before he could un-holster a pistol and cock it. His gun was cocked but that would only buy him another metre or two at most. The anger from that missed kill had played over and over in his mind for a month. He was just getting over it when the urine throwing incident occurred. Jason shook his head at how fast the world seemed to be deteriorating. *Why couldn't people just follow the rules?* At first he had only seen crimes that needed punishing from time to time, now they were everywhere. It seemed to be getting worse.

It was 10:31 AM when Jason parked the forklift and headed to the staff room. The morning tea break went from 10:30 till 10:45. Even though everybody else seemed to go a few minutes early, Jason thought that was unprofessional. He stepped into the staff room and sat down in the corner. He never ate the complimentary biscuits nor drank coffee, and to the mild confusion of everyone else, seemed content to just sit and be quiet during the allocated break. Jason amused himself with his thoughts as he watched the clock on the wall. The digital clock had just hit 10:44 when his boss, Rick Groundstreom, came and asked him to come into his office.

'There goes Mr Personality,' said one of the men from IT sitting at the main table in the staff-room. Several people chuckled in response.

'What's with that guy anyway?' asked the work-experience kid.

'Gay,' said one of the truck drivers matter-of-factly as he took a sip of coffee.

'Are you sure?' said a woman from sales, 'I've

talked to him a couple times, I think he's just shy.'

'Shy and gay then,' said the truck driver.

'He's not gay,' said one of the women from admin, 'I've seen him staring at Jess.'

'Ask her to take him for spin and find out for sure,' said the man from IT. 'She would.'

Jason heard the laughter that followed through the wall, though he had no idea what had prompted it.

Jason followed Rick, a skinny beanpole of a middle-aged man who seemed to think that if he wore clothes two sizes too big it would encourage his emaciated frame to grow into them. He walked down the corridor, staying a few feet behind him and wondered what this could be about. Once they were within the privacy of Rick's office, Rick dropped the casual smile that had accompanied his 'hey mate, can I just talk to you for a minute in my office' question. He now had a different expression on his face. It took Jason a few seconds, but he recognised that expression. It was guilt. Rick was going to tell him something that he didn't want to. He scratched at his receding hairline with his left-hand as he opened his mouth to speak.

'Mate I'm afraid I've got some bad news.' Jason hated being called 'mate' or 'buddy' by someone he didn't consider to be his friend, but now wasn't the time to focus on that. 'As you're no doubt aware the company isn't doing very well and we've made the decision to let most of the casuals go.' On some occasions Jason found reading between the lines was easier than others; he had gathered that he was in the 'most' slice of the casual pie.

'Even though we don't have to give any notice to casuals I thought the right thing to do would be to let you know as soon as possible. We won't be able to give you any shifts after the end of next month.'

Jason supposed that was rather considerate of them. He didn't argue, the decision had clearly already been made, and he didn't want any unnecessary confrontation. He nodded.

'I've always tried to think of this workplace as a family,' Rick added, 'and I just want to let you know this isn't necessarily the end. I'll call you if our situation changes and we can take you back.'

Jason didn't really know what it felt like to have a family, but he was fairly certain it wasn't like this workplace. The same indifference he had felt all his life. The snickering about him behind his back. The bitching and backstabbing he couldn't help but overhear from his co-workers. If that was family, Jason thought he hadn't missed out on anything, only he knew very well that he had. He also didn't like his chances of Rick calling him back, but there wasn't much he could do about that. He thanked Rick for giving him the extra notice, shook his hand and went back to work.

A couple of the other casuals who had been let go stopped bothering to come back to work at all, but Jason turned up to his remaining shifts. He had made a commitment to keep them and he would, even if his usual enthusiasm and attention to detail was gone. He had always looked down on his co-workers who slacked off and took breaks when they weren't supposed to. *Rules were meant to be followed,* he had always thought. Without even realising it, Jason was caring less and less for the rules. The thought that administering punishment to horrible people was also against the rules had previously crossed his mind, but it hadn't taken much to convince himself his actions were justified. He was stepping up to fix a problem when nobody else would.

When he finished stacking all the crates that morning, instead of looking for more work like he usually did, Jason found himself heading towards the staff room to sit down. It was 9:56 AM. Jason stopped when he saw Jess crying there alone. He felt the urge to comfort her but didn't know how to do it. As he stood in the doorway she saw him and made a clumsy attempt to cover up what she had been doing.

'Sorry!' Jess wiped at her eyes with a tissue.

'It's okay,' said Jason. He didn't have an awful lot of experience in comforting people, though he had found people considered him to be very good at it. Jason just sat quietly and listened, like he did whenever people talked. Apparently that was all you needed to do to be good at comforting someone. Sometimes, it seemed, people just needed to talk.

'Did they let you go as well?'

'Oh you too?' Jess replied. 'Yeah they told me a couple days ago. It couldn't have come at a worse time. I've got a lot of my own stuff going on right now.'

Jess was one of the clerks. Jason didn't know exactly what she did at her desk, but clearly it wasn't of vital importance to the company. Only about half a dozen of the thirty-odd employees at the company were women, and Jess was one of only two that were around Jason's age. She was pretty. Jason had talked to her whenever the opportunity arose, which wasn't too often. She got plenty of attention from all the other men at work, and she seemed to enjoy it. Yet despite her popularity, she never ignored him like many of the other workers did. 'Smile Jason!' she had said more than once, apparently noticing the lack of expression on his face. Her smile had made it impossible for him to resist returning the gesture. He particularly liked her smile, but there wasn't much about her he didn't like. Her long blonde hair, her green eyes, the way her ever so slightly too small work shirt and pants hugged her slender frame. He was far too shy to ask any girls out, and Jess was far too extroverted and popular for him to even fantasize about dating, as much as he would have liked to. Even if he'd found the courage, and even if for some reason she was interested in him, which he was sure she wasn't, there was no point. She had a boyfriend. He had overheard her talking to him on the phone from time to time when he walked past the office cubicles.

'Want to talk about it?' Jason didn't know much about women, but he knew that was a question that was likely to unleash the floodgates of everything she had on her chest.

The next thirty minutes was like a blur for both of them. Jess did have a lot going on by regular people's standards, Jason thought. He always had a hard time relating to the problems of middle-class people. He remembered Rebecca who he sat next to in science in year twelve telling him how hard things were at home because her parents were divorcing. That sounds real tough, Jason remembered thinking. *Why don't you see how well you handle having scars burnt and cut into your chest?* Of course, he hadn't told her that, he hadn't told anybody that. He had just listened and tried to comfort her. Just like he was doing with Jess now. Giving people their metaphorical bowls of comforting soup could be even more satisfying than volunteering at the kitchen. It was all the same really, undoing one injustice at a time. Making the world an ever so slightly less depressing and dangerous place.

Jason supposed he could empathise with how

frustrating it was for her to lose her job only a couple months after taking out a loan for a new car. But he didn't feel sorry for her. He had always thought borrowing money was a bad idea. He didn't like having to rely on anybody else for anything. But borrowing money on a casual wage, for something that depreciated in value, was just silly. His interest piqued when she started talking about her relationship problems, though. The man she had been seeing for the past several months wasn't her boyfriend after all. Apparently he only wanted something casual, while she wanted more. Jason couldn't fathom why you wouldn't want something serious with a beautiful woman like Jess. As she talked about what was wrong with the relationship Jason couldn't help but feel she was holding back the extent of how bad things really were. He was harassing her she said. How so Jason asked. After sheepishly staring at her feet for a few seconds, Jess told him she had sent nude photos of herself to his phone and now he was threatening to send them to her friends and family. Jason couldn't begin to understand why you would send photos like that to anyone. Just voluntarily giving someone else that much power over you. He asked if this guy had sent her anything like that of himself. Apparently he had, but Jess had deleted them some time ago when she was angry with him. That was something else Jason didn't understand, throwing away that leverage. When Jason had asked her why she thought he was doing this, she had told him he had always been abusive and manipulative. Jason resisted the strong urge to ask why she had decided to date him in the first place.

Throughout the conversation, he was worried that the two of them would be interrupted. He was surprised they had the entire staff room to themselves for so long. It was fast approaching morning tea time though. The staff room would soon be flooded with people and they wouldn't be able to talk about anything this important. He hadn't connected with anyone like this in a long time. He couldn't let the conversation end here. Jason felt his heart racing. He hadn't been this nervous, since, since … *since my first kill,* he realised.

'What are you doing tonight?' he asked. He had no plans. There were no assignments anymore, and it was his night off from the soup kitchen. Jason always expected the worst. He braced himself for the disappointment that would come when she told him she was busy. He could hardly contain his glee when she said 'No plans.' Her eyes said more than that. Jason fumbled with suggestions for where to go and what to do. Thankfully, Jess picked up the ball.

'Meet me at The Belleview at nine for drinks. You know where it is, right?'

'Sure do,' he lied.

Thank Christ for Google, he thought as he headed back to work.

The Belleview turned out to be on Victoria Road, not too far from work. He must have walked past it a thousand times on the way to work, though it was on the opposite side of the road, and he'd never felt the need to take notice of where the local watering holes were. Stepping into the bar, Jason felt out of place. The Belleview was an upbeat, classy establishment. The few people in the bar were dressed in office attire. The barman, polishing a cocktail glass behind an elegant looking hardwood counter, was actually wearing a bow-tie. Jason was wearing his regular street clothes. He had omitted his glasses. He tolerated the extra attention the clear lenses attracted as he was walking home from work, but in here they were likely to be a conversation starter. Having to talk to some drunken stranger about them was the last thing he wanted. He had left his ballistic vest in his footlocker as well. If anyone hugged him or casually patted him on the back while he was wearing it, he would have some explaining to do about why his torso felt like stone. It had only happened once before when a university acquaintance had tapped him on the back to get his attention. He had stopped after the second tap, started feeling across Jason's back with his hand and had said 'Dude, what are you wearing?' Jason had told him he was wearing a back-brace due to a sporting injury. His classmate had seemed to accept the story, yet to Jason's annoyance, it had led to more questions about the nature of the injury and the expected recovery time. Fortunately, most people didn't know him well enough to touch him at all, which suited him just fine.

Meet me at The Belleview at nine Jess had said. Jason looked at his thick, military styled G-Shock watch as he sat in one of the booths in the pub. It was 8:23. He had been nervous sitting at home waiting.

He hated running late – but also wanted some time to scope out the place. He had observed the building from the front, and also from the laneway behind it. After entering and casually searching the accessible areas, Jason had established which windows would be easy enough to break out through in case of an emergency, and also where the staff room was if he needed to try and make an exit via the building's rear. Once he knew where all the exits were or could be made, Jason allowed himself to relax a little.

Another advantage to being so early was the pick of where to sit. Jason claimed the booth in the back corner. Having his back firmly against something meant one less direction he could be attacked from. By 9:35 his nervous anticipation had turned into annoyance. Jess was supposed to be here by now. Scenarios ran through his head, ranging from her being mugged on the way here to laughing with her friends about standing him up. Every scenario he came up with seemed unlikely to him, but he still couldn't shake the thoughts out of his head. Jason was also feeling increasingly uncomfortable just from his surroundings. He could barely tolerate it back when he was getting paid to be in a bar. There was a table several metres to his left where three men dressed in suits were sitting. He had noticed one of them nod in his direction and say something to the other two. The other two had both smirked and nodded. No doubt a joke at Jason's expense. Check out G.I. Joe in the corner with all his friends, Jason imagined the man saying. He had heard similar things in the past. He was only moderately aware of how out of place he looked. Dressed in military styled clothes, staring straight ahead, without a drink, by himself. He was practically begging people to talk about him. Jason was entertaining a detailed fantasy about splitting laughing man's head open. In his fantasy he walked over to the table, picked up the one unoccupied seat and swung it directly into the man's head. *Let's see how funny they think it is when their friend's skull gets caved in.* He wasn't going to of course. Jason had noticed the security cameras when he had scoped out the building, but even if there hadn't been any, there were still too many witnesses. Jason wasn't stupid enough to get caught punishing someone, even if they deserved it like this man did. Jason did think it was odd that he could be perfectly content one minute and planning to kill someone the next, although the issue didn't particularly bother him. He wondered if other people felt the same way, but it wasn't the kind of question you could ask.

His thoughts of murder disappeared the second he saw Jess. In a short, form-fitting purple dress she was turning heads. Jason's initial admiration and desire was quickly replaced with feelings of inadequacy. She had dressed to impress. *It's Friday night, of course she would,* he thought, feeling like an idiot. He did own a nice pair of suit pants and a collared shirt for job interviews, and he wished he'd worn them instead. As vulnerable as he felt leaving the house at night without his bullet-resistant vest on, he was now glad he had. The fabric vest still concealed his pistol. There was no way he would leave home without that under any circumstances. Taking his bulky jacket off, he could at least try and compensate for his lack of style with his physique. His work shirts covered up his muscles and tattoos, but the army undershirts he usually reserved for wearing under his vest didn't. He had just folded up the jacket and placed it next to him when she spotted him and waved. He stood up as she came over to meet him.

'I'm so sorry I'm late. I would have texted you but I forgot to take your number.'

'It's all good,' Jason replied. It was all good he thought. He didn't even feel the need to ask her why she had been running late. He was mesmerised by how green her eyes were. Much more striking than at work; it must have been the eyeliner. He didn't like girls who wore a lot of makeup, thinking it looked tacky and fake. But if there was a perfect amount of makeup to wear, as far as he was concerned, Jess had found it. The thin black eyeliner, lip gloss, and just the faintest hint of blush.

'What are you drinking?' she asked Jason. It was one of his least favourite questions, and it diverted him from thoughts of Jess' perfection. *Already*, he thought. His opposition to alcohol had caused him more than a few socially awkward moments over the years. The question always led the conversation down the same inevitable path. He would say he didn't drink. She would be taken back and ask why. He would want to tell her the truth, that his mother had been an alcoholic and that had really put him off drinking. In his experience telling people that led to awkward silences, so he'd try something more casual, like saying he just never got into it. Playing the designated driver card had got him off the hook in the past, but Jess knew he didn't own a car. He worried that she would be disappointed to be the only one drinking. For some reason Jason didn't understand, people didn't like drinking alone. She would probably try some form of peer pressure. Being a woman, it was more likely to be friendly peer pressure, though even when it was friendly Jason found being pressured to do something he wasn't comfortable with unbearable.

But he didn't want the night to go badly. He had been looking forward to it all day. More importantly, he didn't want to turn into that weird guy she had met for drinks once. He had a brief flashback to Lisa. This is how he had ended up with her. His one girlfriend. She had asked him out when they had worked together at the bar. Nobody had ever asked him out before, or since. In his attempts to impress her he had tried drinking with her on a handful of occasions, before realising it wasn't for him. He tolerated her drinking for as long as possible, but after a few months he had broken up with her. He had wondered at the time if he was the only nineteen-year-old who wasn't interested in drinking till the early hours of the morning. After they had broken up, with the exception of the obligatory staff Christmas party for the cleaning company he worked for two years ago, Jason hadn't been in a bar since.

Now he was back in a bar and about to betray his principles again. Jason shrugged defeatedly; making people smile did, after all, usually require a form of personal sacrifice. Of course, pretending he was someone he wasn't hadn't worked for him the last time – history could very well be repeating itself he thought – but just maybe things would be different this time. He hoped so at least, as he swallowed his pride.

'I haven't really decided yet. What are you having?'

She was having some kind of foreign cider he had never heard of. Jason ordered two from the bar. As he apprehensively tried the first sip, he was pleasantly surprised to find it had a sweet flavour. It didn't have that awful bitter taste he remembered beer having when he had dated Lisa.

The two of them talked, or rather, Jess talked and he listened. Jess had finished an arts degree at the University of Sydney several years ago. Jason felt slightly better about himself when he realised that Jess hadn't managed to do anything with her degree either. As the conversation progressed, he wondered if Jess was aware he was only saying one word for every thirty of hers. On more than one occasion he had thought of something to say, but couldn't gauge when it was his turn to speak, and before he knew it, the opportunity was gone. Regardless of whether she noticed his lack of input of not, she clearly didn't seem to mind. Her smile only got bigger as the night went on. By the time she had finished her first drink, Jason wasn't even halfway through his. She had called him a lightweight. He had actually smiled. It was a small smile, but a genuine one. She had told him he had better catch up while she went and got the next round. The guilt of betraying his principles came back while she was gone, but that didn't stop him from finishing his cider. The guilt disappeared as soon as she returned.

Jason felt the effects of the liquor about three quarters of the way through his second drink. He knew that being a non-drinker meant he had a low tolerance for alcohol. Jess was considerably smaller than he was but she didn't seem even the slightest bit inebriated. She had probably even had a few drinks before she had come out. Jason felt the surge of panic rise above any feelings of relaxation the alcohol itself might have given him. He tried to put a figure on how much his reaction time would be slowed right now. Ten percent? Fifteen perhaps? He wasn't very affected by alcohol yet, but if someone started a fight with him here, he needed all the advantage he could get, especially without half his armour. Thankfully, he had a plan.

When Jess finished her drink, he had suggested they get cocktails next. By her reaction, you would have thought he had come up with the best idea she had ever heard. When he went to the bar he asked the bartender for two fruit cocktails, one without alcohol.

'I'm the designated driver,' he added when the bartender raised his eyebrows. The non-alcoholic version of the cocktail was still surprisingly expensive. Twelve dollars. *I just paid twelve dollars to not get drunk.* Jason thought it was well worth it.

Midnight came before the two of them knew it. Jess had enjoyed talking; Jason had enjoyed listening and admiring her. This was called a symbiotic relationship, Jason thought, recalling a lecture on the subject he had attended in his first year of biomedical science. He gave a small laugh at his own wit. When Jess asked him what was so funny, he had quickly said he was just pleased with how well the night was going.

'When I went to work this morning I wasn't expecting I'd end up here.'

'Well the night's still young, who knows, it might get even better for you,' she said with a flirtatious smile that wasn't wasted on him. She put her hand on his thigh, ostensibly to help herself get up as she excused herself to go to the bathroom. Jason could see from the way she was walking that she was under the influence of alcohol now. His own mild intoxication had long worn off. She had downed three cocktails. Jason had offered to buy the second round with her money to keep his charade up.

She had surprised him when she came back by asking him if he wanted to come back to her place to watch a movie. He figured even if it was a chick flick he would enjoy spending more time with her.

The taxi ride was short, taking them to a small duplex in Summer Hill. Jason had been left to pay when she got out as soon as they pulled up. As she stumbled up her driveway Jason thought it must have been an oversight rather than a way to dodge the bill. She was drunk. He thought it would be a good idea for her to sit down and maybe have something to eat. He was disturbed when the first thing she had done, after spending a good couple of minutes trying to get her front door key to line up with the lock – Jason had offered to help but she had insisted she could do it – was open a bottle of white wine.

'Don't you think you've had enough?' he asked. She scoffed at the suggestion, poured him a glass without even asking if he wanted one, never noticing that he didn't touch it. She was drinking more than enough for the two of them.

Thinking back on the conversation the next day, Jason couldn't pinpoint the moment when the topic changed suddenly. One minute she was stroking his arms, running her fingers across the fine grooves the tattoo needles had left on his skin and complimenting him on how good his arms looked for the third time that evening. The next she was ranting about the man in her life. Thomas was his name apparently. Jason was surprised she hadn't brought him up yet. He had considered asking her about it, but they were having such a good time at the bar and he thought it might bring her down. For whatever reason, she was doing a good job of bringing herself down on her own right now. She talked about how much effort she had put into the relationship, and how little she had gotten back. She had a drink. She talked about how he had led her on for months, telling her they could be a couple, then she had realised he was just using her for sex. She had a drink. She talked about how he constantly treated her like she was an idiot, even though she was a university graduate and he had dropped out of high-school. She had a drink. She told him how he had kicked a hole in her wall and overturned her dresser while they were having an argument. She had a drink. They were on her couch in front of her television. She had been alternating between staring at it, though not really watching it, and looking at him during her spiel. Now she was giving him her full attention. As he stared back into her eyes, Jason felt like his heart was being pushed into a bed of nails. Her eyes had been so vibrant and green at the beginning of the night, but now they were swollen and red. He was surprised her eyeliner wasn't running like it tended to do in films, though she had smudged parts of it by dabbing at her misty eyes with tissues while she talked. Behind the puffiness in her eyes Jason saw something else. A look he recognised. He had seen it in the mirror as a teenager. She wanted someone to confide in but she didn't have anybody. Jason had a very good idea of what she wanted to confide. He swallowed deep and asked.

'Has he ever hurt you?' The answer was in her eyes immediately. By the time it reached her mouth it was a euphemism so tragically timid, Jason found it hard to hold back his own tears.

'Sometimes, when we have sex … I don't have a choice.' Her lip was trembling and it looked like it was taking every ounce of her willpower to maintain what little composure she had left.

'It's okay to cry,' he told her.

He had heard the line in a documentary film once. A wounded soldier in hospital was trying to talk to a medic about his friend who had been killed in action. His voice was cracking and high pitched and every few words he had to stop to try and compose himself. The medic had spoken that line and the soldier had just broken down and wept. Jason had never seen a man cry that hard before. Jess was crying harder than that now. She reached out and threw her arms around his neck and buried her face into his shoulder. She wept for a good ten minutes. Jason tried to think of some other comforting lines, but all that he could say was, 'It's okay Jess, it's okay.' He put his arms around her and held her while she got it all out. He closed his eyes, leant his head against her, and smiled faintly. Comforting a sobbing rape victim, he felt more at peace than he could ever remember.

By the time the crying stopped, her head had slipped down to his chest. It stayed there for several minutes before the feeling of her hand gently stroking his abs slowly drew him out of his bliss-like trance. At first he thought it might just be innocent cuddling. That thought disappeared when her hand found its way down to his crotch. He turned his head down to look at her just as she turned hers up to look at him. Jason had only slept with two women. Lisa, his ex-girlfriend, and Amy, the one night-stand he had had after the breakup with Lisa. He had felt dirty after the one night-stand. He hadn't felt any connection with Amy emotionally, not like the overwhelming emotion he was feeling for Jess right now. He had finally found someone who might be able to understand his pain. He had tried to hint at the kinds of things that had happened to him as a child to Lisa, but hers was a sheltered upbringing. She could only feel sorry for him and Jason didn't want sympathy, he wanted someone to understand him. The possibility he had found someone who might be able to understand his pain brought him the joy he had yearned for all his life.

No words were spoken. Clothes started to come off within seconds of them kissing. He helped her take her dress off, she struggled with the buckle on his tactical belt and he had to unlatch it for her. The time-consuming task of unlacing his combat boots caused a second awkward break in the otherwise smooth flow of events. She straddled his naked body and eased him into her right there on the couch. He had felt bad when he had climaxed after only a few minutes, but she seemed just as satisfied as he was. They laid down and cuddled together afterwards, covered in a throw blanket that had been resting over the back of the couch. They made some small talk, Jason couldn't even remember what about. It occurred to him that there was only one question he needed the answer to.

'What's Thomas' last name?'

'Williams, why?' she replied with only mild curiosity in her voice.

'Oh I just thought I might know him, don't worry I don't,' Jason lied.

Jess had already mentioned the major real-estate agency Thomas worked for, though not the specific office. It should have been easy enough already to find him, but it never hurt to have too much information. Jess fell asleep. Jason stayed awake for a long time. The warmth of Jess' skin against him mingled with his plans for Thomas. It was a feeling he wanted to savour.

Chapter 9

Howard frowned. It had happened even faster with this one. Scarcely more than two days and already there was no fight left in her. She'd stopped resisting. Stopped entertaining him. The exhilaration had almost all been in the planning. The capture hadn't disappointed. Nor had the first conquest of her body. And this time he had anticipated each subsequent conquest to give less and less of a rush. But already? How could she look so lifeless in such a short time? She wasn't even really looking at him anymore. It was like she was staring right through him. Howard could feel his manhood starting to go limp inside her.

'You love it don't you you fucking whore?' Howard smiled, the smile that came with knowing he was now confident enough to taunt his victims, but the expression soon faded. She didn't react. He grabbed her by the neck and shook her.

'Look at me you filthy little slut!' Nothing. Nothing at all. He may as well be shaking a rag doll. Her eyes were dead. Howard looked at the ceiling and screamed in rage.

Maybe the first one had actually lasted longer than average. Maybe most of them would entertain him for a paltry amount of time. He tightened his fists. The thought of so much effort for so little reward infuriated him. He slid his naked body off hers and got off the bed. He checked her restraints before he went upstairs. They were as secure as they had been two days ago. He didn't want her breaking free now that he was about to kill her.

Rochelle Delfiki wasn't going anywhere. Severely weakened by the attack, and more so by not having been given anything to eat or drink since then, the single mother and part-time liquor store attendant might not have even realised if her cable ties had been removed. Her last coherent thought had been about her two-year-old daughter Lani. Her mother babysat the nights she worked. She had been on her way home to see the two most important people in her life. Pretty much the only two people in her life since her boyfriend realised he wasn't going to talk her into an abortion and left. Her mother had told her it was all you could expect from a man. Her father had disappeared years ago. It was just the three of them. They would always have each other. Until two days ago, that had been true.

Rochelle heard him opening the door and coming back down the stairs, but her brain failed to attach any meaning to it. It may as well have been white noise. Her brain did register the kitchen knife in his hand. She realised she was about to die. She hoped he'd do it quickly.

Let's see how long I can make this whore suffer, Howard thought, as he pressed the tip of the knife against her temple, hoping the feel of the blade would elicit a response. Nothing. Pushing down slightly he relished the sense of the blade seeming to decide whether it was going to break her skin before the threshold was crossed. A thin trail of blood slid down her face and a faint moan of complaint came through her duct taped mouth. Disappointing. He felt a sudden urge to slit her throat, but suppressed it. *I'm stronger than that,* he thought to himself. His mouth curved into a sardonic smile as he spoke.

'Have you ever tried double penetration?'

Her look of dull confusion gave way to one of sheer horror, realisation.

'That got your fuckin' attention didn'it?'

Pinning her down with his left hand he forced himself back inside her, getting a few thrusts in while he tried to hold her head steady. She managed to turn her head to the side, though that suited him just fine. He brought the knife down through the side of her neck. The sound of her choking on her own blood was particularly satisfying, but it was the look in the eye turned towards him that was the real winner.

Her head convulsed wildly, and Howard struggled to keep the blade inside her as she moved. He wondered if she knew she was just causing even more damage. The blade was only a couple inches inside her, but the entry wound just got wider every time she moved her head. Howard laughed. Now this was a game he liked. Here was something he could get used to.

Only he knew it wouldn't last forever, but that didn't mean he couldn't make the most of it. When her frenetic movements showed signs of slowing he pulled out the knife and brought it down again.

Looks like there's still plenty life left in you after all eh?

There was more life, but not nearly enough. The fourth stab to her butchered neck failed to register any change in her eyes, only the sound of her short-ragged breaths filled the room. Howard was about to finish her when he had a better idea. *Let the bitch fuckin' bleed out.* He pulled himself out of her, wiping the last dribble of semen from his cock onto her thigh before he turned and climbed the stairs. Before he'd gotten her back to his house he'd already decided he was going to dump this one at the foreshore somewhere. Not until the middle of the night of course, she was fine where she was till then, but he needed the body found soon enough. His work needed the attention. Centennial Park had been all well and good, but he needed to keep things interesting.

Still naked, Howard rinsed the knife in his kitchen sink's cold water before putting it back in the rack with the others. He'd salvaged something good from an otherwise disappointing victim, but it still wasn't enough. Something was missing and Howard couldn't place what it was. He scratched at his temple, oblivious to the fact he was spreading the blood on his fingers to his head in the process. He needed a way to make this more exciting. More of a rush. Two girls at once? That seemed like a good idea. Howard had enjoyed the one time he had picked up two whores, even if their services for the night had cost him damn near a whole week's wage. But kidnapping two girls at once did seem rather complicated.

As he stared out his kitchen window, Howard caught sight of a young girl and boy jumping on the trampoline in the backyard of the house behind and to the right of his. Howard couldn't see the trampoline, but he could see the young girl's midriff and short shorts as her body bounced above his view of the fence line. She couldn't have been older than nine. Howard liked how young girls dressed these days. He had many images of young girls dressed like that on his computer, and many more with them wearing nothing at all. He kept them in a folder separate from all the other erotic images on his computer. They were different. He seldom looked at them, reserving them for when the images of regular whores just weren't exciting enough. Everyone had pornography these days. It was so much easier than when Howard had been a child. He had once swapped about a hundred football cards for one old and partially torn pornographic magazine with an older boy at school. Today images like that were free, and only a few clicks away. But the images of the young girls, you weren't supposed to have pornography like that, Howard knew. There was a particular thrill that came with having something that wasn't allowed.

Gripping the edge of the sink, Howard grinned as he leaned closer to the window, watching. It seemed so obvious now. The young girl smiled with glee as she jumped even higher, trying to outdo her older brother though not quite able to reach his height. *I got somethin' else you'll really enjoy you dirty little whore,* thought Howard. But no. It couldn't be her. She was too close to his home, and he didn't want the police snooping around near where he lived. He'd have to go out and find another. But that was fine. Most of the fun was in the hunt.

Howard whistled as he flicked the button down on his kettle. He had skipped his morning coffee ritual for the little treat he had in the basement, but now that he was done with her he still had an hour before he had to get to work. Or so he thought. The shrill call of his phone ringing drowned out the sound of the water starting to bubble. He walked over to the wall and lifted up the receiver.

'Uh, hello?'

'Howard, can you please explain why Mrs Hindmarsh just called me to ask why only her front room carpets were cleaned?' The voice demanded.

Fuck! Howard hated speaking to the old prick at the best of times. And now the miserable bastard knew he'd skimped out on his work.

'Ah, Mr Reed, I'm so glad you called.'

'Don't bullshit me, answer my question!'

'Well uh, I thought she only wanted the front rooms done, and uh, well, I uh …'

'Howard, do you think I'm an idiot?'

'Oh no, no, Mr Reed. Look I, uh, I'm real sorry about that. If you like, I, uh, I'll head back down and finish the job.'

'Oh you'd do that for me would you Howard? How fucking kind. Get your stupid ass down there right now and I'll consider not firing you.'

'Oh yes, thank you Mr Reed, I'll get on that right now, yessir, Howard's all over this one like–'

His boss hung up.

'Fuck!' Howard screamed. 'Miserable stupid fuckin', fuckin' … fuckin' fuck!' He picked up his empty coffee mug and smashed it into the wall. He stormed to the bathroom and stood in the shower. Usually he had to play with the taps for a couple minutes to find the elusive warmth between its two predominant temperatures, freezing cold and scalding hot. But today he just turned on the cold and stood with his head down, watching the blood melt off his skin, taking all the magic of the morning with it as it went down the drain. Half a minute later he stepped out and dried himself, and after finding yesterday's overalls on the floor among the other clothes in his room, dressed and begrudgingly got in his van to go back to the Hindmarsh residence. As he reached across to the passenger's side to grab the remains of a half-eaten candy bar he had just spotted, Howard caught a glimpse of himself in the rear-view mirror. He thought he looked tired, weak even, nothing like how he'd felt earlier in the basement. He scowled at his reflection, and was relieved when he leaned back into his seat and out of the mirror's gaze. *It isn't fair*, he thought. *If only he knew, if only they all knew, how powerful I really am.*

Chapter 10

The sweet smell of Jess' hair was the first thing Jason noticed when he woke up in the morning. Next he realised how numb his left arm was, having been wedged under her half the night. It wasn't bothering him enough to move though. He stroked his right hand down from her shoulder to her stomach, feeling a little giddy as two of his fingers caressed the edge of her breast. He would have been happy to stay like this all day. He'd already decided he was in love with her, that he'd die to protect her. He felt closer to her already than he had to Lisa at the peak of their three-month relationship. He let himself daydream about where this new relationship with Jess would take the two of them. He nuzzled his nose into her hair, and kissed the nape of her neck.

Jess stirred. 'Hey,' she called out. Jason didn't pick up on the apprehension and curiosity that tinged her tone.

'I didn't realise you were awake,' he whispered into her ear as he smiled.

'Jason?' This time Jason could tell from the tone

it was a question rather than a statement, though that was just silly. Clearly she just wasn't much of a morning person, I mean, seriously, who else would he be?

Jess reached up and started rubbing her temple with her hand. 'Jesus Christ I don't even remember coming home,' she said.

'We got the taxi remember?'

'Yeah … of course.' Jess ran her hand through her hair. 'I have to go to the bathroom,' she said, untangling her limbs from his and sitting up. Her detachment from his body made Jason feel like he had lost a limb of his own. Head in her hands, Jess spied her knickers on the floor and put them back on before she stood up. As she turned to head towards the bathroom she glanced at him then covered her breasts with one arm, which struck Jason as odd. She definitely hadn't had a problem with him seeing them last night. His confusion eased moments later when the sound of Jess vomiting interrupted the silence. Of course, she had a hangover, no wonder she was acting strangely.

Jason had only thrown up once that he could remember. He had been twelve and had eaten an entire half kilo bag of macadamia nuts from the cupboard in his foster parent's home. He remembered how unpleasant the sensation had been, and felt a world of compassion for what he could hear, even if it was her own fault. He wanted to help her, but he couldn't remember what he would have wanted the time he had been vomiting.

'Can I do anything for you?' he called out. Jason thought that was the best question to ask. In his experience, most people would have asked something along the lines of 'Are you okay?', which he thought would be a particularly stupid question. Throwing up wasn't what people did when they were okay.

'I'm fine!' came the curt reply.

Jason's expression changed from concern to genuine hurt. He didn't like it when strangers were short with him, let alone somebody he actually cared about. He sat up on the couch wondering what to do. His clothes strewn across the lounge room floor were bothering him. Gathering them and putting them back on solved both the issue of untidiness and the feeling of vulnerability that was returning to him. Jess' home was unfamiliar territory, after all, and it always paid to be prepared. He felt a surge of panic when he saw his pistol still in its holster at the back of his pants. Had Jess seen it? No, he thought. She would have reacted for sure. Thankfully the way his pants had fallen to the ground concealed the holster from view. He had still been careless though. Jason tried to imagine what excuse he could have come up with had Jess discovered it, but nothing seemed plausible. It was exactly the kind of lapse of judgement Jason could berate himself for all day. However, he was still riding the high of what he had discovered with Jess, and quickly pushed the thoughts aside. Once he had finished dressing he collected Jess' bra and dress from the floor. He folded the dress and put it on the arm rest of the couch, then placed the bra neatly on top of it, before putting the throw blanket back over the couch the way he remembered it being when he first saw it.

Everything now back in order, Jason sat attentively on the couch, for about thirty-five seconds until his restlessness got the better of him. He went to her fridge, perusing its contents before selecting a bunch of grapes, then wandered back over to the TV. Jess had a rather large collection of DVDs in the cabinet below her TV. He opened the cabinet's glass doors and smiled. Being a minimalist he didn't own any DVDs himself, but he was perfectly happy to enjoy watching someone else's. He sat cross-legged in front of the TV and started sorting through the collection. In the distance he heard the sounds of a shower being turned on and smiled. He hoped it would make Jess feel better. Over the next several minutes he made a pile of nine films he wanted to see. He was eagerly searching for a tenth, hoping to make a nice even figure when Jess came back around the corner draped in a towel. He smiled at her. She stared back at him.

'What, are you doing?'

'Well, we never did watch that movie,' he said with a smile before putting a grape in his mouth.

'What movie?'

'Umm, you invited me back to your place to watch a movie.'

Jess raised her eyebrows and Jason's smiled faltered. 'Would you like to get something to eat first, or something?' he suggested to break the silence.

Jess took a deep breath. 'Look, Jason, I don't feel very well and I've got a lot of stuff to do today

...' her voice trailed off and she made a circular gesture with her index figure.

'Can I help you with any of it?'

'What?' Jess asked. She scrunched up her eyes and cocked her head slightly to the side. 'Look, no, umm, I just want to go back to sleep okay? I had a great time and you're a nice guy, I'll talk to you at work okay?' She turned before he could reply and went to her bedroom.

Jason's heart sank as he heard her door close. The various plans he had for the day – breakfast, a movie, more talking, more movies, more sex – came crashing down, shattering around him as if they were in a glass jar pushed off a high shelf. He sat there awkwardly for a minute, taking the news in. He suddenly felt unsure of what to do with his pile of DVDs. Or the half-finished bunch of grapes in his hand. Did you put down the food you were eating when you were asked to leave? Or did you take it with you? Jason searched his memory for the social etiquette for this situation. He stared blankly at the TV, taking no notice of his reflection in its cold, dark surface. He was fairly certain Jess wasn't coming back from her room. Was he supposed to show himself out? The host was supposed to show guests out. Jason was sure of that etiquette, though he couldn't say he understood the reasoning for it. He particularly hated it when people stood at the front door and watched him as he left. Was there something interesting about him walking to their front gate and turning one way or the other?

Confused, Jason eventually decided to show himself out. Jess didn't even hear him close the front door behind him. She was already asleep.

Jason walked to the nearest cross street and quickly recognised where he was. He had been walking around this city his whole life. He absent-mindedly finished the bunch of grapes as he slowly walked home, his mind a confused mess trying to figure out what had gone wrong.

Chapter 11

The rest of the weekend went very slowly for Jason. After walking home he decided to watch Judge Dredd, his favourite film, on his laptop to cheer him up. The concept of a policing force where each officer was the judge, jury and executioner just seemed so efficient Jason couldn't fathom why the governments of the world hadn't adopted it years ago, but he mainly liked the film for its cheesy action and comic relief. But today he could only manage a weak smile where he normally chuckled heartily. He read an entire chapter of the latest book on his kindle, before he realised he hadn't attributed any meaning to any of the words and didn't have a clue what was going on. He often found concentrating difficult, but now it was damn right impossible. It had taken him his whole life to find someone he thought would understand him, and the prospect of waiting till Monday to see her seemed unbearable.

He could empathise with Jess' hangover pain, in theory at least as he had never suffered from one himself. Over the years he had heard plenty of people complaining about how much they hurt. Why these people kept subjecting themselves to the pain weekend after weekend, knowing full well the consequences, Jason didn't understand. There were a lot of things Jason didn't understand. Sometimes he felt like he was the last sane person alive.

Today he couldn't understand why Jess wasn't making the effort to spend time with him. He would have made the effort to keep her happy, no matter how much pain he was in. But he knew most people weren't as considerate as he was.

Saturday dragged into Sunday. After an early morning workout Jason seriously considered going over to Jess' house to see if she felt up to doing something yet. After debating the issue with himself for well over an hour he decided against it. He didn't want to come across as too eager, even though he was. Sunday seemed to take twice as long as Saturday to end, but the thought of seeing her at work the next day kept his spirits high.

Jason was disappointed when Jess didn't turn up for work on Monday, confused when she was still absent Tuesday, and deeply worried when she hadn't come in on Wednesday. On the morning tea break Wednesday Jason approached Rick and asked him if he knew where she was.

'Man I've got no idea, she didn't call in sick so I guess not turning up was her way of letting me know she didn't want the last few weeks of work here.'

'Can you call her?'

'Already tried, she didn't answer. I did call her emergency contact, you know, duty of care and all that, they just said she's fine. So my responsibility is covered, that's all I care about.' Rick let out a short laugh and went back to reading the newspaper.

Jason didn't see anything to laugh about. He could understand her not wanting to work there anymore. Counting down his final days of guaranteed employment wasn't exactly enjoyable. Ironically Jason was working there on a full-time basis now. One of the other casual forklift drivers had quit upon being given notice and Jason had been given his shifts. As they said, the candle sometimes flickered brightest before it went out. But Jess had told him she would see him at work. Jason cursed himself for not asking for her phone number. To be fair he had been seeing her practically every day at work for the last eight months and had no reason to think that would change, but it never hurt to be over prepared. Jason knew that.

What was really bothering him was that Jess hadn't made any effort to contact him. They had had such a good time together! And she could easily get in contact with him through someone at work. He was aching to see her, surely she must feel the same way about him. She had to. They were meant to be together.

Weren't they?

The more he thought about it, the more he worried something had happened to her. It seemed like the only rational explanation. Sure, Rick had said she was okay, according to her emergency contact anyway. But who was that? What if it was Thomas? And what if Thomas was lying?

He couldn't leave it another day. When he finished work that afternoon he decided to walk to Jess' home. Her duplex in Summer Hill wasn't far from the warehouse in Marrickville. A twenty-five-minute walk according to Google Maps; Jason did it in just under nineteen, concluding that Jess was just being lazy by driving to work. He felt a little self-conscious to be walking so fast. He would have run, but from experience as a teenager running in public drew an awful lot of attention. Unless you were dressed for jogging of course, and Jason wouldn't have been caught dead wearing his gym clothes outside of the gym.

Stopping outside her house, Jason observed for signs of trouble, and found himself strangely disappointed to not find any. Her car was in the driveway. Lifting up her mailbox he found it empty – it had either been collected today or she hadn't gotten any. This all meant nothing though. Jason knew first hand just how easy it was to conceal a murder, for a while at least. He approached the front door, hesitated, then decided to knock.

'Just a minute.'

Hearing Jess' voice brought on a flood of emotions. He was relieved she was okay, but the fact she was raised more questions. As he stood there searching his brain for answers he didn't even realise it had taken Jess more than a couple minutes to open the door. It eased open the four inches the inside chain would allow. Jason hadn't been concerned when the first expression he had read on Jess' face through the gap had been surprise. He began to feel anxious when that surprise gave way to one other than happiness. Jason was having trouble reading the expression on her face, but he sensed it wasn't a positive one.

'Jason?'

'Hi Jess,' Jason smiled, hoping Jess would give him one in return. She didn't.

'What are you doing here?'

Now it was Jason's turn to be taken back. What was he doing here? What did she think he was doing here? Trying hard to control his frustration, he attempted to answer her perverse question.

'Well, I, you said you'd see me at work and when you didn't show up I was worried ...'

Jess said nothing. Jason still couldn't read her expression.

'I didn't get your number so ...' he continued.

'Yeah well I decided I didn't want to work there anymore.'

'Okay. Well, um, would you like to do something tonight? I just finished work.'

'I have plans tonight Jason.'

'Ah, well, what about tomorrow?' Jason saw the frown develop on Jess' face. That must mean she was busy tomorrow as well. 'Or Friday,' he added quickly, 'actually any night is good with me really.' He was rostered on to work at the soup kitchen Friday and Saturday night, but he would have cancelled that in a heartbeat to spend time with her.

Jess was silent for a while, then she sighed and spoke. 'Look, Jason, last Friday was fun, okay, but that's all it was. You're a nice guy but I'm not looking for anything right now. I've got a lot of things to sort out and I need to get back to it.'

If there was one thing Jason had felt a lot of in his life it was pain. The pain he felt now was different from anything he had felt before. He felt it welling up inside his stomach. He didn't know whether to cry, beg or scream. But he knew he had to try and ignore it. Just for now. He had to stop this conversation from ending and he was only going to get one shot at it.

'But, well, can I get your number? Maybe once you sort some things out and you are looking for something we could catch up.'

'I don't think that's a good idea. Look I have to go now.' She took a last look at him, and Jason sensed some sympathy in her expression. 'I'm sorry,' she added as she closed the door.

* * *

'Who the fuck was that?' The voice was dazed and clearly unhappy to be awake.

'Mormons,' Jess said, thinking fast as she turned around to face him.

'Hmmph, fucking cunts.' He sat on the lounge and turned on the TV.

'Did you still want to get pizza for dinner again?' Jess asked, hoping to completely change the subject. The last thing she needed right now was another jealous rant. She wouldn't have heard the end of it if he had found out who was at the door. Thank god he had fallen asleep after sex.

'Yeah, and this time try not to forget to order something to drink.' The voice was condescending as usual.

Jess dialled the pizza store. This time she didn't 'fuck up' the order, as Thomas had so eloquently put it when the pizzas had arrived last night. Deep down Jess knew he was just freeloading and using her for sex, but she pushed those thoughts away. She was good at doing that. She was also good at clinging to the hope that he would change.

She sat down beside him and he casually threw his arm around her shoulder without looking away from the football match on TV. Jess closed her eyes and smiled. These were the times she liked most. He was content. Content meant there wouldn't be any drama. It was always her fault when there was drama. Thomas had successfully drilled that into her, or rather, he had built on the groundwork Jess' father had laid many years before by treating her mother like a doormat.

Jess spared a thought for Jason before she snuggled into Thomas. She did feel sorry for the guy, but there was something not right about him. She just couldn't put her finger on what it was.

Chapter 12

The two of hearts. The two of motherfucking hearts. Who the fuck does this guy think he is? This is the kind of thing that happens in bad cop shows. People just don't do this shit in real life.

It was the week after Jess rejected Jason on her front door step that Detective Ames found himself shocked for the first time in his career since that whole debacle with the McIntosh kid. Brad McIntosh had been six years old. Brad McIntosh had a particularly bad case of attention deficit disorder. Brad McIntosh had proved just too stressful for his father to deal with. At least that's what the forensic psychiatrist had said. Brad McIntosh had been found face down in the family swimming pool with bruising on the back of his neck, indicating he had been held under water. His father had only gotten eight years. Anxiety disorder. An abusive childhood of his own. Low frustration tolerance. Apparently that was mitigating circumstances to drown your son. *Low frustration tolerance*. What the fuck did that even mean? Why don't we just call it what it really is.

You're an angry fuck of a father who can't handle his shit. Goddamn shrinks were coming up with pretentious names for all kinds of horse-shit psychological conditions these days. The prick would be eligible for parole next year, and for the last seven years he'd had cable TV and three meals a day. A lot more than he deserved, as far as Ames was concerned. Like a lot of cops, Ames was all too often disappointed with the lenient sentences these monsters got. Sometimes he wished someone would do society a favour and just kill the sick bastards.

They could start by killing whatever sociopath had butchered the poor girl they'd found naked on Maroubra beach three days ago. Found by a pair of surfers at dawn, the evidence showed she'd been dragged to the sand from the south end carpark. The similarities couldn't help but remind Ames of that Steiner girl they'd found three months ago. The profile wasn't a perfect match though. Kelly Steiner had been found face down, clothed and with her purse, though the boys at forensics seemed to think she'd been dressed post mortem. A collection of bruises, particularly around the neck. Cause of death: strangulation. Injuries to her wrists and ankles indicated she'd been forcible restrained for several days.

That last factor had been one of the few similarities with the new girl. Aside from the glaring fact that they'd found another young woman dead in a public place. This one was naked and face up. No ID. And she didn't have bruises around the neck, she'd upgraded to multiple stab wounds there, her obvious cause of death. They both, however, were found with their limbs unevenly splayed, indicating they'd just been dropped after they were dragged. That told Ames the victims were unknown to the killer. He'd had seen it more times than he cared to remember, the wife stabbed in a jealous rage once her extramarital affair was discovered, the mother beaten to death with a hockey stick because her drug addicted son needed the inheritance now. When the killer loved the victim on some level, they almost always gave the corpse some form of dignity. Laying them down gently, placing the hands by their sides so they looked like they could be sleeping, closing their eyelids. This girls' eyes were wide fucking open. Ames had found himself staring at the gaping holes in her neck whenever he looked at her, anything that would take the attention away from the twisted expression of horror in her eyes as they stared right through him.

Still, murder victims not knowing their attackers wasn't too unusual, but Ames knew it had to be the same killer. What were the odds there were two similar psychopathic murderers in the one city?

Even before the autopsy report had been completed, his suspicions had been strengthened when they called him about the playing card. He'd reached his peak threshold for shock by the time they told him about it. When they clarified they'd found it in her vaginal canal, he took the additional news rather placidly.

When the full report had come the next day, they'd matched the rope fibres on her ankles to the same type of nylon found on the other girl. The wrist wounds were made with the same sized cable ties. The playing card came from at least the same deck design as the last one. More than enough to convince a jury they were committed by the same killer on their own, even if there was nothing terribly unique about any of it. The ropes and ties were the kind available at any hardware store. The cheap playing card design had mass-produced written all over it. But none of that mattered, because the semen was a perfect match. If the killer had wanted them to know it was him, the semen itself was sufficient. But no. Apparently he had to leave something else on them. Some kind of perverted reverse trophy. Ames pictured a deck of fifty cards in this sick fuck's house, just waiting for new victims.

The girl had been quickly identified. She matched a missing person's report filed by her distraught mother the day after she disappeared. Ames had quickly pulled the video footage from the petrol station across the road from the liquor store she worked at, the last place she had been seen. The video camera footage from inside the store showed her locking up, but unfortunately there was no camera in the car park. They didn't know why she hadn't been able to make it from the front door to her car only fifteen metres away. The footage from the station, however, showed a white van entering the liquor store car park at 11:08 and leaving at 11:42. Rochelle Delfiki had locked up at 11:31. If the van hadn't taken her, the owner should at least have seen something. Unfortunately the footage had been too far away for a licence plate check, or even a look at the driver. It was a plain white van, but at least it was a start.

Dr Ryan Edwards, a police psychologist, was brought in to address Ames' team now that they knew they were dealing with a serial killer. 'This killer's pattern is already clearly established, subsequent victims will almost certainly fit the same profile. Late teen to early twenties, slim attractive women,' Edwards had said.

Oh gee that's helpful, thought Ames, *I guess we'll just keep an eye on everyone who meets that description and we'll catch him the next time he strikes.* Thinking that most of the officers actually would be thrilled with the prospect of being assigned to keep an eye on all the good-looking young women in the city, Ames had laughed out loud in the middle of the briefing. When Dr Edwards gave him a scolding look and questioned what was so funny, Ames only shrugged.

'We're looking for a man who clearly has a lot of resentment towards women,' Edwards continued, 'he's sexually immature, likely to be in his mid-twenties, by physically fit and live at home with his parents. He probably owns a large collection of violent pornography.' Ames closed his eyes and tuned out. Edwards sounded like he was reading straight from some kind of catch-a-psychopath manual, and even if this bullshit turned out to be true, it wasn't particularly helpful until they actually had suspects to match the profile with.

Ames had held the press conference a couple hours after yesterday's psych brief. When he'd stated the same murderer had also killed Kelly Steiner, it had turned the event into a circus. Looking at the headline in today's issue of *The Daily Telegraph*, Ames wished he hadn't disclosed the information about the playing card. He couldn't help but feel responsible for the nickname the sorry excuse for journalists at that paper had come up with. Jack-knife Joker. Whatever they were paying the journalist who had pulled that one out of his ass, it was clearly too much. Ames hadn't even told the media what playing cards had been found on the victims, it was important to hold some key information from the press, but naturally the newspaper had gone with the most provocative choice in the deck. But jack-knife? They didn't even know what kind of knife had been used on the second victim – forensics said it could just be a kitchen knife, and a reasonably blunt one at that – and the first victim hadn't even been stabbed. Not that the tabloids ever really cared about coherency. Besides, it was the only paper who had used the name. Ames hoped it wouldn't catch on.

At least the murder was all over the news. The killer's DNA and fingerprints weren't in police records, and they didn't have any witnesses yet, but with any luck, the publicity might jog someone's memory enough to give them a lead.

'Well looks like we're taking a break from waiting around for a lead, they need us to take an initial look at a shooting death at an apartment in Paddington,' said Detective White as he approached Ames' desk, 'GDs said it's hardly worth our effort, place was locked up tight from inside, single occupant lived alone, left a suicide note, the shotgun he put in his mouth is registered to him, but, you know …'

Ames sighed. 'Yeah, I know.' It fell under their jurisdiction until forensics made their assessment, which meant they had to go out there and follow procedure, basically just put a tick in another fucking bureaucratic box.

'Another day in paradise,' said White, 'wanna head now?'

'Yeah yeah just give me a minute.' White nodded and turned to leave.

Ames closed his eyes and started rubbing his temples. Of all the creative ways that people found to take the coward's way out, a shotgun in the mouth was his least favourite. They'd turned up to one last year and to be fair the guy had actually had the common decency to arrange a heap of towels in a circle around himself first. It had ensured the blood had only pooled within the neat circle, not that it had made much difference in reducing the mess overall. Blood, brains, skull fragments and a few other former body parts that couldn't be neatly slotted into those three categories with the naked eye alone were streaked against the wall over a space of about five meters. The man had actually owned a rifle as well, though it had been neatly stowed in his gun safe. If he'd really wanted to make things less unpleasant for the police, the paramedics, and the cleaners for that matter, he could have eaten a bullet out of the rifle instead. It would have guaranteed the same result, though with about a quarter of the mess.

Ames managed a brief smirk. *Guarantees the same result, with only a quarter of the mess.* In his mind's eye, he could see it as a jingle in a public awareness campaign that would never get approval from the advertising standard's board. He knew it was morbid, but still, he genuinely thought the world would be a nicer place if the people who decided to end it all would at least put some research into how to do it properly. The worst one he'd seen had been his second year on the job. Some fuckstick had put a sawn-off shotgun in his mouth and angled it almost parallel to the ground and somewhat to the right, which had only resulted in blowing out half his face. He'd managed to get it right the second time with the shell in the other barrel. Yeah. Some people actually needed multiple attempts to even blow their brains out properly.

Ames looked over at the documents on the dividing wall next to his desk. He could just make out the bottom of the photograph of him and his father under the mess of notes that had been pinned above it. It was one of the few photographs he had of the two of them. They were standing together after his graduation ceremony from the police academy in

Goulburn. His father was actually smiling. Not much of a smile, but any form of emotion on the face of Norman Ames was a rarity. Norman had still been in the police force himself at the time. Thirty-two years, the overwhelming majority of it working for the highway-patrol. In his late-teens, Ames had actually thought becoming a police officer would give him and his father something to talk about. His father, however, had greeted the news with his usual indifference to anything Ames did. Sure there'd been a pat on the back and a joke about laying down the law together, and then it had gone back to watching the TV in silence. Ames had wondered more than once if his career choice had been motivated entirely by trying to connect with his father by following in his footsteps. Well, kind of following in his footsteps. Giving out speeding fines full-time was considered the bottom of the food chain within the police force. Ames had set his sights several rungs higher on detective from the get go. Not that his father had seen him make it that far. Non-Hodgkin's lymphoma was a cunt of a disease. The doctors had given him six months. Norman had held out for two years, which Ames sometimes thought had been purely out of spite. The man had never exactly liked adhering to other people's schedules. Ames knew his promotion definitely wouldn't have brought the two any closer though. He'd actually been worried about resentment from his father for being overtaken in rank. He had to admit, there was something about that that just seemed to disturb the natural order of things.

Kind of pathetic really, isn't it Brendan? Some men might have joined to continue their father's legacy, but all we really wanted was some kind of approval. And we didn't even get that, did we?

'Get fucked,' Ames said under his breath to the thought in his mind.

He stood and started following after White, feeling content to leave the photograph buried where it was.

Chapter 13

Thomas. He had to be the problem, Jason thought. He was still hurting Jess, placing such a drain on her that she wasn't free to be with him. It was the only logical explanation he could think of. Even if Jess had told him she still wanted to be with Thomas, Jason wouldn't have believed her. The only logical explanation for that would be that Thomas was making her lie. And, of course, there was only one permanent solution to solving this problem.

'You look stressed mate.'

Jason broke out of a blank stare. He had been sitting on the forklift looking dead ahead for a few minutes. He turned to Rick, who was standing a couple feet to his right. How long he had been standing there watching him, Jason could only guess.

'Um, I guess so,' Jason mumbled.

'Yeah well those crates were supposed to go on the truck, not back on the shelf.'

Jason looked at the crates he had last set down. *Shit*. Rick was right. If there was one thing Jason couldn't stand, it was incompetence, even worse when it was his.

'I, I'm sorry.' He put his head in his hands.

'Geez it's okay mate.' Jason picked up on the change of tone in Rick's voice. That was sympathy.

'Worried about not having a job much longer, hey?'

Relieved to have been handed an out, Jason nodded.

'I know it must be hard mate. I wish we could keep you on, but to be honest I don't think we're going to be open for business much longer at all. Why don't you take the rest of the day off? Just finish putting those crates on the truck and you can go. I'll still mark you down as finishing at five.'

Jason looked at his watch. It was 12:36. 'Really? Hey thanks.' Jason felt a brief surge of happiness for the first time all week.

'Don't mention it. Take it easy mate. See you Monday.'

An almost three-day weekend stretched out ahead of him. It didn't take him long to decide what he was going to do with it. The most effective way to get violent thoughts out of one's system was to act on them. He knew that from experience. If he didn't get it out of his system, it would take weeks to slowly ebb away, and Jason didn't think being angry for such a long period of time was very healthy. He started walking to the main road, quickly finding an internet café. For the second time in his life, he was going to do some serious hunting. Just the thought of it brought back all the memories of the first time.

Chapter 14

It had taken thirteen years before Jason made a concerted effort to find Peter, thirteen years since that night in Peter's apartment when he was a child.

Jason had no idea what he wanted to do with his life at the time, he still didn't, but the uncertainty of the future had kept him awake at night more often and for longer back then. It had been two years since he'd finished high-school and moved out from foster care into his apartment. Dead-end jobs kept him occupied and alive, but they were getting him nowhere. He focused on Peter, telling himself that once he had destroyed him, things would hopefully make more sense.

By the time he decided he was actually going to do something, he had a serious problem. He didn't know where Peter was. He didn't even know his last name. The only thing he knew was Peter's former address. Jason didn't expect Peter to still be living in the rundown flats. Still, he didn't want to simply knock on the door and see who answered. He was worried he wouldn't be able to control himself when he finally came face to face with the monster, and he needed to be careful if he wanted to get away with murder.

Jason didn't remember the exact address, but he did remember it being a couple blocks from his primary school in South Strathfield. He walked around the area and one by one forgotten memories came drifting back, invading his thoughts like unwanted guests. The corner of the school yard where the other kids in his year had circled him to make fun of the fact his shoelaces were tied back together in the places they had snapped. The piece of pavement down the corner where he'd tried to carve his name into the fresh cement, until the bigger kids had chased him off. The window of their apartment that his mother had smashed in a drunken stupor. It had been fixed long ago, but Jason could still remember the pangs of pain that came from coming home and seeing the piece of cardboard propped in where the glass had been, as if that could cover up what had really happened. *Fucking, just fucking leave me alone.* Jason scowled as he curled himself into the corner of the bus stop just across from the flats, waiting until the occupants from No. 3 returned home. Sure enough, it wasn't Peter. An African couple with three young children lived there now. Jason felt bad for the family, his identical flat there had been being barely big enough for him and his mother.

He didn't like his chances, but he decided to knock on the doors of all the flats and ask if anybody remembered Peter. Jason smiled, gave a fake name, and an equally fake story describing Peter as a long-lost uncle. He got an odd stare and a shaking of the head from the first occupants. The door slammed in his face from the new occupant of his former flat. In his frustration he had even knocked on the door of the African family. Maybe they had moved in directly after Peter and had known him. No such luck, though at least they had been polite to him. Jason approached the last of the four flats, knocked, took a deep breath as he heard footsteps approaching, and gave his now well-rehearsed speech when the bespectacled old woman opened the door with an eager smile.

'Hi there. Sorry to bother you. My name is

Daniel. I'm trying to track down my uncle Peter who lived at No. 3 some time ago. It was a long time ago, over ten years. You don't know him by any chance do you?'

'Peter.' The old lady repeated pensively, breaking eye contact with him and staring up and slightly to the left as if she were trying to look at the short snow-white curls of hair hugging her scalp like a tea cosy. 'Yes, the electrician right? I remember him. That was a long time ago dear.'

Jason nodded, gambling. His story wouldn't hold up if he didn't even know what his uncle did for a living. Now that she mentioned it, Jason remembered Peter wearing a tool belt at times. Electrician seemed likely enough.

'Yes! That's him,' he replied.

'Come on in dear, I'll make some tea and see if I can help you.'

Jason stepped inside. He was impressed with how homely the lady had made her little apartment. Photo frames with kids, her grandchildren no doubt, adorned the walls, along with a picture frame of a sheep being shorn in a barn. Jason knew he'd seen that picture before but he just couldn't place where. He took a seat at the small table in the kitchen and found himself inundated with several different types of biscuits to choose from. The lady shook the tray in front of him. Jason didn't like sugary foods, but couldn't say no after looking at the woman's eager eyes. He took a scotch finger. And a chocolate cookie when her gestures made it clear that one wasn't enough.

The woman smiled eagerly, and Jason got the impression she didn't get many visitors. Sylvia Andrews, she said her name was. She'd been living here for fifteen years. Jason's pang of guilt for not remembering her was promptly replaced by the fear she would remember him. But the fear soon passed. His appearance had changed somewhat since kindergarten. He found himself very curious to see what Sylvia would have had to say about his mother, but it was too late for that now. He had chosen a cover story and he needed to stick to it.

Sylvia remembered Peter living there for two

or three years, a good deal of time before and after Jason had lived there himself. Jason thought he'd only lived at the flats for about a year at most. His mother had moved frequently after his father left. He couldn't remember why.

Sylvia distinctly remembered Peter being an electrician. He had repaired a blown fuse for her once. And changed the fluorescent bulbs in her kitchen that she couldn't reach. 'Such a nice man,' she said, 'he never even charged me for it.'

I bet they're all nice on the outside, thought Jason. *That's how they get away with it for so long. Nobody suspects them.*

'Are you alright dear?'

Jason looked up at Sylvia, suddenly aware that he had been staring out the window with a scowl on his face, his head jerking to the side. 'Ah, yeah, just got a bit of a headache.'

'Oh that's no good pet. Drink your tea,' she suggested with a smile.

Jason drank his tea. He listened intently as

Sylvia kept talking. She hadn't kept in touch with Peter and had no idea what he'd be doing now. But he had an occupation. It wasn't much, but it was more than he'd had when he left his apartment this morning. Jason struggled to find a question that would give him some more information, but he couldn't exactly ask Sylvia if she knew where Peter was from, or what his last name was without giving away that he wasn't really his nephew. It was then that Sylvia volunteered the biggest piece of the puzzle.

'I wish I could be more helpful dear. Have you tried looking in the phone book?' she asked. Half a second later she answered her own question. 'Oh, I suppose that's no good. There'd be an awful lot of P Jones' in the phone book wouldn't there?'

'Jones,' Jason repeated, immediately realising he'd said it a little too curiously. 'Yes, ours is a very common surname,' he added quickly. It could have been worse. Jason supposed his name could have been John Smith.

Jason's mind seemed to start screaming several things at once, each voice competing with the others till his head was filled with white noise. His hands started tingling and he started pumping his fists, hoping to get the circulation flowing. He supressed the urge to rush out and continue his search, mindful that leaving in a hurry may have drawn suspicion.

He barely heard the next half hour of her chit-chat, but a sliver of attention remained, enough to know when to nod and smile at the right times as she talked. Sylvia had given him what he had wanted, and he figured the least he could do was give her some company. Besides, looking at how happy she seemed talking to him did give him that same small familiar buzz he got from volunteering.

Eventually Jason told her he had to go to work. She eagerly told him he could drop by any time. He smiled and nodded but felt a small pang in his heart, knowing full well he wouldn't be back. Jason walked straight from the flat until he found an internet café he hadn't used before. He didn't want the search for Peter to be traced back to him in any way. Searching for 'Peter Jones' and 'electrician' and the names of the surrounding areas yielded no viable results. He widened the search to include the entire state of New South Wales, and then Victoria and Queensland for good measure, though to no avail. Jason wanted to scream in frustration, instead he scowled at the oversized computer monitor as he hunched his shoulders over it. He had initially been worried he would have too many results. But it was the mid 2000s, social media hadn't yet taken over and many businesses did not have an online presence. Jason abandoned the computer search for a more traditional approach.

Jason photocopied the electrician adverts from the Yellow Pages at the local library. He also took the time to look up Jones, P in the regular phone book, though the number of results looked far too daunting. He photocopied them anyway, hoping he wouldn't have to resort to using them. The electrician adverts were more than enough to keep him busy. He had about twenty pages.

Jason considered how to go about calling the numbers. He couldn't leave a paper trail with his own phone records. He considered a pay-phone, but he needed privacy. And he was worried it would take him several hours to go through all the numbers, and what if somebody else wanted to use the phone? He imagined how angry he'd feel if he needed to make a call and some asshole had been holed up in the booth all day. He ended up buying the cheapest phone he could find and a new sim card, giving the phone company he had to call to activate the phone a fake name and address. He panicked when the operator asked him for his driver's licence number, and cursed himself for forgetting they had asked him for his own when he had set up his regular phone account. Despite not having any interest in learning to drive, Jason had obtained his learner's permit in the last year of school. He had taken a handful of lessons from his last foster carer before he had moved out, but hadn't made any effort to continue them now that he was on his own. He took a gamble, assuming the phone company weren't actually going to check the licence number was valid. They didn't. They told him the phone would be ready to use within the hour. He bought $100 worth of phone credit, the maximum that could be bought at once. Jason assumed he would need all of it. As it turned out, $10 would have been sufficient.

Jason started calling the electricians one by one, always with the same approach, saying he wasn't sure if he had called the right one but he was looking for an electrician named Peter Jones and was wondering if he worked there. He was rather taken back when only on the second page, the response changed to 'Yeah you've called the right place, I'll just go and get him.' His heart raced, and Jason froze for a moment. When he heard the faint clunk indicating that the receiver had been placed on a table, he hung up the phone. It had happened too quickly. He wasn't prepared for what he would do when he actually found Peter.

Jason looked down at the ad that had brought his success. Walker Electrical. Jason wondered where they had come up with the company name. There was nothing unusual about the ad, though he noted there was no address, which meant no place for him to go and scope out. He decided to wait a few days before he called again, hoping the man would have forgotten his voice. He searched the internet for more information on the company, but they didn't have a website. There was nothing else he could do but wait. It was a long three days. The same male voice answered when he called back. 'Walker electrical,' it said again. Jason noticed that the man didn't give his name.

'Hi there,' said Jason, 'I was hoping to have some lights installed all throughout my new house, would you be able to do something like that?'

'Sure would,' said the voice, 'what exactly do you have in mind?'

Jason needed to know where they worked. 'I have a few ideas printed off, would I be able to bring the pictures down to your office and talk about options?'

'Uh well we don't actually have an office,' said the voice with just enough embarrassment for Jason to detect it, 'we just kind of operate on call, coming directly to you.'

Jason knew what he wanted to ask next, but the voice started up again before he had a chance. 'We can come to you now and take a look if you like. Whereabouts are you?'

Jason grimaced. He pawed at his temple with his free hand.

This. Isn't. Thewaythiscall'ssupposedtogodammit!

He tried his best not to raise his voice as he attempted to steer the conversation back on track.

'Oh, so you, uh, do all the work yourself do you?'

'Well today it would just be me,' the voice said jovially. Jason tightened his grip around the phone. *That answer isn't helpful asshole.* He needed to know if the person he was talking to was Peter, and if not, how many other people worked there. There was a silence along the phone. When Jason heard the man draw breath on the other end, he knew had to say something.

'Today's no good,' he blurted, instantly regretting how loud it had come out. 'Uh, let me see when I'm free next.' He began ruffling the photocopies he had made at the library while he decided what to say, hoping it would come across the phone like he was sifting through his day planner. 'When are you free till anyway?' Jason added.

'Well mate I can do anytime till about 5 PM today, my offsider might be able to do after hours but I'll have to check with him first.'

Jason's grimace turned into a smile. A smile that did not reach his eyes.

'Oh, so it's just the two of you then?'

'Yep, just me and Pete, I'm Craig by the way, Craig Walker.'

Jackpot. Jason didn't know how he was going to use this new information. He needed time to think. 'Uh, I've got another call I have to take, I will look into when I'm free and get back to you.'

'Yeah righto mate,' Craig said before hanging up. Jason detected what he thought was relief in the man's voice.

Jason put the mobile down. He had the information he needed. He just needed to formulate a plan with it. He figured it wouldn't be too hard to arrange a booking with Peter instead of Craig. He couldn't kill Craig after all. For all he knew Craig was completely innocent. He couldn't make the booking to his apartment. Even if Peter took the booking there was a chance he'd write down the address somewhere Craig or someone else could find it. Or Jason's neighbours might hear the commotion. And how would he get rid of the body? Jason pondered his predicament for most of the night before a plan hit him all at once. The abandoned house.

The abandoned house was about halfway between Jason's apartment and his then job at the supermarket in Annandale. He walked past it almost every day. He walked past a lot of unoccupied buildings in this neighbourhood, but he knew right away which one he wanted to use. Most of them had all the tell-tale signs. Graffiti. Broken windows. But this house still looked respectable from the outside. Jason only knew it was abandoned because the junk mail and newspapers were never collected. The overflowing letterbox was spewing its contents onto the sidewalk. That could have meant the occupants were either lazy or just plain filthy, but there was an old rolled up newspaper leaning against the front door of this house that never moved. Once Jason realised nobody lived there and was going to clean up the mess, he felt the need to do it himself. About six months earlier he had picked up all the junk on two occasions, after making sure nobody was watching him.

Picking up the junk was only a temporary solution, it seemed to give the junk mail peddlers carte blanche to start all over again. But the mail kept coming regardless of whether he cleaned it up or not. For a reason he just couldn't fathom, new junk mail kept appearing at the house no matter how obvious it was that nobody was collecting it. Jason always considered himself to be a problem solver. He purchased a small plastic 'No Junk Mail' sign and superglued it to the house's mailbox. He had felt uncomfortable holding the sign in place while the glue dried. He hoped passing motorists just assumed it was his house. The junk mail had decreased following the sign's placement, but not nearly as much as he had hoped. Most of the people who delivered it either didn't notice, or didn't care. He considered waiting for the offenders to strike and see exactly what the problem was, but decided against it. He wasn't sure what he would say to the person, and he seemed to be getting into more than enough awkward conversations with lowlifes at work as it was.

Jason left his apartment fifteen minutes early the next day, cutting his morning workout short to have enough time to scope out the house. Arriving at the front gate, Jason turned into the footpath leading to the house. The only step up to the front veranda creaked under his weight as Jason walked up to the door. He knocked, figuring that was the best way of seeing how solid the door was without seeming suspicious. It was all hardwood; no weak spots. It was the kind of door Jason would have wanted. Front doors with aesthetic glass panels were absurd. It was as if the door's designers were deliberately building in a weak spot for criminals to exploit, something to break so they could reach for the handle inside. The bars on all the front windows looked solid as well. Jason continued to work, but first he cleaned up all the junk mail again and dumped it in the garbage bin near the padlocked side gate. Junk mail he had put there several months ago was still at the bottom.

He returned under the cover of darkness after his shift. With his leather gloves on, Jason crept over the yellowing clumps of overgrown lawn and jumped the side-gate. It was five-foot tall, but Jason was athletic and over it in a second. The alleyway that separated the house from the fence next door led to a small concrete backyard, barely big enough for the clothesline and shed there. It was what you expected from a backyard in this part of the city. Jason turned on his tactical flashlight. He had switched it to the red filter as it cast a fainter glow than standard white light, and was less noticeable from a distance, while still providing enough light for the user to get a good look up close. He would have preferred a night vision monocle, but such things were out of his budget. At the time, he was saving up for some Kevlar shoulder armour. The shed was unlocked though empty except for a small pile of bricks, a few offcuts of wood and two tins of paint. For no particular reason Jason nudged one with his foot. From the amount it shifted, he reckoned that it was empty or just about. Turning around he looked at the back of the house. The windows there were barred just like the front, and the back door looked almost as sturdy as its counterpart at the other end, though this one was safely out of public view. Jason smiled, realising he was going to get a chance to do something he'd always wanted to. He planted his left foot on the concrete and lifted his right, giving a moderately forceful kick next to the door's lock, having read in an urban survival guide that this was the best way to kick down a door. The door shook in its frame. Confident he had the technique right, Jason repeated the movement, this time with as much force as he could muster. The door swung open so violently it hit the inside wall and came rushing back at him, reminding Jason of one of those inflatable clowns at kid's parties that always stood back up after being knocked over. He barely had time to catch the door from slamming shut, before he realised he needn't have bothered. The lock was shattered and wouldn't latch now. He left the door ajar, placing a brick from the shed on either side of it to stop it from banging against the wall and making any more unwanted noise. He then left the way he had come, conscious of the possibility someone may have heard the sound of the door breaking and called the police. He calmly walked home. There was no need to rush. His mother had called the police once after his father had beaten her. It had taken them over an hour to arrive. They had taken his father away but he was back a few hours later, and had beaten her even harder.

The following night he found the door just as he had left it, and guided by red light, he entered the house for the first time. The back hallway passed an empty room which would have been a laundry back in its day, and opened up into a kitchen that was equally as empty save for three bar stools by the wall mounted bench. They were quite sturdy and expensive looking and he wondered why the previous occupant had left them behind. Aside from being dusty and sprouting cobwebs, the house was in good condition. Passing through the adjoining living room Jason walked down the long hallway that led to the front door. Two doors on one side led to bedrooms. The two on the other side contained another bedroom and a bathroom. Finding all the rooms empty, he moved to the front door. He opened it a couple inches then closed it again, checking it worked even though there was no reason to expect it wouldn't.

Satisfied he knew everything that he needed to about the house, Jason left, leaving the back door ajar again with the bricks. The only thing he could foresee going wrong now was somebody finding the back door busted, but they would have to jump the side gate as he had. The view of the backdoor was shielded by the shed on one side, and the back fence was topped with so much wisteria it effectively turned the five-foot fence into a seven-foot one. Nobody was going to be peering casually over that. The fence on the other side would only afford a view of the door from the very back corner, and it was unlikely anybody would be looking from there. Jason had his kill zone prepared. Now he just needed to lure his victim.

The next day Jason called Walker Electrical from his burner phone. As it rang he looked over the printouts of light fittings he had gotten from the internet café. If they asked exactly what needed to be done, he wanted to be prepared. He had been holding his breath without realising it, and breathed a sigh of relief when the phone was answered half way through the sixth ring. 'Walker Electrical,' a voice said. It was a different voice this time. Jason's heart skipped a beat. He didn't remember Peter's voice – it had been too long – but who else could it be on the other end since the company only had two employees?

'Yeah hi,' Jason said quickly recovering. 'I called the other day and spoke to Craig about having some light fittings installed, he said his offsider might be able to do that for me.' It was stretching the truth a bit, but his main objective today was making sure it was Peter who turned up for the job. If for some reason Craig turned up, Jason supposed he would have to pretend not to be home, then he'd have to go to the effort of finding a whole new plan.

'Oh ok,' said the voice, 'yeah that'd be me.'

'Are you available today?'

'Well actually I'm pretty busy right now but I could swing by around a quarter to five I guess. Did you have everything ready to go?'

Jason was almost about to correct him, to insist on his story of wanting to discuss the options on arrival, but then he realised Peter had given him a story that was less complicated. 'Sure do, Craig said it all sounded good to go.' Jason briefly worried that Peter would ask detailed questions about what was going to be installed, but he had his printouts, plus he could always fall back on saying he didn't really know anything about lights or electricity. Which he didn't, but wasn't that why you'd call an electrician in the first place?

'No worries, so what's your address?'

Jason gave him the address and clarified he needed lights fitted in all three bedrooms and the kitchen when Peter asked.

'Ok, well I'll see you just before five then,' said Peter, who still hadn't given Jason his name yet. It struck Jason as unprofessional that neither man had answered the phone with their names. When Jason had started his second job at the electronics store the previous month his manager had given him explicit instructions on how to answer the phone. Begin with either 'Good morning' or 'Good afternoon' depending on what time of day it was, followed by the name of the shop and his own name. He had frequently found himself losing track of time, still saying 'Good morning' sometimes well past one o'clock. After having annoyed himself with this mistake several times, Jason had solved the problem by answering the phone with 'Hi there' instead, which he thought worked at any time of day. One size fits all approaches were just so much easier.

'Sounds good, it's Peter isn't it?' Jason asked to clarify what he already felt in his gut.

'Yep that's me, sorry what was your name?'

'Daniel,' said Jason. Later it occurred to him that he should have used a different fake name than the one he had given to Sylvia.

'Cool, well I'll see you later Daniel.'

Jason noted the time on his phone as he hung it up. 10:16 AM. After waiting a lifetime for this day, he supposed another seven hours wouldn't hurt, though he was suddenly glad he had thought to pack a sandwich. He looked out the front window of the abandoned house through the small gap at the end of the curtain. His adrenaline hadn't let him sleep last night. His alarm had been set for 3 AM, but he had still been awake running his plan through his head for the thousandth time when it had gone off and he had begun his journey here. He couldn't risk being seen arriving during the day. He was thankful it was his day off from both his jobs. He wasn't going to be getting a day off both for at least another two weeks, and he wasn't sure if he could wait that long.

He felt naked without his standard tactical gear on, but he knew enough about forensics to not want to leave any traces of fabric from his clothes here, or to take any traces of anything from the apartment with him when he left. He was wearing a cheap but respectable enough looking pair of blue jeans, a long sleeve t-shirt and a black hoodie he had bought from an opportunity shop. A backpack containing a second pair of jeans and a hat and sunglasses, all purchased at the same shop, waited for him in the kitchen. The shop unfortunately hadn't had any shoes in his size, so he had bought two pairs of the cheapest sneakers he could find elsewhere. He had paid cash. Rule No.1 of committing a serious crime: Don't leave a paper trail.

The irony wasn't wasted on Jason that when he needed them most, his best weapons and tactical clothes were at home. But it couldn't be helped. Rule No. 2: Everything you take with you must be disposable. His regular clothing and weapons were obscure and their purchase may have been traced to him. He did have plenty of untraceable knives, purchased from various army disposal stores over the years. He currently had one attached to the cheap belt he had bought at the opportunity shop, and another strapped to each of his ankles. Jason figured that if he was tackled to the ground, no matter which way he fell or was pinned, he would be able to reach at least one of his knives.

His primary weapon, tonight, was the half inch thick piece of steel pipe he had concealed under his hoodie between his pants pocket and his armpit. He easily had several hundred dollars' worth of weapons in his trunk, and now he was carrying something he had found in the gutter instead. Despite its crudeness, he had no doubts of the damage it could inflict.

As he sat in the empty bedroom he fantasised about how the afternoon would unfold. He looked at the time on his phone every few minutes. By 5:30 PM, he was well past the point of worry. He'd been peering out the slot beside the curtain for over an hour. The van finally pulled up at 5:38. It was emblazoned with the company's faded name on the side. *Typical for a tradesman to be late*, he thought sardonically, though he had never actually called one before. Jason stepped back from the window and walked towards the front door, taking off his latex gloves on the way. He waited with anticipation. A thought so horrible yet seemingly obvious now suddenly occurred to him. What if it wasn't the right Peter Jones? Before he had time to ponder the predicament, the knock finally came. He waited a few seconds, then opened the door with his jumper sleeve, conscious to not leave any fingerprints now that his gloves were off.

The thought that he didn't have the right person vanished the second he saw Peter. He was briefly confused by the man's age. For some reason he expected Peter to look exactly as he remembered him. But it was definitely him, even if his short brown hair had more grey in it, and the once average sized man had gone up at least one clothes size. Finally face to face with the man he held responsible for ruining his life, Jason was surprised at how calm he felt. He had worried he would be overcome with rage and strike out right there on the doorstep, but he found himself eerily still, in the calm before the storm, a storm that had been building for over a decade.

Jason saw no sign of recognition in the man's face. His appearance, after all, had changed a lot more over the years than Peter's had.

'Daniel?' Peter questioned.

'Yes, come in,' replied Jason, trying to sound as casual as he could and hoping he was succeeding. He opened the door the rest of the way and gestured down the hall. 'I've got all the stuff waiting in the kitchen.'

'Cool beans,' said Peter as he stepped past Jason and moved up the hall. Jason scowled involuntarily at Peter's casual demeanour. He closed the door and followed, his hand already resting on the pipe. The steel felt icily cold against his sweating hand.

'So you just buy this place or something?' asked Peter. Jason hated small talk at the best of times but right now it would serve a useful distraction. He needed a few more seconds to get out of the hallway and into the living room where his attack would be most effective. The hallway didn't allow enough room for a full swing from the side and he worried a swing from above would be too easy to dodge, even with the element of surprise. Always aim for the centre point of mass Jason recalled, having read the advice in a marksmanship book. Granted the book was referring to shooting, but Jason figured the same principles applied to bludgeoning. The torso was a bigger target no matter what you were attacking it with.

'Sure did,' said Jason. He turned slightly to the right as he started pulling out the pipe to conceal what he was doing if Peter glanced over his shoulder, but Peter's gaze remained firmly ahead as he stepped into the clearing of the living room. He stopped three steps in and turned towards Jason. By that time Jason already had the pipe in full swing.

A sickening crack almost completely drowned out the simultaneous wet thud of metal on flesh as the pipe connected dead on with one of Peter's ribs, just below his chest. Peter let out a sharp, brief cry and fell. A screwdriver bumped up out of his tool belt as his rear hit the floorboards. He looked at where the metal had ripped open his work shirt. And a couple inches of flesh underneath. From the expression on his face, Jason thought Peter might never have seen blood before. Jason saw no fight in the man's spirit. He brought the pipe up above his own head, intending to cave in Peter's. Peter could only raise his arm in defence. The pipe created a crescendo of three cracking sounds like some kind of twisted percussion show. It continued on its downward journey, knocking the cracked forearm out of the way and finding a new point of contact with the top of Peter's head. Peter's head and torso, which had been propped up with the help of his right hand, reeled back. His head slammed into the living room floorboards.

Jason stepped in close. He squatted down in front of Peter and met his gaze. Peter could only stare back, a single tear rolled out of his left eye.

'Do you remember the little boy you molested in the Mooney St flats?'

Peter's eyes widened. Jason had seen enough films to know it wasn't a good idea to stop and make a victory speech. That one question was too much an indulgence as it was, but he needed Peter to know. The fear and realisation he had seen in Peter's eyes were enough for him. There was no need to drag this out now. He brought the pipe down on Peter's skull again. The first blow almost certainly killed him. Jason lost count after about eight. When he stopped, the right side of Peter's skull was caved in. A squashed eyeball lay on the floorboard, still tethered to a mash of red mass by a couple inches of a wet pink cord-like substance.

Exhausted, Jason took a couple steps back until he felt his back hit the wall perpendicular to Peter's corpse. He slid down, his feet straight out in front of him. The pipe fell from his grip and rolled away. Despite his fatigue, he still had the clarity to put on his second pair of latex gloves before his hands touched the floor. He retraced his movements in his mind, and was pleased to discover he hadn't touched anything besides the pipe while his hands were uncovered. The pipe. Jason picked it up again. It was dripping with blood, and he looked at the floor where it had left a foot-long patch of red, like some kind of defective paint roller. It didn't matter. He didn't care if the police found out what he had used to kill Peter. They'd never be able to trace it to him.

Jason spent the next several minutes trying to get his breath back. For the first few minutes he felt so drained he couldn't have resisted if the police had arrived. When he could stand again, he made his way, pipe in hand, to the kitchen sink, avoiding the pool of blood slowly spreading across the floorboards. He washed the pipe clean, only concerned with his fingerprints but also removing the blood in the process. He admired how fresh and shiny it looked. No one would guess what it had just been used for, were it not for the corpse in the adjoining room. He left it in the sink.

Jason looked down at his hoodie. The dark fabric looked like it could have been sprayed with anything. Cola, soy sauce. Perhaps water even from a distance, but the jeans were clearly stained with flecks of red. Jason took off his hoodie, jeans and shoes. He donned his replacement jeans and shoes along with the yellow baseball cap and sunglasses in his backpack. Like the long sleeve bright green shirt that he had been wearing under the hoodie, the yellow hat was something Jason would never have worn. Bright colours were far too ostentatious for his liking, but if anyone saw him leaving the house he needed the police to have a description of someone who looked nothing like him. He stuffed the dirty clothes into the bag and made his way to the front door. He repressed a sudden urge to spit on Peter's corpse as he stepped around it. It would have defeated the purpose of being careful not to leave his DNA anywhere at the scene. He reached the front door and exited calmly without looking back. He stepped out into the world with a content smile on his face. Jason had pondered what he would do with both the body and Peter's vehicle long before the murder, quickly deciding the answer to both those questions was 'not a damn thing'. He didn't care if the murder was discovered, as long as he wasn't there when it was. Jason threw the backpack in a dumpster a few blocks away on the way home. It was a dirty old tattered thing, chosen deliberately so nobody would think twice about seeing it thrown away. He dumped both pairs of disposable gloves, the printouts of light fittings and his burner mobile phone down randomly chosen drains. He went home, showered, got changed and threw the gaudy clothes he had worn home into a dumpster around the corner.

When he came home, he sat at his desk and put on Judge Dredd. Jason swelled with pride for several days. He had gotten his revenge, and he had done the public a service by removing a predator. He wondered how many children he had saved by taking out just one paedophile. Maybe a dozen children wouldn't spend years racked with guilt, confusion and anger because of his actions. For the first time he could remember, he almost slept soundly. Almost. A dull ache in the back of his mind slowly progressed to a sharp stab, and Jason thought he knew what it was. Having been robbed of the chance to kill his own father, he had gotten his revenge on the other son of a bitch who had hurt him. But whatever; they were both out of Jason's life. Right? Everything was supposed to be good now. Except it wasn't. He still felt like he had work to do. Only now, after fulfilling a lifelong dream, he didn't know what it was.

Chapter 15

Occupying the only seat at the bank of computers in the internet café, Jason chuckled and shook his head. Hunting Peter had been challenging. This was just too easy. The first result when he googled 'Thomas Williams' and the real estate company's name was Thomas' profile on the company website's Leichhardt branch. Opposite a photo of Thomas sporting wavy red hair, a thin beard and a big shit-eating grin, was a stalker's gold-mine of information. The address of the branch he worked for, how long he'd been there, what he specialised in. Auctions apparently, and according to the auction tab at the website, he was doing one this Sunday. The agency profile even listed his mobile phone number and email address. Jason had more than enough information to work with before he even searched for Thomas' profile on Facebook.

Despite the relatively common name, it wasn't hard to find the right 'Thomas Williams' once he added the search parameters of age and location. His profile picture showed him and another man his age at a nightclub, each holding a beer. He looked somewhat less professional here Jason thought. There was nothing too embarrassing on his profile, but there was certainly a lot there. His hometown – born and raised in Sydney it would seem. What high-school he went to, which of course neglected to mention he had dropped out in his final year – Jess had told Jason that. Favourite music, TV shows, films. Jason flipped the page of his notepad and continued writing. Knowing things like Thomas' favourite sports team might help Jason strike up a conversation with him and lead him into a trap. He didn't think such an approach was likely, but at this stage he didn't know where the kill would take him.

Jason put his pad and pen away after taking three and a half pages of notes. He thought Thomas had to be some kind of idiot to just give away this much information about himself. The time display in the bottom right-hand corner of the screen read 1:13 PM. Like they say, there was no time like the present. Jason paid the $1 for his twenty minutes of internet time and headed towards the real-estate branch.

Situated between a computer store and a bakery, the real estate office looked like any other.

Windows filled with pictures of properties for sale framed a glass door. Jason stepped inside into a tiny waiting room and reception counter minus the receptionist. Thomas' grin beamed back at Jason from the business card holder. Picking up the card, Jason didn't see any information he didn't already have. It was even the same photo as the one on the company website. He put it back down, wiping his prints off it with his jacket sleeve in the process. Just as he was wondering what to do next, the receptionist came from around the corner. A short and slightly overweight brunette, she greeted Jason with a smile.

'Hi. Can I help you?'

Jason looked at the stack of rental papers advertising current properties for lease on the counter next to the business cards.

'Oh, ah, I was just after the rental properties list, because I'm, looking for a place to rent.' He picked up the list and showed it to her as if she had never seen it before.

The receptionist giggled. 'No worries,' she said, eyeing him with pleasant curiosity. Jason stared at her for a couple seconds, mechanically spun around and left, looking over his shoulder as he opened the door. The receptionist was still smiling at the cute, awkward young man she had just spoken to. Jason tightened his fists, grimaced and jerked his head to the side as he crossed the road. *Idiot. Fuckin', just leave me alone.* He should have had a plan of what to say before he went into the office. Now there was a chance that the receptionist was onto him. Well it couldn't be helped now, he'd just have to be more careful in the future. He stopped and stood at the other side of the road. A middle-aged couple stepped around him while he wondered where to go. He needed a good understanding of Thomas' routine before he attempted anything, and that required an observation point. He looked around. There were chairs and tables outside the bakery next door to the real estate, but if he sat there all day the shop owners would expect him to keep buying things. He kept looking. The bench just to his left looked promising. It was conveniently almost directly opposite the agency, but unfortunately it was facing the wrong way. Jason sat at one edge of it, lent his back against the side rail, planted one foot on the ground and rested the other on the bench. He thought he looked pretty casual, and he could get a good look at the real-estate agency with a cursory glance to his left. Jason could see the clock tower of Leichardt Town Hall poking above some trees in the distance, giving the time as 1:45. Jason checked his watch a second later and confirmed the clock tower was accurate. Realising he was hungry, he took his sandwiches out of his satchel bag. He figured it was probable Thomas was on his lunch break – Jason would have been on his if he had still been at work – and would return shortly.

2:08 PM. Jason spotted Thomas walking up the street towards him. He was wearing a black suit with a white shirt and a grey striped tie. A portfolio in one hand and the remains of a kebab in the other. As he got closer Jason felt his heart beat faster and faster. He worried he would lash out as Thomas walked past, and was relieved when he turned onto the zebra crossing and headed into the real-estate agency. Jason pulled out his notepad. On a fresh page he wrote the time and date, followed by 'Subject returns to work with kebab.' Jason hadn't written Thomas' name anywhere in his notes. He didn't want to make things obvious for the police if he got caught. Naturally he would eat his notes if he was cornered, but it never hurt to be too careful.

Jason waited. He had never really done reconnaissance before. He had failed to anticipate how boring it would be. When he started doing this full-time after his final week at work he would have to bring his headphones, which he didn't usually carry as they made it less likely to hear someone sneaking up to mug you, or even a maniac driver while you were crossing the street. Sitting here on the bench in broad daylight, however, he thought it would be safe. Not only would it alleviate his boredom, it would make also him look more casual without distracting his gaze like reading a book would. He also needed to visit an opportunity shop and buy a couple jumpers. Jason knew people commented on his never changing style of clothing, he just didn't care what they thought. Here, during reconnaissance, looking the same every day would be a weakness. He didn't want anybody to remember him.

Jason didn't spot Thomas again. Having taken note of the agency's opening hours – nine till five – Jason was surprised when by 5:15, none of the staff had left through the front door. A minute later the receptionist came to the door, switched the sign hanging there from 'open' to 'closed', fiddled with the lock, then turned around and disappeared from view. Jason guessed what was going on now. He gave it a few minutes then walked around the block. Each business had parking spaces behind them. Jason found the car park behind the agency, now devoid of vehicles. Evidently the staff all parked here and entered and exited from the rear. Good to know. Jason made a small entry in his notepad.

Jason killed the next few hours at an internet café. He initially searched for information on Thomas outside of the company website and Facebook, but found only a news article at *The Sydney Morning Herald*'s website where he was quoted about a new housing development. The headline article on the site, however, drew his attention instantly. 'Serial killer loose in city'. Jason's heart skipped a beat. He wondered how he had been found out. When he opened the link to find the story wasn't about him, he was relieved, but the relief soon turned to anger. A Twenty-year-old girl's body had been found dumped at one of the city's beaches. Stabbed repeatedly. The police said they'd found a playing card on her, leading them to believe it was the same murderer who had killed Kelly Steiner five months ago. Jason remembered people in the office at work talking about that. He had picked up the paper on the staff room table and read the front-page news about it. What the fuck was wrong with some people? And now apparently this sick bastard had struck again. Why? According to the paper, Kelly had been a nursing student, like Jason had been briefly, and the new victim had a steady job and a child. Jason shook his head. It was barbaric, but more than that, it was confusing. There were so many people out there worth killing, and someone was focusing their effort on the innocent instead. He hoped the police would find the culprit.

Jason resorted to playing video games at the internet cafe to pass the time, and to try and stop the injustice of the murdered girls from playing over and over in his mind. When it was dark, he returned to the rear of the agency. It didn't take long to discover there were no security cameras. A sensor light came on as he approached the door, but there was no one in sight, and even if there had been, Jason wasn't breaking the law yet. He hadn't broken or climbed over anything, and it wasn't legally trespassing until you had been asked to leave. Not for the first time, he felt relieved he had spent so much of his teenage years researching laws like this.

The back door of the agency was solid, and was preceded by a sturdy screen door. Jason placed his gloved hand around the door's handle. Locked as expected. The sole window at the back was not barred, but the glass looked thick and a sun-faded sticker warned of an alarm, which Jason supposed may or may not have been still active. He shrugged, turned around and walked home. There was nothing to gain from breaking into the agency, but it was good to know what kind of security he would be up against if he had to in the future.

Despite being an uneventful day. Jason was neither bored nor consumed with homicidal thoughts on Saturday. He had a plan now, and as long as he had a goal to work towards, he was content. On Sunday he put on a blue jumper, one of several items he had bought from the opportunity shop the day before. He felt moderately uneasy about leaving his jacket behind, but he still had his boots and tactical pants. And the protection of his vest. He only needed to alter his appearance slightly since he wasn't planning any direct contact.

It took two buses to get to Ryde, where the auction was to be held. A short walk after the hour-long ride brought him to the destination. The block of units stood in front of him. Unit two was going under the hammer and Jason could see a small gathering of people at the far end of the unit's driveway. Today was a day when being too early might not be a good thing. He wanted to blend into the background, but he didn't think the crowd was big enough yet, and he had nearly forty minutes before the auction was due to start. He took out his headphones and continued with the audio book he had been listening to on the bus and while he walked. *The Chrysalids* by John Wyndham. Unabridged of course, abridged audio books were just the pits. Jason did prefer real books, but owning any was trumped by his minimalism. His library, as prodigious and impressive as it was, was confined to a mixture of digital and audio books. All legally purchased; stealing was a crime after all. As the narrator voiced the characters, Jason felt like he was surrounded by old friends. In many cases, he had gotten to know the characters in his books better and better over more than a decade. Jason had always felt particularly close to David, the main character in *The Chrysalids.* He was different from everybody else in his society, and he rebelled against an oppressive and delusional authority figure, his abusive zealot of a father, Joseph. His favourite part of the book wasn't when David, Sophie and Petra found their promised land. It was earlier, when Joseph got the death he deserved.

Returning to the auction site twenty minutes later, it occurred to him that this was probably the first time he had ever been happy to see a crowd. The car park behind the units had attracted more people than he had expected, which served his purposes. Jason took a spot up the back and looked around. There were young couples, old couples, parents with children, but also several people here on their own. He didn't think he would look out of place at all. The job was getting more intel on Thomas, but Jason couldn't help but feel a little excited to be here. He'd never been to an auction before.

Thomas was standing on the rear balcony of a

ground floor unit, presumably number two, which conveniently was about a metre off the ground and overlooked the car park. Jason had expected him to have a gavel – everything he knew about auctions came from films he'd seen – but the only thing in his hands was a clipboard. Thomas addressed the crowd with a big smile and a strong voice, radiating the kind of charisma Jason supposed you needed to make it in this profession, and a lot of others for that matter. Jason frowned bitterly. That smug bastard in his fancy suit just seemed to have it all.

'Thanks for coming today everyone, it's nice to see such a large turnout,' said Thomas, 'I recognise a lot of familiar faces, I appreciate some of you coming such a long way to be here. Some of you have even come from as far away as the flat upstairs,' Thomas said jovially, gesturing to a man in the crowd. The man, interested in purchasing the unit just like everybody else, laughed heartily, as did those around him.

Jason snapped back to what was going on in front of him, realising that Thomas had made a joke of some kind, and felt his face contort into even more of a scowl. Thomas didn't deserve to be happy, not with the amount of misery he had caused. But Jason was going to fix that. He liked fixing problems.

'Let's start the bidding at $350,000,' said Thomas.

Jason was surprised at how informal the bidding process was. Nobody had a card with a number on it like he had expected, they just put their hands up. After a number of bids, the apartment sold to a young couple. They seemed thrilled, embracing each other before shaking hands with the people around them. Jason couldn't understand their happiness. They had probably borrowed an exuberant sum of money to place their winning bid. He shuddered at the thought of being burdened for a lifetime by a loan of that magnitude. He didn't owe anyone a damn thing.

The crowd dispersed quickly. Jason followed the slow shuffle up the driveway. He stopped at the unit's mailboxes, pulled out his mobile phone and pretended to be speaking to someone. It was a simple cover, but an effective one.

About twenty minutes later Thomas drove up the driveway. Thomas paused his vehicle at the end of the driveway to check for traffic. Seeing Jason leaning against the mailboxes, he casually waved. Jason returned the wave; he couldn't afford the luxury of being rude and leaving even more of an impression. He wrote down the colour, make and model of the vehicle – a white Toyota Rav4 – but he kept the vehicle's number plate in his mind. It was safe there. Jason was good at remembering numbers and codes. It had been fifteen years, but he still remembered his friend Carmelina's landline number. Carmelina had been Jason's friend during his six-month stay at his third primary school. She had been his only playmate and he still had fond memories of playing Nintendo and handball at her house after school. Sometimes he considered calling the number and seeing if Carmelina or her family still lived there, but he never did. Or would. Jason put his audio book back on and walked to the bus stop. He knew what his next move with Thomas would be.

Chapter 16

Seventy minutes. A thirty-minute walk to Thomas' work. Ten minutes to place the tracking bug on his car. Only thirty seconds if the coast was clear but Jason had budgeted for extra time just in case. Another thirty minutes to walk back. It would make him slightly late back to work, but it was the best he could do. The smart thing would be to wait until next week when he didn't have a job anymore, but a whole week of inaction was going to drive him insane, and if he did this right today, Monday, he'd have a week's worth of solid intel with which to plan the hard work.

Jason fondled the tracking bug, safely concealed within one of his oversized pants pockets. The device had been sitting in the electronics box in his footlocker for over three years. It was one of several gadgets Jason had bought but never actually used. They had all looked like they would come in handy but so far they hadn't. The tie with the hidden camera built into it; the solar powered USB charger. Jason's electronics box looked like it couldn't decide whether it was for a spy or a survivalist.

There were cheaper, smaller tracking bugs on the markets now, but this one still worked just fine. It synced to the smartphone he had bought yesterday afternoon. He was planning on retrieving the bug once it had served its purpose, but just in case he couldn't, he didn't want the police to link it with his own phone. He had set up his new phone on the internet, punching in a fake address, name and driver's licence number, which the phone company's website had all accepted. Things were so much simpler these days. Lying to a computer was so much easier than lying to a person.

When Jason reached the real-estate agency car park, Thomas' 4WD was there between a red hatchback and a blue sedan. He stood across the road and looked around cautiously. This was the part he was worried about. It was broad daylight. One of the other employees could come out to their car, or another car could return at any moment. Variables like this couldn't be predicted. Jason knew this wasn't the best time of day for this. While Thomas had come back from lunch via the front entrance on Friday, one instance was not conducive of a pattern.

He hadn't done anywhere near enough surveillance to establish a routine. But that was about to change.

Jason took a deep breath. It occurred to him that if he had placed the bug when he first got here he would have been done already. He took one last look around him. A black hatchback was approaching from about fifty metres away. He waited for it to pass, walked directly to Thomas' car, knelt down and attached the magnetic side of the bug to the metal frame under the driver's side. He stood and turned in one fluid movement feeling the tension in his muscles as he briskly walked away. If anyone yelled out he was planning to run.

If he had been spotted, he considered it unlikely they'd suspect him of placing a bug. Perhaps they would think he had been looking to steal hubcaps, or was just plain crazy. But nobody noticed. He took one last look from the end of the street, making an awkward 360 degree turn as he continued to walk away. He walked a couple blocks then checked his smart phone tracker app. Perfect. The tracker bug's location was marked by red concentric circles continuously spreading out and fading from a point on the map. Jason switched the phone off. He wasn't going to be getting any calls on it, and there was no need to constantly monitor the bug. The app kept a log of where it had been and for how long.

He was only six minutes late to work. Nobody noticed. Despite the discomfort of being late, he was feeling good about himself. He had a purpose. He worked that little bit harder until he thought he had made up for the time he had missed.

Jason checked the app's log later that night. It showed a seventeen-minute drive just after 5 PM from the real-estate agency to a residential address in Croydon Park. He turned the phone off and went to bed. It was presumably Thomas' address, but he needed more data. Tuesday the app showed the car leaving the residence at Croydon Park at 8:35 AM and arriving at the agency at 8:53. The return journey after 5 PM was interrupted by a short stop at a supermarket. Wednesday was much the same, with a quick stop at a petrol station. Jason was convinced it was Thomas' residence.

Thursday, however, after a brief stop at his own home, Thomas had driven the several kilometres to a house in Five Dock where his car had stayed the night. The following morning he drove from there directly to work. Jason had no way of knowing who lived at the house or why Thomas had gone there. Google street images showed an unremarkable house, just like Thomas'. Was it his parents' house? A friend's? A girlfriend's?

Another rape victim?

Jason clenched his teeth as he considered that possibility. Every day he didn't do something about Thomas was another day Thomas could hurt someone else. The social responsibility to fix this mess felt like the weight of the sky on his shoulders; after all, nobody else was going to fix it if he didn't. Jason felt the rage building. He needed to get out and cool off, and he knew exactly where he wanted to go.

The walk to Thomas' house took well over an hour, but that suited Jason. He felt like a long walk, and he needed to know something. Checking his tracker app and making sure Thomas' car wasn't there for at least the tenth time, Jason rounded the corner and into Thomas' street. When the house came into view, Jason felt relieved to see the lights off. The brick house with its spacious veranda was nice enough, but not exactly anything to write home about. Jason had expected someone who worked in real-estate to have a grander home, but he supposed Thomas was still in his twenties and this was the best he could afford at the moment. Beyond the front fence a stand-alone garage was visible in the backyard. It was open and empty. There were no cars out the front. It would seem the predator lived alone. Perfect. Jason was tempted to get up close to the property, perhaps even break-in, but he didn't want to raise suspicions or get caught doing anything yet. Tonight's mission was a simple one. Familiarise himself with how to get to Thomas' residence, and to see if anyone was home when Thomas was not. Satisfied he had achieved both of those objectives, Jason turned around and walked home.

Friday. Jason's final day at work could almost have been any other. An uneventful shift. Rick assured Jason he could put him down as a character reference. He gave Jason his personal number to put on his resume, telling him quietly that the warehouse would shortly close down, and accordingly, the landline number to his office would no longer be operational. Jason smiled politely and thanked him. He didn't know how to feel on his walk home. He hadn't particularly liked his job, or felt close to anyone he had worked with. Besides Jess of course. But there was still a degree of sadness at the loss of what had become a comfortable routine, and the knowledge that it was gone forever.

Unlike the previous night, Jason recognised the new address where Thomas had parked on Friday night. When he checked his tracker app and realised where Thomas was, Jason clenched his phone so hard it felt like the screen would crack. He was right. Of course he was right! Thomas was still hurting Jess.

Jason gripped the sides of his head and started pacing the length of his small apartment. *Just, fucking, leave me alone!* He pulled his bullet-resistant vest out of his trunk and put it back on, feeling the instant relief of its embrace. He ran his hands over his chest, relishing how smooth and sleek the vest felt, unlike the scarred and raised tissue concealed underneath. He closed his eyes, feeling the weight of it against his body, which somehow seemed to relieve the pressure as always. But tonight, his vest wasn't enough to completely ease the pain. He started putting on his outer armour as well.

Jason's bullet-resistant vest was designed to be

concealed. The rest of his armour was not. He took the six by nine-inch bullet-resistant plates out of his regular vest, and transferred them to his plate carrier. A military body armour system, the plate carrier was a bulky item. It had light Kevlar lining around the neck and torso, protecting the areas the plates didn't cover. The plates were designed to stop multiple rounds from an assault rifle. The Kevlar lining could only stop small calibre pistols and shrapnel, but he still felt twice as secure with its added protection. His Kevlar lined shoulder attachments and groin and buttock panels connected directly to the plate carrier. The rest of his armour he had to attach separately. Kevlar greaves protected his legs from the shin to above the knee. Quadriceps pads, which he had custom ordered from a person he had talked to on a survivalist internet forum, protected the gap between his greaves and groin armour. Only his bulky elbow pads protected the gap between his shoulder armour and the Kevlar forearm pads he was now putting on. The elbow pads only offered protection from blunt trauma. Despite spending a considerable time searching, Jason hadn't found anywhere that made elbow pads from ballistic resistant material. His armour, like all sets from medieval times till the present, had its weak spots.

From the front the only parts of Jason's body that wouldn't stop a bullet of some kind were his feet, hands and head. He couldn't do anything better for his feet and hands than his regular army boots and a pair of black tactical gloves, but there had been several options for protecting his head.

The bullet-resistant helmet was a given, it fit snugly as Jason strapped it on, but choosing how to protect his face had presented more of a challenge. He had found two items specifically designed to fit under such helmets. The gas mask proved not as practical as he had first thought. The filters only lasted a few hours and when society inevitably broke down and chaos ruled it would be difficult to find replacements. Other doomsday prepper's he had found on the internet thought the downfall of society would be caused by anything from an alien attack to some kind of zombie virus. Jason had no time for such fantasy. It would probably be an invasion from Indonesia, or some kind of new and improved black plague, but it was coming, and when it did, he would survive, just like he always had. Hell, it could only be an improvement on life as he knew it now.

Jason preferred the second option, a ballistic face shield. It resembled a thick hockey mask, and offered protection from ballistic threats while concealing his identity. Unfortunately even the best available ballistic protection wasn't good enough. While it was designed to stop bullets from penetrating the body, the force of a round impacting on it could still cause significant tissue damage. In the torso, this may mean a broken rib. But the delicate bones of the human face? A round hitting armour there was still almost certain to take him out of the fight, if it didn't kill him, and if it was one thing Jason dreaded, it was the thought of being captured alive. Eventually he settled on a balaclava to conceal his identity and his everyday ballistic glasses. He'd seen an advertisement for them on a military website. The ad showed a combat soldier in Iraq whose face had been peppered with light shrapnel. You could clearly see where the glasses had protected his eyes. Seeing the near perfect outline of where they had been, surrounded by small wounds and caked blood was almost funny to look at, kind of like the outline a cartoon character leaves after running through a wall. Jason had wanted the glasses immediately. He hadn't realised exactly how vulnerable his eyes had been until he had seen the ad. The frames had interchangeable lenses. He wore polarised ones during the day and clear ones at night, keeping whichever lenses he wasn't using in his jacket pocket. The clear lenses drew some odd looks at night, though the invulnerability was worth it. Jason figured if they were engineered to stop shrapnel they'd be good protection against fists and other blunt weapons as well.

Like so much of the tactical gear he had bought over the years, the gas mask and ballistic face shield had been resold on the internet. Jason liked having one armour set to suit every occasion, just like he liked having one set of clothes. It made things so much simpler. This was his armour, and once he settled on every piece of it, it would not change.

Jason looked at himself in the mirror. Decked out in his jet-black full armour, he looked like a tactical police officer. Indeed most of his armour was made by the same suppliers who outfitted the police and military, although he usually bought stuff from other armour enthusiasts rather than the manufacturers, who typically didn't sell directly to the general public. Jason couldn't help but love the way his armour looked, but that had hardly been why he'd bought it. As he felt it cocooning his entire body, kissing every inch of his skin, the ever-present fog of vulnerability dissipated. Nobody could hurt him now.

Jason sat down. It was a cool night, but even so the heavy, bulky armour made him feel like he could have been halfway into an inferno. But it had helped calm him down. No longer burdened by his job, he was now free to dedicate his time to more important things. As he sat there Jason considered his next move with Thomas. He sat there for a very long time.

Chapter 17

Thunder boomed several seconds after giant white veins cut into the night sky. The thunderstorm had rolled into the city the following afternoon, creating the perfect conditions for what Jason had already decided to do. The thunder, wind and rain would not only cover the noise of his attack, it would also reduce the traffic and potential witnesses.

His tracking bug showed Thomas had come home from Jess' around midnight the night before. Did that mean Jess had finally kicked him out of her life? Probably Jason thought, but that didn't mean the man didn't still have to be punished. Today Thomas had only driven to a local pub around 11 AM and retreated home when the storm broke a few hours later, where he remained.

Jason had spent the day coiled with anticipation. He hadn't been half this nervous while waiting to kill Peter, the only kill so far that he had planned well in advance. In between pacing his bare apartment, alternating between sitting on his chair and his footlocker, and doing random bouts of push-ups in a fruitless attempt to let off steam, Jason wondered why he felt so much angrier about Thomas' abuse than he had Peter's. Peter had robbed Jason of his innocence. He had hurt him personally. But Thomas had gone a step further. He had hurt someone Jason cared about. Jason thought that was why he felt so mad, never considering the possibility it was because Jess had still let Thomas into her home after she had shut the door in Jason's face. Or maybe it was because he knew Thomas was still active, still hurting people. Jason felt like he had protected other children by killing Peter, but his prime motivations were revenge and punishment. Only after he'd killed Peter had Jason taken some happiness from the idea he was protecting others from a predator. Everybody he had killed since had been mostly about social responsibility, of ensuring standards of behaviour were maintained. There was a degree of punishment, sure, but mostly he did it for the same reason he volunteered at the soup kitchen, just making the world a better place one step at a time.

This time Jason couldn't decide which of the three motivators were the strongest, the desire for punishment, the protection of society, or the fact it was personal. He was sure of one thing though. He wouldn't have shot Peter even if he'd had the gun then. Shooting some piece of shit in the back of the head was a simple and effective way of getting rid of garbage, but there was a satisfaction to beating Peter to death that Jason hadn't enjoyed since. Jason decided that with Thomas he wasn't going to use his gun. Not unless he had to. He didn't know what kind of firepower Thomas had access to, so taking the pistol with him just in case was still a given.

When the tracking bug had showed Thomas' car still at his house as the storm continued into the night, Jason knew for sure that tonight was the perfect opportunity. He was wearing the rest of the items he had bought at the opportunity shop last weekend. The second jumper, this one was red and black, jeans, some scruffy old work boots and a faded red baseball cap. The work boots weren't as sleek as his combat ones, but with their steel caps, Jason thought they would be just as deadly. He searched through his knife collection for his primary weapon. The pig sticker was the ultimate knife for such an assassination. Many of Jason's survival knifes had everything from compasses built into the handles to serrated edges. A serrated edge was great for a survival situation, but thrusting it into flesh could get it caught in tissue and bone. He didn't have to worry about that with the pig sticker. It was eight inches of cold, tempered steel. Straight in, straight out. Jason wiped it for prints before he concealed it in the pouch for his hands at the front of his jumper. He strapped a spare knife to each boot, which were concealed by his jeans.

Jason had bought the hat purely to obscure his appearance, but as he trudged through the back streets and pounding rain towards Croydon Park, he was grateful of how it protected his face. The strong winds ensured his face was just as saturated as the rest of his body, but between his clear ballistic glasses and his hat, he could at least see where he was going. Jason's jeans were sticky as the wet denim clung to his skin. His jumper felt like a wet dead-weight over the top of his bullet-resistant vest. His teeth chattered in the cold. His rage, however, had not cooled a bit.

Jason stopped twice on the way, under a bus stop shelter and under the awning of a takeaway shop. Out of the rain he checked the tracker app, confirmed the car was still at Thomas' home, and continued en route. He had considered the possibility that Thomas might have been picked up by a friend, or had taken a taxi somewhere, but that would have suited his purposes just as well. He didn't think he'd have too much trouble breaking into the house under the cover of the storm, and the prospect of waiting a few hours, or even an entire weekend for Thomas to return didn't concern him.

Rounding the corner into Thomas' street, Jason immediately saw that the lights were on. The car was in the garage at the end of the driveway; the garage door was still up. Jason stopped directly in front of the house under a large tree on the sidewalk. The wind was howling through the deserted street and the nearest streetlight was three houses up. He wasn't worried about being spotted as he stood there, steeling himself for what was about to come. Jason took a deep breath and put on his latex gloves. He pushed the front gate of the yard open, walked up the path, climbed the four steps up to the porch and stood directly in front of the door. The lights were off in the window to Jason's right, but the one to the left exhibited a bright glow. Through the tiny slits in between the venetian blinds he could glimpse what was inside. A male figure walked across the room and appeared to sit down just outside of his view. Jason stood at attention in front of the door and continued his watch.

* * *

Thomas was on the couch in his house. Or the house Thomas' father had bought in his name at least. His father had lent him damn near half a mill, what it cost to even buy a run-down shack of a house in Sydney these days, and he had lent it to him interest free. Not that his old man couldn't afford to, it had probably only put a moderate dent in his bank account. If anything, Thomas thought his father should have just given it to him scot-free, but he supposed he couldn't complain. He had it better than most of his mates.

He turned the TV back on. Images of a women's soccer match (*right, women's sport, how pointless*) changed to fishing (*I'd rather watch paint dry*), some sappy country music song (*Forever begins tonight? No thanks*), the cooking channel (*if I wanted good cooking I'd eat out*), a 'Friends' repeat (*wasn't funny ten years ago, not funny now*), the news (*no thanks*), world news (*even more pointless than the local drivel),* financial news (*nobody gives a shit about the Dow Jones index)* and an infomercial *(fuck you).* Thirty channels and he couldn't find anything decent to watch. He settled on a repeat of a rugby match and went back to swiping through Tinder profiles on his phone looking for something new. Thomas always had a few prospects lined up on the dating app. He preferred picking up girls the old-fashioned way – getting them drunk at a nightclub – which was pretty much a regular weekend activity for him, but he'd found more than a few girls that were worth his time on the app, and with the rain still sheeting down it was the only way he was going to pick up tonight. Seeing an attractive young woman's face, he clicked to open her profile. It showed a second picture of just her face, then a third, then a picture of two small dogs. Thomas rolled his eyes and closed the app down. *Fat bitch.* Close ups of faces and no body shots meant she had something to hide, and that was probably that she was in dire need of a gym membership and someone to motivate her lazy ass to actually use it.

Thomas couldn't believe his bad luck. Russell, his regular wingman, was away for a week on a course, and Thomas had always believed going out to clubs by yourself was pathetic. The weather wasn't helping. Even if he found someone to fill Russell's shoes, waiting in line at a club for an hour in this weather? Fuck it. To make matters worse, the three girls he was currently screwing were all unavailable. Mary had gone to visit her sister for the weekend, Susie's boyfriend was back in town. Two weeks on at the mining site and one week off meant Thomas could only tap that resource once her boyfriend pissed off again in another four days. *Stupid prick,* thought Thomas. He wasn't *too* picky when it came to finding girls to fuck, but he did get a particular thrill from sex with girls who were already taken. He was surprised someone hadn't caught him sleeping with their girlfriend years ago. He was sure his luck would run out sooner or later, but he planned to make the most of it in the meantime.

His third girl, and least favourite, was giving him the silent treatment again. The bitch always seemed to be on her period over something. Last night had been a new issue though. Having already scored twice with Jess, he'd decided he was keen for a third round. Jess had passed out by this stage, but that was no problem. She'd wake up and start enjoying it. She always did. Or had. Last night after he'd finished with her, the crazy bitch had gone into another one of her crying fits.

'It's not okay when you do that.'

'Do what?' he had asked.

'Have sex with me when I'm passed out, what do you think?'

Thomas laughed. 'Oh come on, you loved it.'

'Did I? Did I look like I was enjoying myself Thomas?' Jess' voice was high pitched and breaking.

'What the fuck is this all about? You always liked it before!'

'No I didn't!'

Here we go, bitch just wants to start a screaming match. 'You never complained. What's the fucking problem now?'

'I was too afraid to complain!'

'Afraid of what?'

'I don't know.'

'Oh of course you fucking don't. I don't have time for this shit.' Thomas started pulling his pants on and was looking around for his shoes. 'And if you didn't like it, why didn't you ever say anything?

Huh? Huh?'

'I shouldn't have to!'

'Oh fuck me!' Thomas headed for the door, carrying his shoes in his hands. In his haste to get away, he had forgotten to grab his jacket. But it didn't matter, he would get it back in a couple days. Jess was crazy, but she always came crawling back to him. It was pathetic really. With the exception of her mood swings, Thomas was pretty happy with what he was getting out of the relationship. For good measure, he kicked over her coffee table on his way out then slammed the front door behind him. Whatever. He was done with her for the night anyway.

After driving home drunk – Thomas knew his luck not getting caught drink-driving would run out one day as well – he had a couple more beers and passed out in front of the TV. A trip to the pub for brunch and a couple beers had staved off his hangover, but he was feeling the effects of it now. *Probably a good thing I didn't go out after all*, he thought. He turned off the lounge room light and headed for bed. A few steps down the hall he was startled by a firm knock on his front door.

'Who the fuck …' Thomas' voice trailed off as he thought who it could be. Jess seemed like the only possible answer. A sly smile spread across his face as he turned the light back on. 'I knew she'd be back for more,' he muttered to himself. *Thought she'd still be pissed for at least another day or two though.* Thomas put his hand on the handle and unlatched the lock. A split second later the door came rushing straight towards him.

Thomas barely had time to register what had just happened. Crying out, he stumbled backwards into his TV cabinet as his attacker came inside. Thomas took one look at the man, quickly realised he didn't have a fucking clue who he was, before he noticed the look in the man's eyes. He looked possessed, miserable, in pain, but also like he'd done this a hundred times before. Who the hell was he? And what the fuck did he want?

As his attacker took his second step into the living room, Thomas' fight or flight response kicked into full effect. This was his home. He pulled his right fist back and rammed it hard into his advancing opponent's stomach. His hand cracked in response.

'FUCK!' Thomas screamed more in anger than

in pain. What the fuck had just happened? Thomas felt like he had tried to punch the Terminator. He reached to grab his broken right hand with his left.

Unhindered by the punch, Jason took a third step forward, grabbed Thomas by his shirt collar and hurled him across the room. Thrown completely off balance, Thomas landed chest first on his coffee table, cracking the cheap pine frame and one of his ribs in the process. Jason advanced towards him with the same strange calm that seemed to have settled on him from the moment he kicked in the door. He didn't even want to use his knife yet. Once the knife was out this would all be over.

But Thomas wasn't done. With a ferocious speed Jason wouldn't have thought possible after suffering three heavy blows, Thomas picked up his broken coffee table, and spinning around he swung it at Jason's face. Jason barely had time to raise his left arm in defence. The table connected with his shoulder, bounced off and lost one of its two remaining legs as it hit the ground. Thomas felt the softness of Jason's shoulder as the table connected with it. So his opponent wasn't superhuman, he was just wearing some kind of armour over his chest.

'Christ!' Jason screamed as he staggered to the right, clutching his injured shoulder and suddenly wishing he had worn his full armour.

Thomas stood up straight and faced-off with Jason. 'I don't know who the fuck you are or what the fuck you're doing here, but I am going to fuck you up.'

Thomas' confidence and adrenalin overtook his pain and fear. A rugby union forward until his auction work on weekends had conflicted with too many of his B grade matches, he charged forward and threw all his weight into Jason as he tackled him around the waist. Jason didn't feel the impact through his vest, but he started falling backwards like his body had been hit by a runaway semi-trailer. He wasn't hurt when his back connected with the wall behind him either, his vest soaking up all the damage, but he sure felt it when his head snapped back under the momentum and connected with it. Thomas, with his clear size advantage was now on top of Jason, and Jason felt pure fear for the first time since he was a child.

Thomas, who had tackled his fair share of front-rowers, barely felt his shoulder connecting with

Jason's armour. He laughed at Jason's feeble attempt to push him off. He had this sucker now. He had both the upper body strength and the mechanical advantage on his pinned opponent. Still aware of the pain searing through his broken right hand, and the fact this psycho had a cast iron plate or something strapped to his chest, Thomas reeled back with his left arm and slammed his fist into Jason's face.

Crack.

'FUCK!'

Thomas screamed out again. Both the glasses and one of the bones in Thomas' left hand now had a hairline crack in them. The reinforced glasses took most of the brunt, but Jason still got a decent share of pain spread across his face. The pain, however, only served to bring Jason back into the fight.

Frustrated by the failure of his punches, Thomas pulled Jason up by his jumper and slammed him back into the wall, the pain searing through his injured hands with the impact. He didn't notice Jason reaching for the knife in his front jumper pocket.

Pinned half against the wall and half against the floor, Jason only had a few inches to swing the knife. He plunged it into Thomas' stomach, where it penetrated only an inch and a half. Thomas screamed. He saw his wound, then the object that had made it. He froze. He had been in more than his share of fist fights, but had never been confronted with something that could kill him so easily. The fear swelled inside him as warm blood trickled out of his stomach and down his pants.

Jason took note of Thomas' reaction. It didn't make sense. The wound wasn't that deep, it didn't justify his horrified response. It was almost like the moron had never been stabbed before. He shoved Thomas back with his left hand – the bastard seemed to want to be pushed off him now – and swung back with his right as he stood up. The second swing, a full one, found its way in-between Thomas' ninth and tenth rib. He grabbed Thomas' shirt with his left hand and pulled him towards him, ramming the knife in as far as he could.

Jason watched Thomas grasp for breath. He heard the harrowing, frothing coming from the new wound. *Ironic,* Jason thought, *how do you like being penetrated with something you didn't want?* Thomas tried to push feebly against Jason's hand and the knife it held. Jason rammed the knife in an extra quarter inch in response, as far as it could go before the hilt hit skin. Thomas looked like he wanted to scream, but that would have required more oxygen than he currently had. Instead, he fell backwards.

Knowing the fight was won, Jason held the knife in as Thomas fell. It seemed to slow his descent, but still slid out with a pleasant ease. Thomas hit the ground with a thud. He gasped for air with lungs that couldn't hold on to it. Jason leaned forward. He saw the fear in Thomas' eyes; the knowledge he was going to die and could do nothing about it. He remembered his final moments with Peter. There were only two things to do now. Let Thomas know why he had been punished, then finish him.

'I bet you regret raping Jess now.'

The expression in Thomas' eyes changed but not in the way Jason expected. In Peter's eyes, Jason had seen realisation, the horror of acceptance. In Thomas' eyes there was only confusion and pain.

Rape? Jess? What? Thomas felt a confusion rise up through his pain. He had never raped anyone. Rapists slipped drugs into girl's drinks, or held knives to their throats. *What the fuck was this guy ... wait.* Was this about that bullshit Jess had blown up about last night? Who the fuck was this guy? How could he know about that already? And what the fuck was wrong with it anyway? That wasn't rape.

Right?

Jason waited patiently for Thomas to understand, but he just seemed more and more confused as he faded from consciousness. *No! No! No! You can't die yet! You need to understand first!* Thomas had to know why he was being punished. Jason had made it perfectly clear. What part of it didn't he understand?

He knelt down, placing his knees on either side of Thomas' chest. He grabbed Thomas' collar and lifted his head off the ground, holding the pig sticker – still dripping with blood – in front of his face.

'You raped her! You hurt her! You ruined her!'

Jason shook Thomas violently, as if each shake strengthened his argument.

'No … didn't … when?' Thomas said in a weak voice in-between ragged gasps. His lips trembled, struggling to speak against the pain.

When? WHEN?!? Jason didn't know when. Did it matter when? What mattered was that he did it at all.

'Yes you did! I LOVE HER AND YOU RAPED HER!'

'...... no ...' Thomas seemed surprisingly calm, which only infuriated Jason further. Blood was coming out of his mouth now. Jason looked into Thomas' eyes. He still didn't see any understanding. And now there was no fear either. This bastard wasn't just a rapist, he was a liar as well. Frustrated with Thomas' failure to acknowledge what he had done, Jason tried to put the fear back into him. He raised the pig sticker up high. Thomas' gaze followed the knife, for a moment anyway. Lack of oxygen was overcoming him. His eyes rolled back a second before his head did.

'No!' Jason shook Thomas again with his free hand. Thomas gurgled faintly in response.

'Arrghhh!' Jason's scream coincided with a clap of thunder, as if the gods were drowning out his anger with a mocking cry of their own. It wasn't supposed to be like this. It was all going wrong. Why? *WhyNoNotsupposedtobelike JUST LEAVE ME ALONE!!!*

Jason rammed the knife down. It penetrated about five inches straight through Thomas' right eye.

Jason thought he might already be dead but Thomas' body gave a series of short twitches. Jason derived no pleasure from what should have been the highlight of his evening. Sitting on Thomas' chest, he suddenly felt very tired. He had looked forward to this moment all week, he had the feeling it might resolve something deep within him. But now that it was done, he felt even less satisfied than before he had started. Empty even. He didn't understand Thomas' repudiation. He knew he was going to die, so why couldn't he just admit what he had done?

Jason couldn't help but notice that the front door was wide open. A brief panic crept up his spine. He rushed to the door. Looking out into the darkness he heard only the storm and saw no signs of life, save for the lights on inside most of the houses across the road. He closed the door, and made sure the venetian blinds were tilted all the way shut. Taking his hand off the blind cord, Jason noticed he had left a bloodstain on it. His latex gloves were covered in blood, and he had a good amount on his clothes as well.

A thought occurred to Jason. He rushed down Thomas' hallway and found the bathroom. He looked in the mirror. Good. There was bruising around his eyes, where his glasses had been rammed into his face, and no doubt there was worse bruising on his shoulder as well, but he was not bleeding. Not leaving any fingerprints was easy. Not leaving any DNA was a little harder. Had Thomas' punch connected directly with Jason's face and skin, there could have been DNA left on his fist, and that would have required cleaning. But he hadn't. Jason had been lucky.

He returned to the living room. Even without the bloodied corpse with the knife sticking out of an eye like a mini flag placed on a conquered mountain, the place was a mess. There was no point in trying to cover up what had happened here. He could, however, throw the police off what the motive was.

Jason searched Thomas' pants for his wallet and smartphone. The phone may have had a GPS tracker, so he left that, but he placed the wallet next to his body before he slipped off Thomas' watch, a Seiko that looked like it was worth at least a couple hundred dollars, and added it to the pile. Making this look like a robbery gone horribly wrong wasn't an original idea, but it was probably the most likely to throw the police off the scent.

He went through the house opening draws and emptying their contents, pulling things off the shelves and throwing them onto the ground. He had no intention of profiting from his mission, but he was going to take everything of value. He found a small backpack in the spare room next to a heap of camping equipment. There were sleeping bags, ropes, rappelling equipment. It seemed Thomas was quite the outdoorsmen. Jason was tempted by the loot, some of the equipment would come in handy eventually, but he wasn't stupid enough to keep anything that could have linked him to the scene of the crime.

After turning the house upside-down, the backpack contained a laptop, gold chain, dress ring, a very expensive looking silver money clip and a hip flask. Returning to the living room Jason added the watch to the bag before he went through Thomas' wallet. Credit cards, drivers' licence, some business cards, an unopened condom, and $120. Jason pocketed the money. Thomas sure as shit wasn't going to be needing it anymore. He figured it was untraceable and he could use the extra cash. He threw the wallet into the backpack then opened the TV cabinet and added Thomas' PlayStation 3. He considered taking the knife but then decided to leave it. He liked it just where it was.

Confident he had taken enough things, Jason closed the front door behind him and retrieved the tracking bug from Thomas' car before he walked towards his home. Once he was a sufficient distance away, the items in the backpack started going down stormwater drains one by one until the only thing left to throw down the next one was the pack itself.

By the time Jason reached his apartment the storm had washed away any visible traces of blood on his soaking clothes, but he put the boots, jeans and jumper in the garbage bag he had set aside earlier all the same. Jason normally only stayed in the shower for a minute or two, any more was a waste of water, but tonight he huddled on the floor for several minutes until he stopped shivering and then for another twenty for good measure, staring at the tiles until the water finally went cold. Standing up slowly he turned off the taps and shuffled to the bathroom mirror. The bruising around both his eyes was quite apparent now, and the one on his shoulder looked horrific, an uneven border that spread over several inches. Jason gently rubbed the area. It was painful to touch, but he didn't think anything was broken. He had broken his forearm falling from a tree as a child and was reasonably certain that by comparison this was just a lot of soft tissue damage.

He picked up the ballistic glasses he had dropped on the floor as he undressed. He was impressed with how well they had protected him from the punch, while injuring his attacker at the same time. The crack down the front didn't actually look too bad, but no doubt the structural integrity of the item, and the protection it afforded, had been compromised. *Just fucking great,* he thought. Now he'd have to go and buy a new set of clear lenses. He wouldn't feel comfortable leaving the apartment without the protection his glasses offered. But then again, he wasn't going to be leaving his apartment for a few days anyway. The bruises around his eyes would draw attention he didn't need, but more importantly, his shoulder was damaged. He was not currently 100% combat effective. He couldn't leave his apartment until he had healed. Fortunately, Jason had planned for a situation like this. He had contingency plans for all sorts of things that could go wrong. He had filled the cupboard above his sink with enough canned food to last for a couple weeks. Jason opened a can of beans, ate them straight from the can, eased himself into his sleeping bag on his good shoulder, and curled into the foetal position. His palms pressing hard into his forehead as he shook softly, he hoped sleep would come quickly.

Chapter 18

When he woke just before midday, Jason tried to intellectualise the situation. He told himself that he should be happy. Jess' rapist had been taken care of. He'd done society a service. Still, he couldn't shake the feeling that the issue was unresolved. The only thing he could put it down to was that Thomas had been too much of a liar and a coward to admit to what he had done.

Jason only left his apartment once that day, and only after considerable internal debate. The desire to dispose of last night's clothes, which could have been used to identify him, or may have even had a minute trace of blood somewhere on them, eventually overrode his hesitation about being out in public. The clothes had gone in a dumpster a couple blocks away. The pain and swelling in his shoulder had been so great Jason had struggled to put his bullet-resistant vest on for several minutes. Shortly after getting out of bed, Jason had done something that he hadn't done since he was a child. Taken painkillers. There were plenty of painkillers in Jason's survival kit for emergencies, and he decided this was one. Just because certain drugs were legal, didn't mean taking them wasn't a form of weakness. He'd always thought people who took them at the first sign of a headache were just pathetic, and was only moderately successful in convincing himself that his injuries justified taking such medication himself. The tasteless pills had been somewhat bitter to swallow emotionally, but he soon felt better after his body had absorbed them and they were working their magic. Every couple years he had to replace his emergency stash as it neared its expiry date, just like he had to do with his collection of canned food. Today, he was very pleased with himself that he had kept both stores up to date.

After downing the recommended doses of the strongest over-the-counter painkillers and anti-inflammatory drugs, Jason checked his armour for damage. His body would heal, that gave him little concern, but Jason wasn't sure how well he'd handle replacing part of his vest. It wouldn't be the same, as if he could just order a replacement part for something that had begun to feel like an extension of his own body and pretend like nothing had ever happened.

Fortunately, as expected, his heavy armour was completely intact despite Thomas' best efforts. Jason let out a short chuckle as he remembered the look on Thomas' face when he had punched the armour. Priceless. That couldn't have gone better. Replaying the events over and over in his head, Jason knew where he had gone wrong. His flawless victories over the last five opponents had made him over-confident. He shouldn't have used his fists last night, he should have been more professional, shot Thomas twice in the chest and once in the head and left. Especially since he now knew that some people couldn't be reasoned with and were obstinate to the end with their lack of shame. It was good to have a reality check, and the night before had been an important one. He wasn't going to let his personal feelings get in the way of what needed to be done. It would be for the best. Jason was strong and fast, but he had no delusions about his limitations. He wasn't exactly Bruce Lee. If he hadn't had the protection of his armour, there was a good chance he would have lost.

He looked in the mirror again. The bruises

around his shoulder didn't look any different, but his eyes looked even worse. Part of the bruising was still visible even when he wore his ballistic glasses, which now had the polarised lenses in them. New lenses were already on order, but Jason would have to wait until he was fully healed to buy a replacement knife. He had to buy that in person, and with cash. If there wasn't any paper-trail to any of the knives he owned, he wouldn't have to worry about losing them in action, or leaving them protruding from people's heads. Knives were cheap. Jason didn't mind replacing them. It was better than using them again and again. He knew the forensics teams could match knife wounds to certain styles of blade. It was bad enough he had to carry around one weapon linked to several murders. It was a shame he couldn't adopt the same principles he applied to knives to firearms. Not only were pistols expensive, Jason had no idea where to buy another one. He'd noticed the media had picked up on his pistol being used in the last four murders. It had worried him from the start. He didn't want to be linked to his kills. He wanted to be completely anonymous, to work in the shadows. Most importantly, he didn't want to be caught. But it couldn't be helped. The efficiency of the firearm outweighed the attention it generated. And anyway, being caught for one murder would have the same result for Jason as being caught for all of them. Jason couldn't stomach the idea of being in prison, surrounded by criminals. He had no plans of being taken alive. He often wondered if he put his gun in his mouth and pulled the trigger, would he have time to feel any pain before he died?

Jason amused himself for the next several days with a combination of sketching – after several attempts he had a sketch of Jess sleeping that he was pleased with – playing video games and reading. He called the soup kitchen and told them he had the flu. Margaret wished him a speedy recovery. In three years of volunteering he'd never called in sick before, so he figured they'd cut him some slack. By the end of the week, he was as close to catching up on all the reading and all the video gaming achievements on his mental 'to-do' list as he could ever remember being. Jason had never had no plans for an entire week before. He found the concept foreign at first, then salubrious, but still, he was looking forward to being able to see Jess, thinking about all the things they could share together. He would confide in her about his abusers, just as she had with him. They would watch films, read together, maybe she liked video games as well – he hadn't thought to ask her yet. And he would finally have someone to show off his collection of weapons and armour to. But for now, he just wanted to hold her in his arms again.

In between his novels, games, and sketching, Jason searched the news websites for any information regarding the murder. The kill before had hardly gotten any attention. Jason hadn't been sure if he should be happy about that. He didn't want any attention, but he did want everybody to know there was one less criminal to worry about. It had been good to put a name to the face. Scott Vickery. It was nice to know the police hadn't been making a big deal out of the last kill. That must mean they were on his side.

But they were making a big deal about Thomas. The first article had appeared late the following night. Limited details at first. Stabbed. Signs of a struggle. And robbery. The first article hadn't even mentioned Thomas by name, just the suburb he lived in. A more in-depth article naming

Thomas appeared the next day. Co-workers had apparently been worried when he hadn't turned up for work. *They wouldn't have been worried if they knew what the bastard had done,* Jason told himself. Police weren't stating a motive yet, but according to the news, preliminary investigations indicated it was a robbery that had gone wrong. Perfect. At least some things went according to plan. Jason sat back and smiled, feeling proud of himself. He wondered how good Jess must be feeling to know her abuser was dead.

* * *

Jess stared at her vomit in the kitchen sink, the coarse feeling of stomach acid eating into her throat mingled with the aftertaste of regurgitated toast and coffee. It was the first time she had vomited since the morning after her night with Jason. Only this time she didn't have any alcohol in her system. You didn't need to have any alcohol in your system to vomit when two detectives turn up and tell you your kind-of boyfriend's cause of death was multiple stab wounds. Knowing she wouldn't make it to the bathroom in time, she had instead rushed to the kitchen sink.

'Are you okay Ms Little?' asked the detective.

'... yeah, yeah I'm fine,' Jess struggled to lie. She felt like some vomit was lodged in her sinuses, her head was still over the sink, looking at the business card she'd dropped in there just a few seconds ago. It was splattered with sickness, but still entirely legible. Detective Brendan Ames, it said.

'May we come in?' asked the younger detective, whose name she'd already forgotten.

Turning around, Jess made a half-hearted welcoming gesture with her hand. The detectives came in and sat on the couch Jason and Jess had slept on.

'Ms Little, Thomas' family didn't really have any idea who he was dating, we found you via his phone records,' said Ames, 'if you don't mind me saying so, the text messages indicated your relationship with him seemed a bit volatile.'

'Yeah, yeah, that's putting it mildly,' answered Jess as she shuffled over to her recliner and took a seat.

Volatile relationship or not, after forty minutes of questioning, and half-assed improvised consoling, something neither of the detectives were particularly good at, Ames and White didn't feel like they had any new leads. Jess had been the detectives' first logical point of interest after informing the family and asking them for leads, of which they could supply none, and then questioning the neighbours, who hadn't heard a damn thing.

But this was just another dead end. It was early days though. Ames thanked Jess for speaking with him, told her to call him if she thought of anything she thought they should know, and accompanied White to the nearest pub for a steak lunch.

Jess was used to feeling sick, but not like this. The guilt sat in her stomach and she felt it spreading through her. She had given Thomas the silent treatment, again, and hoped in vain that he would reach out to her. Again. She had hated him all weekend for ignoring her, and now she knew why he had. She never considered the unlikelihood of Thomas contacting her even without the three ounces of steel penetrating from his eye through to his hypothalamus.

Jess had spent a lot of time thinking about the future. The city really wasn't working out for her. She had only moved here for university, and only stayed once she had graduated because her unskilled office job was, unfortunately, probably a lot better than she could have expected to find back in Gloucester, her home town, population 2,500. She thought there'd be a better selection of men in the city as well. But like back home, she seemed to only attract destructive relationships. Knowing the relationship with Thomas wasn't going anywhere, she had decided to do something she rarely did. Stand up for herself. She thought if she finally confronted Thomas, he might have listened. *Yeah, right.* In retrospect that seemed about as likely as him pulling out a ring and proposing. Her older sister, Becky, had been trying to convince her to move home for a while now. Partially, Jess thought, so Becky wouldn't feel so bad about getting pregnant at sixteen and never leaving herself. With her credit cards maxing out, Jess had worried that moving back in with her parents was going to be her only option soon. *Nearly thirty and moving back in with my parents. Does it get any more depressing than that? Jesus Christ.*

Now that Thomas was dead – something that made absolutely no sense to Jess – there was truly nothing keeping her here. Jess couldn't even bring herself to continue her lacklustre efforts to find a new job anymore. She needed time to recover. She called her mother. Her father drove the 250 odd kilometres down in his small truck two days later. They spent the day packing then she followed him home in her car. She gave her notice to the real-estate, without caring about having to pay four extra weeks rent. She couldn't stay in Sydney a single second longer.

* * *

By Friday the bruising around Jason's eyes had gone down. The bruising around his shoulder was still evident but he'd regained almost all the movement in it. He felt safe enough to leave the apartment. A session at the gym confirmed to him that there was no permanent damage, and after replenishing his canned food supply, he spent the rest of the day planning what he would say to Jess. Now that he'd taken care of her problem, she'd no doubt have the time to see him. He thought about telling her that he was the one who had fixed the issue for her, but decided against it. Jess hadn't had the mental preparation that Jason had. She may not react well to the information. Most people weren't strong enough to commit murder, some weren't even strong enough to talk about it. Maybe he'd tell her one day, once they were settled and happy together. It would be a surprise.

Her car wasn't in the driveway when he got there. Still, there was always a chance she was home. Perhaps it was at the mechanics for repairs, or something.

Jason stopped on the second of the three concrete steps up to Jess' front door. He had an eye for small differences. The difference was the tacky dreamcatcher that hung from her veranda. Or rather, the lack of it. Jason cautiously approached the kitchen window and cupped his hands around the glass as he leant into it. He should have been able to see a whole heap of clutter on the kitchen counter, and the blurry outline of the couch and TV unit beyond that. Instead, the inside of her house looked even barer than his own.

Standing there in silence, Jason felt his heart racing. He started shaking his head violently. *No. No no no. This isn't right. It's not supposed to be like this. She's supposed to be here waiting for me and we can be happy now.* Jason grabbed at the sides of his head. If his hair had been long enough to get a hold of, he would have pulled it out in clumps. He sank to his knees. *No, not again, just leave me alone!* Jason could feel the tears coming. They hadn't come for a long time. He felt one roll down his face and the shame of it made him even more depressed. Crying was a sign of weakness; his father had taught him that. His father had taught him a lot of things.

Everything seemed heavy all of a sudden. His mind clouded and searing with pain, Jason dropped to his knees, then simultaneously sat back on his ankles and brought his head down towards the ground. He hadn't felt the need to do this since he was a teenager. It always seemed like the only position his body would accept being in when the pressure got too much. Jason gritted his teeth; his eyes were squinted tight as he sobbed loudly, trying hard to resist the urge to scream and also repeatedly hit his head into the ground like he had every other time he had found his body in this position. The urge was strong but somewhere in the back of his mind he knew the attention such behaviour would bring would only make his situation worse.

He rocked back and forth on his knees, losing track of time before he felt able to stand again.

Standing, however, brought no clarity to the situation. After staring at Jess' door for nearly half an hour, he turned around and started walking. His brain wasn't even letting him make wild guesses at what had happened to her. It didn't even seem to be steering his body.

Jason felt like he was walking on autopilot. He walked two blocks in the direction of his old work before he realised he actually wanted to go home. Half-way to his apartment and waiting at a set of lights, Jason didn't hear the frantic chiming letting him know he could cross the street until it was almost over. He started shuffling across the intersection. A car beeped its horn.

'Take yer fuckin' time why don't ya asshole?'

Jason had never liked abusive men. He pulled out his pistol, aimed it in the direction of the driver's seat, and still looking straight ahead, pulled the trigger twice. He saw the spray of blood and the figure slump forward before the vehicle disappeared completely from his peripheral vision. He put the pistol back in his holster and walked the rest of the way home, mainly staring at the ground. After a block or so it occurred to him to start checking no-one was following him, but there was only the occasional passing car. All the same, he turned into the backstreets. Part of his brain was telling him he needed to pick up the pace and get off the streets entirely, but the larger part was telling him it just didn't fucking matter anymore. When he got to the steps in his apartment he looked up. He didn't feel up to climbing two flights of stairs, but he sighed, and took on them on all the same. Each time he lifted his legs he felt like they were made out of lead.

Seated in his chair staring aimlessly at the technicolour spirals on his laptop screensaver, Jason struggled to understand what had gone wrong. Where had Jess gone? And why now? Now that she was finally safe. It didn't make sense. Nothing made sense. Why were people yelling at him when he was minding his own business? Jason knew that shooting the churlish man in the car had been a mistake. It was broad daylight and someone may have seen him do it, but it wasn't like the man didn't deserve it. How hard is it to not yell abuse at people?

As the hours of Jason's self-pity rolled by, a thought kept recurring. This was all supposed to happen. If Jess was still here, Jason would be happy.

Content. Maybe he wasn't supposed to be content. When he was content, he didn't feel the need to get justice for others. He didn't feel the need to protect the innocent. And wasn't that what was really important? He had a job to do, a job nobody else was willing to take on, and Jess would have been a distraction. An enjoyable one, but a distraction nonetheless. And he didn't need to be distracted from his purpose in life.

And this was his purpose. Wasn't it? Killing the guilty and obtaining justice for those who hadn't gotten any themselves. *Is this why I'm still here?* But if he was supposed to protect women and children by taking down their abusers, wasn't his transformation supposed to be a profound, life changing event? His family being murdered. Or something like that. The girl he liked – whether she was his soul mate or not – up and leaving just didn't seem to fit the bill. At least it wouldn't have in a film. Or a book. Jason had seen more than enough films and read more than enough books to know how this was supposed to work, and something about his personal problems just wasn't adding up high enough for him.

Well maybe in real life you didn't need a single

catalyst. Maybe he needed to stop waiting for his destiny and instead meet it head on. Maybe he had everything he needed already. The satisfaction of knowing Peter and Thomas couldn't sexually assault anyone else was good motivation. And finding the pistol had been a pretty important moment in his life. Jason couldn't help but feel his father had left it specifically for him. A gift to make up for all the abuse and pain. His job ending. His degree leading him nowhere. Maybe you didn't need a single defining moment. In books chapters ended, in films the scenes changed, jumping ahead anywhere from hours to years. In real life, time went slow. You collected your experiences one at a time and you learnt from them. Jason thought he was beginning to get the message.

Over the next two days, the thought that he was here to punish the guilty bored deeper and deeper into his mind. A growing satisfaction from killing Thomas, and the thought of the next one, got him through the otherwise bleak days. Starting back at the soup kitchen only reminded him of how annoying both the patrons and the other workers could be. He worked out at the gym twice a day to make up for the time he'd taken off, having to force himself through his usual work-out routines. He knew it was good for his body – he needed his strength now more than ever – but the usual euphoria that came after his workouts was missing.

Jason checked the time. His volunteer shift started in twenty-five minutes. It normally took thirty to walk there from the gym. It was his only commitment these days, and somehow he had still managed to be running late for it.

Having made up his mind about what he was going to do with his life, Jason spent the walk to the soup kitchen wondering where he was going to start. Sure he could walk around and just take what he could find, but there had to be a better way. Jason had gotten lucky with Jess' disclosure, but he didn't like his chances of somebody else confiding that kind of information to him any time soon. And he couldn't exactly take out an ad in the paper asking for victims to come forward.

Jason didn't notice Caroline look up and smile when she saw him come in, but he did register her voice.

'Hey Jason,' she said.

'Hey.' He barely looked at her as he walked to join her behind the counter, and made no comment about her hair, which was now jet black with red streaks in it.

'Another night in paradise huh?' she chirped.

'I guess so,' he said, not even looking at her at all this time and failing to see her smile fall into a frown.

After the initial rush of patrons, Jason began to read a copy of *The Sydney Morning Herald* which someone had left behind.

'So what's news in the world?' Caroline asked.

This time Jason didn't hear her at all.

'Fine then,' Caroline muttered under her breath as she went to restock the disposable cutlery.

The front page of the paper called for any witnesses who may have seen the murder of Dean Jordan, gunned down in his vehicle the day before yesterday as he waited at the traffic lights. Police wanted to speak to a man in khaki pants, army boots and a motorcycle jacket, who was seen leaving the area. *Shit.* Jason looked down at his clothes. He'd have to do something about this now. Maybe he'd order some jungle green and black pants instead, he had tossed up between those and the coyote brown ones to begin with, and maybe he'd stop tucking them into his army boots, just let them hang down normally so they'd just look like hiking shoes. And he could get a hat or two. Still, he didn't think that was enough. He considered his jacket. It was very distinct looking. Jason felt pained, he'd grown so attached to the thing he almost couldn't bear to part with it. But he needed to be smart. He'd go and buy several different coloured jumpers and wear a different one each day, lest other people start recognising a pattern in his clothing. He'd never cared before when people had commented on his uniform, but now he was trying to hide from the police, it was the smart thing to do.

While the article on page one had certainly gotten his attention, it was the one on page three that Jason was really interested in. Community outrage over an alleged paedophile who had been released on bail. Neville Hazelton, seventy-four years old, former vice-principal of a nearby public school. Several of his former students had come forward and pressed charges. A search warrant had been taken out on his residence when he had been arrested two days ago, though police had found nothing to link him to the crimes. This fact, coupled with it being the first offence Hazelton had been charged with, had contributed to him being released on bail. His lawyer told the papers the community needed to be reminded that his client was innocent until proven guilty.

Jason almost hated the lawyer as much as he did the paedophile. How could you make a career defending scum like that? It was almost as sick as abusing the children in the first place. Jason considered whether he should start killing lawyers who defended these sycophants. But first things first. Taking out the source would eliminate the need for them to be defended. Jason took note of the photograph of Hazelton clumsily trying to hide his face as he left the police station. He was easily recognised, thinning wisps of white hair and a complexion riddled with liver spots. And he was clearly guilty. Why else would he try to conceal his identity like that? Thankfully he hadn't been quite fast enough to avoid the cameraman. He knew what the man looked like. But more importantly, where to find him. He re-read the article. 'Mr Hazelton was released on strict bail conditions. He is prohibited from visiting eight residences and must report to the police station on a daily basis.' On a daily basis. Jason looked at the photograph again. He knew where that police station was, not far from the university. He smiled for the first time all day. Life had given him another sign. Now he knew what he wanted to do, and he knew how to do it.

'Hey man, I said can I get something to eat?'

Jason snapped out of his fixation on the article. A man his age, though with considerably fewer teeth and a scar on his cleft was waiting at the other side of the counter. Jason hadn't even seen him approach.

'Oh, sorry.' Jason filled the man's bowl and gave him an extra bread roll as an apology.

'No worries brother,' said the man.

Jason wouldn't have gone as far as to say he was happy, not that he could remember ever being happy for that matter. Maybe his early teens counted, living with indifferent foster carers where his only real concern was finishing the book he was reading. But while he couldn't call this new feeling happiness, having a plan again did at least make the rest of the night bearable.

Chapter 19

Howard took a break from staring out at the local sports ground to read *The Sydney Morning Herald's* front-page article on the new killer in town. Or rather, the older killer who was getting all the attention now. Howard didn't mind the competition. *I admire your work, friend.* Scarcely into the third paragraph, Howard felt something he hadn't felt in a long time. A sense of belonging? No that wasn't quite right, but he definitely didn't feel alone anymore. There was someone out there. Someone just like him. Well not quite like him, Howard couldn't understand the man's work, he was only killing men and even the newspaper couldn't figure out exactly why, but he admired it all the same. Kind of like the abstract print hanging in the living room. Howard didn't know where his father had got the thing, it had been there as long as he could remember. The four different sized rectangles, the shades of red and black. Howard couldn't say he understood the painting, all he understood was that he liked it. You didn't have to understand something to appreciate its beauty.

The bright floodlights lit up the soccer field as if it was the middle of the day, even though the sun had set an hour ago. Any of the sweet little cherubs on the under tens girls' soccer team running around at practice would have suited him. Howard watched as one of the girls, a redhead whose face seemed to have more freckles than a country night had stars, ran joyfully into the safety of her mother's arms. As a child Howard had wondered what it was like to have a mother. He had asked his father about his mother once. The brief explanation, 'the slut had just left', hadn't satisfied his curiosity. He had pushed the matter, until his father's belt cut off the desire for more information. But that was OK. If his father didn't think Howard's mother was worth knowing about, then that was surely for a good reason.

The redheaded girl's mother gave Howard a concerned look as she walked her daughter to her car. She stopped by another couple and their daughter, nodded in Howard's direction and exchanged a few words. Howard suddenly found himself staring at a group of concerned faces. On the outside his own expression remained blank, but he felt a cold chill of fear run through him, like someone had infused ice directly into his spine. He turned over the ignition and backed away, just before the redhead's mother could take down the number plate belonging to the van and the creepy stranger she remembered spotting here last week as well. Howard cursed as he pulled out into the traffic. He supposed it wouldn't be a good idea to come back here next week, but maybe that was for the best. The sports field was too well lit, too well guarded by parents. It was time to find a new hunting ground.

* * *

'Watch out for Corporal Punishment'. Jason stared at the headline article on *The Daily Telegraph's* website. *Corporal Punishment?* He smiled. He kind of liked the name that sorry excuse for a newspaper had given him. Far more than he liked the rest of the article he was reading on his laptop. He jerked his head neurotically and grimaced as he continued to read. Psychopath. Madman. Crazed. *No, it's not like that, just, fucking, leave me alone!* Nobody seemed to understand or appreciate the contribution he was making to society by getting rid of all these cretins. Worst of all, they were comparing him to that brutal monster abducting and killing women. 'Is something in our culture breeding hateful killers like this?' The article questioned, as if the two of them had anything in common. If Jason had any inkling where the real crazy psychopathic madman in town was he would gun him down in a heartbeat. But for now, he'd just have to focus on tracking down Hazelton.

* * *

He's killing people who annoy him. My god it's so simple why didn't I think of it months ago? After some consideration, detective Ames decided not to be too hard on himself. Who in their right mind, after all, would consider such a motive? Sometimes Ames thought being a psychopath would help him in his career. If he knew how these whack jobs thought, apprehending them would probably be so much simpler.

He'd had a strange feeling the ballistics report was going to confirm Dean Jordan's death was the work of their seemingly random pistol shooter. Mainly because the murder had no obvious motivation, and appeared unconnected to any of the others. Ames considered the irony. The mark of this serial killer was his randomness. He certainly didn't fit the mould.

They'd called the resident police psychologist back this morning to address Ames and his team. Dr Edwards had taken the liberty of clarifying that, assuming the motivation was simply irascibility, technically this wasn't a serial killer. Serial killer's plan and hunt. 'What we have on our hands,' he said, 'is a petulant psychopath with a gun.'

Well thanks for clearing that up Dr Fuck-bag. Who the fuck cares what we're labelling him as? He has a gun and he shoots people because he can. It's not rocket science.

Ames had closed his eyes during the lecture and pictured himself punching the good psychologist in the face. Wait and see what he'd write in Ames' next mandatory psych evaluation after that. All the homicide detectives had to have one every year. Make sure the job wasn't getting them too down, and they weren't thinking about harming themselves, or jacking off to the kid's section of the K-Mart clothing catalogue, or whatever the fuck people did when they snapped. Ames thought it was a waste of time. *If you can't handle the heat, just man up or get the fuck out of the kitchen.* He wondered how much money the government had wasted putting this shrink through university, and how much they were now wasting putting him on the police payroll. Money that could have been better spent on another officer. Or a couple of new cruisers. *Hell my own fucking office would be a nice start while we're at it.*

But at least they finally had something to work on now. Two witnesses. Well more like one and a half. A young woman crossing the road on the opposite side had seen it all. She had still been on scene when Ames arrived, clutching a Styrofoam cup of coffee which was shaking slightly.

'I'd uh, I'd just finished crossing the road when a car beeping its horn got my attention, the street was pretty empty so I turned to look,' she said in a thin voice.

'And this was from the vehicle that was later shot into?' asked Ames as he took notes.

'Uhuh,' she nodded, 'as soon as I turned I saw the driver yelling at the man.'

'What did he yell?'

'Um, he was telling the man to take his … effing time.'

'Right. Then what happened?'

'The man, he pulled out a gun and pointed it at

the car. I didn't hear anything, but I saw the windscreen crack and the driver slump forward.'

So he was using a silencer. That wasn't really a surprise to Ames, but it did help explain why there hadn't been any witnesses before.

'What happened next?'

'Nothing, I mean, the man, he just kept walking. I don't, I just don't understand how he could kill someone over something like that and not even care.' The woman's voice was starting to break. She had that look in her eyes that was generally reserved for animals caught in headlights.

'The man, what did he look like?' said Ames, a little louder than he had to.

'Huh? Oh, weird, like, like he just para-trooped in from somewhere.'

Ames raised his eyebrows. 'How do you mean?'

'Army boots and pants, and a big black jacket.'

'Army pants, like camouflaged?'

'No no, they were all the same light brown colour, they just looked like army pants, I don't know how to explain it really.'

Ames nodded. *Tactical pants. Looks like we got*

ourselves a wannabe soldier. 'Did you get a good look at his face?'

'Yeah. Well, um, not really actually. He had short blonde hair and big dark sunglasses. I was across the road ...'

The other witness hadn't been able to give a good description of the man's face either. Actually he'd been pretty much completely useless. He'd admitted he was busy talking on his phone waiting behind Mr Jordan at the lights. Hadn't even noticed something was wrong until the young women had come running across the road, and then had only seen the killer from behind when he was already half-way up the street. *And this is what society has come to. Idiots are too busy yacking on their phones to even notice people being shot anymore.* Well one reliable witness was a good start. Even if they didn't have a good facial description, surely someone would remember a person dressed like that. The newspaper report that the police now believed all five murders linked to the firearm were committed by the same person should jog someone's memory.

Turns out, it had, but not in the way Ames had expected. Plenty of people remembered a man dressed like that, but from everywhere from last week to several months ago. He had several officers at his disposal, but Ames had asked for calls regarding the matter to be directed to him if his line was open.

'I got someone on the line about the shooting last Friday,' the switchboard operator had informed him.

'Yeah righto,' said Ames. A faint click indicated that the call had been put through to him. 'This is detective Ames.'

'Yes, my name is Julie, I'm calling about that shooting in the newspaper.'

'Right, well what can you tell me?'

'Well, I recognise the man the paper described. At least I think it's him.'

'Where do you know him from?'

'Well he used to walk past my house every morning.'

'And where do you live?'

She gave him her address in Marrickville.

'Uhuh, go on.'

'I noticed him because he always dressed like that, the army boots and the black jacket. And the sunglasses,' she added, 'I haven't seen him in a while though.'

'How long's a while?'

'A couple weeks I guess.'

'Can you tell me anything about him?'

'Not really, I just used to see him every morning, or almost every morning. I always read on the porch for a while after the kids walk to school you see, I used to walk with them but my knee started playing up again–'

I don't need your fucking life story lady. 'And what time of day was this?' Ames interrupted.

Ames took down the approximate time and Julie's details. It wasn't much, but it was something. It was particularly interesting that this guy dressed that way every day. It seemed stupid to Ames, like he wanted to get caught. And while this killer was clearly deranged, he didn't strike him as stupid.

There were half a dozen similar calls, though each less helpful than the last. His favourite had been just an hour ago.

'I've seen that guy around!' said the eager young caller.

'Whereabouts?'

'I, I dunno, just around the city, I've seen him!'

'When was this?'

'I'm not sure, a while ago, but I've definitely seen him!'

'That's outstanding sir. Give us a call back if anything else comes to mind.' Ames hung up the phone.

Consolidating his notes with his partner, Ames looked over the information they had. Sure it was at least starting to resemble a puzzle, but rather than having a few missing pieces in a five-hundred-piece jigsaw, it was more like they had only scraped together the first handful. The outline of the dark picture they were forming could have been just about anything. A night sky, or a hole in the ground.

'And you're still certain these killings aren't in any way linked to the Jack-knife Jok–' 'Detective White began.

'Don't you start calling him that, Christ!' Ames interrupted his partner, 'and no I still don't think they're related. One's a brutal attention starved show pony, the other is, at least from what we know so far, disturbingly calm and trying not to draw too much attention to himself. I don't care what the tabloids or the other officers say, these killers are mutually exclusive.'

'How can you say he doesn't want attention when he shot that poor bastard in broad daylight?'

'Well for starters it wasn't planned, he's not trying to turn it into a bloodbath like the other one is. I think his problem is he just doesn't care. He has a gun. If you piss him off, he'll shoot you.'

White looked pensive, running his fingers through his flattop haircut. The hairs bristled under the pressure then snapped back into place, like a thousand little soldiers coming to attention. 'Yeah but are you so sure that's his motivation? I mean, maybe he just wants to shoot someone on certain days and that guy in the car was just the first unfortunate prick he saw?'

'Yeah I don't buy that. Look, the junkie and the dealer, hell half the cops in the city probably would have shot them if they knew they could get away with it.'

I'm not so sure about that, White thought as his partner began yet another of his angry rants. White didn't see the point in interrupting.

'The fat computer geek, what was his name

...' Ames snapped his fingers repeatedly.

'Bryant.'

'Right, Alex Bryant. Hell that guy pissed off so many people I wouldn't be surprised if nobody turned up to his funeral. Maybe our little gunman just caught a smell of him and felt the need to do society a favour. Do you remember how bad his house smelt?'

'Still trying to forget,' said White. He'd only partnered up with Ames the week before that murder. It had been his first homicide investigation. 'So what about the other one? Gary Meredith?'

'Right, well that's the only one I'm not so sure about. But hey, he'd been drinking all night, and was clearly up to no good in that part of town. Maybe he just called laughing boy a wanker or something. I'd say that's about all it takes to set our killer off.'

'Chief wants to see you two in his office,' said one of the senior constables as she walked past.

'Oh great,' said Ames.

'What do you reckon he wants?' asked White.

'Only one way to find out I guess,' said Ames as he stood up and began the walk down the corridor to the superintendent's office.

The superintendent was on the phone as the two detectives entered his office. He gazed briefly at them then at the seats in front of his desk. The detectives sat down. Ames tried to keep his patience as he waited for the phone call to end. He looked at the gold-plated name badge ostentatiously placed in the middle of his boss' desk. 'Superintendent David Malcolm' it read in large, engraved letters. *Yeah, just in case we weren't sure who's office we were in.* Ames wondered if a big-ass nameplate came with the job or if the old man had ordered it himself.

'You wanted to see us?' asked White when the superintendent finally put down the phone.

'Yeah, you wouldn't believe the shit-storm I'm looking at now that the media knows we've got two serial killers operating in the city.'

'Actually Dr Edwards doesn't think the new guy is a serial killer sir, I believe the correct term is–'

'Nobody likes a smart-ass Brendan,' said the superintendent, 'tell me you've got something new to go on.'

'I did get a handy tip from a caller just an hour ago, Mike and I were just about to follow it up, weren't we Michael?'

White nodded, trying to restrain a smirk.

'Aha. Well it better turn into something substantial. I've got these media hounds to deal with and a city full of very concerned citizens. It was bad enough when we only had to worry about the Joker–'

Ames breathed deeply and started to slowly count to ten in his mind.

'–and now to find out we've had a second serial killer running amok for three years?'

'I can appreciate the public's concern,' said Ames, 'we're doing everything we can.'

'I know that, but we need to be seen to be doing more.'

'Well as you know sir we've already increased our uniformed patrols of all the areas we've heard reports of him walking around. They're door-knocking too, but all we've got so far is a handful of people who kind-of remember seeing someone like that walking at some undefined point in the past, nothing useful. Until we get some new evidence I don't see what more we can do.'

'I'm doubling your task force.'

Ames stared at his boss. 'I believe you already did that sir, I've got six detectives running over all our evidence, seeing if new sets of eyes can find anything, but I really don't have anything more for them to do right now. The uniformed patrols are so frequent the only thing they're probably accomplishing is making sure he finds a new area to operate out of, and there's only so many houses and businesses in the area to canvas.' Little did Ames know, in a few days' time uniformed officers would door-knock the street of Jason's former workplace. After seeing the giant warehouse abandoned and the 'For Lease' sign out the front, they would simply tick it off their list and move on to the next business around the corner.

'Well I'm doubling it again anyway. And since you're so fond of Dr Edwards, I'm getting him to focus on developing more in-depth profiles on these bastards.'

Uhuh. Let me guess, he'll tell us they weren't hugged enough as children, Ames thought.

'I don't think that's necessary sir …'

'To hell it isn't! This second killer hasn't even been public knowledge for two days and I've already gotten more media calls than I have in the last three months.'

'I'm sure the attention will die down soon enough sir. Neither of these guys kills too frequently.'

'That's not the point dammit. Look, I know you don't need it right now, but this way I can at least tell the vultures we're putting all our resources on it. And you'll be giving another public statement to the media this afternoon. I want you front centre, and flanked by your entire team, telling everyone what they want to hear.'

Ames sighed. He'd rather stare down the barrel of a gun than into a television camera.

'That will be all,' said the superintendent.

'Well that didn't go too badly,' said White as they walked back down the corridor.

'Easy for you to say. You're not the one who has to take all the media's questions.'

White shrugged. 'So anyway, what do you want to get our new team members to do?'

'Tell them I need a coffee, a decent one. I'm going out for a cigarette.'

Stepping out the front of the station as he fumbled in his pocket for his cigarettes, Ames nearly walked right into someone.

'Sorry ma–' he started, before he realised it was that Hazelton scumbag. *You sick fuck. Hell I'm not sorry at all.*

Neville Hazelton looked at Ames blankly as he stepped around him.

Don't look at me you prick, thought Ames, *how the hell did you even get bail?*

Ames found his cigarettes. He felt the need to smoke increase considerably all of a sudden. He flicked his lighter once. Twice. Four times. Seven.

'Fuck!' he yelled out. A woman walking across from the station with her young son frowned at him.

Isn't this just fucking magical. Ames binned the lighter and stormed off towards the nearby newsagency to buy a new one. He never noticed the young man standing directly across from the station watching. Waiting.

Chapter 20

Jason wasn't concerned about being spotted by the police even though he was right across from the station. He'd already picked up two sets of green and black pants from the army disposals store, and three different coloured jumpers and hats from opportunity shops. He'd wear a different combination each day. He still felt uncomfortable without his jacket and regular pants, but the military-style pants he'd picked up were almost as practical as his old ones, and he still had his weapons, equipment and his vest.

Jason barely registered detective Ames' presence, even his vulgar exclamation hadn't drawn his attention. In any case, he had no idea who Ames was, having only read his statements to the press. When Jason saw Neville Hazelton walk up to the station, however, he may as well have been wearing blinders. He breathed deeply, feeling his heart race and his fists tighten as the adrenaline started to flow, its presence feeling like the embrace of a cherished old friend, returning right when he was needed most. But therein lied the problem, he couldn't use it now. He stood there telling himself over and over that he needed to be patient. The brief feeling of power was quickly taken over as the hormones pooled into a sickness in his stomach, stagnating. Jason took a deeper breath and closed his eyes for a second. *So close, yet so far.* As he tried to maintain his composure, Jason wondered what the police would do if he simply followed Hazelton into the station and sucker punched him in the back of the head. Surely they hated this scumbag too and knew he needed to be removed from society.

Jason had always been in two minds about the police. Most of the time he felt like they were on the same team. Fighting the same fight. Yet he always felt his nerves heighten when they were nearby. *Somehow they must know I have a gun. What will I do if they search me?* Jason didn't know what he'd do. He wouldn't feel comfortable shooting a police officer. That wasn't going to help society. But neither would surrendering. Who would take over his work? Jason knew that the pistol was illegal – he just didn't think it should be for him – and that they would trace the ballistic reports. He was fairly certain they wouldn't let him get away with it just because he was only killing bad people. Fairly certain. Jason had considered, for a long time, approaching a police officer. To try and find one who knew, just like he did, that killing criminals was the only real solution. If the prison system worked, fewer people would re-offend. If only he had access to the files the police did. He could find out where all these vermin lived. He'd start with all the paedophiles, then work his way down the list.

Striking up a conversation with the right officer could be a good move, but what if he got one who disagreed with him? Jason didn't need that kind of attention. He'd given up on the idea, which he thought was a shame. He would be the perfect unofficial partner for a police officer. They had all the info. He wasn't bound by the law like they were. He could do the things they only dreamed about.

Less than two minutes after entering the station, Hazelton exited. He looked just like his picture in the paper. Hell, he was actually wearing the same green wool sweater and grey slacks they had photographed him in last week. As he turned out of the station's entrance he folded up a piece of paper and put it in his pocket. *So reporting for bail is that easy huh? They're not even going to follow this guy and make sure he doesn't hurt any more kids?* Jason thought it was lucky, as always, that he was ready and willing to step up and fix the problem.

Crossing the road, Jason kept pace behind Hazelton. Close enough, but not too close. He'd played this game once before with a man named Bryant. The old man rounded the corner and Jason followed, expecting Hazelton to go back to his car and drive home.

* * *

'Just keep a low-profile Neville, stay home as much as possible, it's the best thing you can do now. I'm still surprised we got you bail. The cops will be looking for any excuse to revoke it,' his lawyer's advice rang fresh in his ears.

'What am I looking at?' Neville asked

'As I anticipated, the prosecutor has told me she's taking this one to the district court. I'm still advising you to plead guilty.'

'I'm not pleading guilty!'

'And that's your choice, but as your lawyer, it's my job to inform you that their case against you is strong.'

'But they don't have any physical evidence. They found nothing in my house!'

'They don't need any physical evidence. They have eight people testifying that you assaulted them, and knowing how these things generally play out, it's likely more will come forward during the–'

'The little sluts were all asking for it!'

Neville's lawyer cleared his throat. 'I'm going to pretend I didn't hear that. Look, as I told you if you plead not guilty you might get twelve years, fifteen even if you're unlucky. We plead guilty now, I can get you off with three to five.'

'I'M NOT–'

'–pleading guilty, yes okay,' his lawyer finished. 'Well Mr Hazelton, why don't you go home and think about it over the weekend, and I'll see what I can do in the meantime.'

Neville had thought about it a lot over the weekend. He'd heard all about what happened to people like him in prison. Fifteen years. Five years. *Makes no difference. I won't survive either,* he thought. *If the other inmates don't get me, my heart will.* Neville unscrewed the cap on his angina medication and took another three capsules dry. The prescription said he was only supposed to take two. *Why did this have to happen now?* Neville bunched up his fists as he walked. Knowing he didn't have many years left, he'd bought the tickets to England. He'd always wanted to see the old country, where his father had come from, but he had wanted to get his affairs in order before he left. *Why did I leave it so late? I would have been gone in four months. Why did the pricks finally grow a pair and press charges now?* To make matters worse, the tickets had been non-refundable. *Well, those little cunts may have robbed me of my chance to leave the country, but we'll see who has the last laugh.*

Neville reached his car and got in. About to turn the ignition over, he realised how hungry he was. He had plenty of food at home, but the bakery he liked was just a walk around the corner. 'Just keep a low-profile Neville, stay home …,' his lawyer's message played over in his head.

'Fuck you,' Neville said out loud as he got out of the car.

* * *

Jason couldn't believe his luck. He had expected to just observe which car was Hazelton's today, and place his tracking bug on it tomorrow while he was reporting for bail again. Hazelton had just saved him a whole day by getting out of his car.

Still standing on the footpath, he waited to see the old man disappear around the corner before he approached the light blue station wagon. He looked around. A few cars on the road, but no pedestrians. The cars wouldn't be able to get a good view from this angle anyway. Jason approached the vehicle and knelt before the front passenger wheel. His hand and the tracking bug disappeared under the vehicle. Jason felt the strong pull as the magnet on the bug coerced his hand faster toward the metal underside. *At least I know it's not going to fall off,* he thought. *Well, all I have to do now is wait.* It was such a nice day, and he knew there was a quiet park nearby. It was a good a place to wait as any, and there was no point in watching the vehicle now that the bug was doing the hard work for him.

He sat on a park bench and turned on his audiobook. Today's adventure was *Starship Troopers* by Robert Heinlein. Another favourite. Jason liked war stories. He had thought about joining the service himself. He'd even attended an open day information session run by the army once. The recruiting corporal had seemed surprisingly impressed that Jason had finished high-school, and asked him if he had considered applying to be an officer. Jason had not. Feeling overwhelmed with the number of pamphlets he'd been given, Jason had taken them home and read over the collection. He didn't like the sound of being an officer at all. Three years at military college seemed a lot harder than the three months at boot camp the regular soldiers got, plus he considered himself, correctly, as too timid and shy to be dishing out orders to the enlisted men. After a couple days, Jason decided against the idea. He considered going back to the recruiting centre, but he'd been worried they'd keep pushing him into doing something he didn't want to. Still, he sometimes wondered what his life would have been like if he had enlisted.

Jason looked up and saw a family sitting down at a bench about twenty metres away. The woman was unpacking a hamper, the father tussling his son's hair. The young girl with her pigtails was the only one who took any notice of Jason. She made eye contact with him and smiled. Jason smiled back before she turned around to join her family in their meal. Jason felt a pang in his heart. He'd always wondered what it would have been like to have normal parents. A sister perhaps. Not so much a brother. He'd never liked the boys at school. They'd been teasing him the day he met Carmelina like they always did, making fun of his creased clothes and how long and scruffy his hair was. Jason had been sitting on one of the logs in the playground surrounded and sobbing when she had come to his defence, calling the teacher and getting all his tormentors in trouble. For the short time before he was moved onto the next school, that brave and bossy little girl with her olive skin and chubby face had felt like what he imagined having a sister would be like.

The mother at the table said something Jason couldn't quite catch over the sound of Johnny Rico describing his Marauder armour – Jason thought he'd finally feel safe if he had an armoured exoskeleton like the lead character in his book – and the children laughed hysterically. He closed his eyes, unable to look at the family a second longer.

Several chapters later, Jason checked the

tracker app. Half an hour had passed since Neville's car had left its current location and come to a stop at a residential address in Rozelle about five kilometres away. An hour's walk. Hardly an issue for Jason's patience or fitness, but he knew if he was going to start doing this full-time he'd need to get a car. A van perhaps. He could outfit it with all kinds of weapons, armour and tools, taking everything he could possibly need for any job with him. He planned how he would arrange all his belongings in the hypothetical van as he walked.

* * *

Neville walked up the steps to his modest wooden home, grateful it was the middle of the day. Fewer of his nosy neighbours were likely to be home. After the very public police search on Friday he knew the neighbours must all be talking about him. Let them talk, Neville thought as he unlocked his door and stepped inside. *They'll certainly have more to talk about tomorrow!*

The faded blue suitcase was covered in a thick layer of dust. He hadn't used it in nearly nine years. Not since the annual school excursion to Canberra for the year six students. Neville missed the overnight school excursions. You could only get away with so much on school grounds. When you had the children for the weekend, it was a whole new world of possibilities. He often wished he could have stayed beyond the mandatory retirement age. His new life was slow and uneventful in comparison to all the pleasures his old job had given him access to.

The bail conditions said he had to report daily, but anytime between 7 AM and 7 PM. Even if he took his sweet time packing, which he intended to – these pricks weren't going to make him rush any more than he had to – Neville would still have thirty hours before he was officially missing. Plenty of time to put some distance between him and the local authorities. They probably wouldn't even start looking for him till the next morning. He'd be well over the state line by then. Neville had no real plan for where he was going, but he was sure going to get there fast. He had plenty of money hidden away. What he didn't have a lot of was time. He figured the money would last until either his heart or the law caught up with him.

The house was still a mess from last Friday. The cops had ransacked the place, turning over everything in the hopes of finding evidence. Neville had been most displeased, after getting bail, to discover they hadn't put anything back in its place. Cupboards open, contents on the floor, the beds stripped, his books all rifled through and laying around the bookcase. Neville had marched right back to the police station and lodged a complaint to a snappy old sergeant who obviously couldn't have cared less, and had gone straight back to his lawyer from there. He was furious to learn even his own lawyer couldn't do anything about the mess in his house. Neville didn't know what he was paying that grinning little bastard for, then he laughed as he realised that he wasn't going to be paying his lawyer after all.

Neville packed the suitcase containing his clothes and toiletries into the car, hoping none of his pissant neighbours would notice. He then collected food into a milk crate, enough supplies to last him a few days before he would need to visit a store. Now there was only one more thing left to get. Well two actually, but they were hidden away together. There was his money. Neville had never trusted the banks. And luckily he hadn't too. The cops would no doubt freeze his account as soon as he disappeared. Well he'd already emptied the last several hundred out of that on the way back from the bakery. Combined with all the money he had hidden in his sock drawer – the cops had found that but surprisingly hadn't stolen it – and his main stash, Neville needn't worry about finances any time soon. And along with his main stash of money were all his prizes. Neville couldn't leave without those.

He looked at the rug in the hallway. It looked like it hadn't been moved at all. Even if the cops had lifted it up, they hadn't been smart enough to lift up the floorboards. Oh no, Ol' Neville had outsmarted the bastards. *Thought they were so high and mighty, to think all they needed to put me away was right under their feet.*

Neville searched his garage for his claw hammer, and returned to the hallway. Straining to pry up the board, Neville worried he might have a heart attack there and then. Not bothering to use the usual finesse in removing it, the board cracked from his effort, but that was no matter, he didn't need to put it back in anyway. Neville wished he could see the look on the police officer's faces when they saw how close they had been to finding it.

Looking in the space, Neville spied the plastic bag with his life savings from teaching. And there was the small wooden container next to it. A warm feeling of nostalgia came over him as he picked it up. He hadn't looked at his prizes in a couple years now. The little bastards had obviously told the police all about the photos. No wonder they'd done such a number searching his house. *But they still hadn't found them, had they?* He took the lid off the container. There they all were. His polaroids. He'd bought the camera especially for these photos, knowing he couldn't exactly take a roll of film to be developed without those nosy bastards at the pharmacy calling the cops.

The top photo was his favourite. Jennifer. She had been so sweet. For a slut that is. They had all looked so sweet and innocent in their school uniforms, but underneath, they were all the same. Just begging to be taken. And it may as well have been him who got them first.

Looking through his photos, he wished he'd been able to take more. It was never enough. He'd forgotten how beautiful they all were. All the memories came back to him, the array cascading through his mind as he remembered how good each one of his sweet little things had felt, had tasted. And they had all wanted him. He felt a faint but warm rush to his loins that he seldom felt these days. Neville unbuckled his belt and stuck his hand down the front of his pants, touching himself right there in the hallway. His weak heart almost gave out when the front door opened behind him.

Jason had seen Neville's car in the driveway. Walking past it on the way to the front door, he observed the suitcase in the backseat and the crate of food in the passenger's side. *Going somewhere?* Jason got the distinct impression he was just in the nick of time. His plan had been similar to his plan with Thomas. He'd knock on the door and wait for the response, except this time it wasn't personal. He'd just shoot the piece of shit and be done with it.

Reaching the front door, Jason reached out and grabbed the handle with his gloved hand. He was surprised to find the door unlocked. And considerably more surprised by what he saw next.

Neville sheepishly took his hand out of his pants when he saw the young man standing in the doorway.

'Stop! What are you doing here?'

The young man said nothing as he started to advance.

Neville panicked. His photos were spread out on the floor all around him. Any closer and the man would be able to see what they were.

'Get out! This is private property!'

Neville stood awkwardly, trying to re-buckle his belt but just fumbling with the clasp over and over. The expressionless man continued his approach.

His belt still undone, Neville took a step forward and pointed his finger in Jason's face. 'I'm calling the police!' His finger was less than a foot from Jason, but Jason wasn't looking at it. He was looking at the floor. *Oh God, too late,* thought Neville.

Jason's gaze met the old man's. His face was no longer expressionless. Neville suddenly felt more afraid than when the eight-armed police officers had barged their way in with their warrant.

'Look, I have money OK, I'll give it to you, just don't tell anyone about this.'

Jason sighed. *Why do they always think they can buy their way out of everything?*

Neville turned towards the plastic bag with the money in it. He bent down, picked it up and turned around to show it to Jason. When he turned around, he saw the young man had something of his own to show him. Jason waited until he saw the item register in Neville's eyes before he pulled the trigger. He had instinctively aimed straight for the forehead, but he let his anger win its battle over his professionalism at the last second. With pressure already on the trigger he aimed it eight inches lower before the faint muffle of the pistol cusped over the silence.

The bullet tore through Neville's throat, deflected off one of his vertebrae and lodged itself in his left lung. The old man sank to the floor. He clutched at his throat with his right hand, his left still holding his bag full of cash. He tried to say something but the only thing that came out was ragged gargling. His lungs filled with blood. He took about a minute to die. A very painful minute.

Jason relished every second of it. It was a bit unprofessional. A sloppy, messy kill. But he didn't care. Sometimes justice was more than making sure the person couldn't hurt anybody else. Sometimes they needed to suffer to repay their debt to society.

He looked at the closest of the polaroids that were surrounding Neville's corpse. The chubby little blonde girl couldn't have been older than ten. Jason reached out, his latex glove running across the pain in her face. He hadn't been in time to save her. There was no way he could have. Judging from the age of the faded Polaroid, Jason guessed she'd be older than he was now. But that didn't make the burden any easier for him to bear. Her entry into a world of pain had been immortalised by this lecherous man's camera. Damaged, just like Jason. Broken. Scarred. Maybe not physically like he was, but scarred all the same. It took Jason a few moments to realise what he was doing. He had shed a single tear four days ago outside Jess' home, this time he was crying. It was ironic, he had all the power he needed to take a life, but there was nothing he could do to ease this girl's pain. He closed his eyes. *No.* He could do something, had done something. She didn't have to live with the pain of knowing her abuser had gotten away with it. He'd gotten justice for her. He was doing this for her, and all others like her. *She'd want me to do this*, he thought. They all would. They needed someone to fight for them.

Jason took a moment to compose himself. The tears dried and left a feeling of determination in their wake. This felt right. Was right.

The bag of money caught his eyes. Jason hadn't ever seen that much money before. It was only a small bag, scarcely bigger than the kind you took your sandwiches to school in, but instead of two sandwich halves it contained two tightly packed bundles of cash. Mainly twenties and fifties, but Jason could see tinges of pink and blue indicating the odd five or tenner. He picked it up. First finding the gun, now this. He couldn't have been given a better sign. This was all supposed to happen. He'd lost his job, but now he had enough money to finance his real purpose in life. He'd kill the next abuser with the proceeds from the last. And so on. He now had enough money to buy all the equipment he needed. That night vision monocle he'd always wanted. A police radio maybe. And a vehicle to put it all in. A vehicle. *Wait.*

Jason searched Neville's pants pockets, finding a wallet with an additional several hundred dollars in it and a set of keys. The set of keys was cumbersome. Jason couldn't understand how one person could own so many keys. He only had one himself, to his apartment door. He'd had two until he replaced the keyed padlock on his footlocker with the combination one. It made life just that little bit less complicated.

He identified the car key from its neighbours, slid it off the ring and tossed the remaining keys into Neville's lap. *Cheers.*

Jason cautiously peered out the front door. Some kids were playing with a sprinkler in the front yard a few houses up. No one else was in sight. Kids. This close to a paedophile. Jason hadn't been able to do much for the children in the photos, but maybe, just maybe, he'd saved those children up the road. He smiled.

Opening the driver's door to Neville's car, Jason again noted the food on the passenger's seat. Convenient. Neville Hazelton was the scumbag who just kept on giving. He'd go through the suitcase in the back later and dump anything he didn't want, probably all of it.

Staring at the gearshift, Jason was relieved to discover it was an automatic. His few driving lessons had been on an auto, even so he felt intimidated to be behind the wheel again. He turned over the ignition and slowly backed the vehicle out of the driveway. Yesterday he wouldn't have felt comfortable trying to drive by himself on his learner's licence permit, but something seemed right about how everything was falling into place today. Nevertheless, he still felt his heart race. He hadn't done this for a long time and he wasn't confident about his driving skill. He took a few deep deliberated breaths before he put the car in drive and started the short journey home. One dead paedophile. Several thousand dollars. A vehicle. And food for the next few days. Not bad for a day's work. Not bad at all.

Chapter 21

She was the one. Howard was certain of it. A little older than he had initially planned on – she looked about twelve – but she was still a keeper. Not literally of course, thought Howard with a smirk, he'd dump her corpse somewhere eventually, but he did have a sneaking suspicion he'd be having a lot more fun with this one than he had with the last two.

It had been difficult to find her. The younger ones always seemed to travel in groups or have a parent with them during the day, and they weren't out at all when he had the cover of darkness. Howard had wasted evenings outside the sports field, then the cinema, and then the shopping mall. But good things come to those who wait. Or so he had heard. When he saw the flyer for the Dulwich Hill girl's dance studio in a home while he was steam cleaning the carpets, Howard had a feeling he'd find what he was looking for there.

And he had. There she was, all alone. Staring at her phone in her skin-tight dance leggings. Howard could just picture the young, budding breasts on her petite frame. Unfortunately they were covered by a jumper, but he'd have plenty of time to see those later. And it was good to leave some things to the imagination. For a while.

Howard felt like it was his lucky day. Why was she standing outside the dance studio all by herself? It was dark and everybody else had left at least fifteen minutes ago. It was like she was waiting for him. Meant for him. Streaks of peroxide blonde danced among her undulating mass of dark brown hair as a strong gust of wind caught it. It was too enticing to watch any longer. He decided to make his move.

* * *

Sonia Marshall checked the last text on her phone. 'Sorry I'm running late sweetie, I'll be there in 5 mins.' *That was fifteen minutes ago mum! And I'm too old to be called sweetie!* Sonia rolled her light brown eyes. Her mother often ran late, but not this much. *Why can't I just get a lift back with Karen's mum? She's the one who brings me here after all.* Sonia had just about given up when she saw her mother's car out of the corner of her eye.

Vanessa Marshall brought the faded red station

wagon in front of her daughter.

'Sorry I'm late honey, how was your class?'

'It was fine mum,' Sonia said as she opened the door, not even trying to mask the annoyance in the voice.

'We can watch *Master Chef* when we get home if you like,' said Vanessa hopefully.

'We're gonna miss the beginning of it!'

'I'm sorry hun, I got here as fast as I could.'

Sonia crossed her arms and pouted.

Vanessa sighed inwardly. She'd never been good at managing time even before she became the breadwinner, and now she was it was getting harder and harder to make time to spend with her daughter after she finished her shifts at the RSL club. Not that her daughter seemed to mind her absences. Vanessa reminded herself that she had been twice as rebellious when she was thirteen, but that did little to soothe the blow. Now that it was just the two of them, her daughter was her entire world. One day, long from now when Sonia had her own children, maybe she'd understand. But Vanessa hoped that unlike herself, Sonia wouldn't have to do it alone.

* * *

Howard had only just opened his door and had one foot on the ground when the station wagon pulled up. He closed the door again as it rolled away, his plans in pieces. He cursed and spat out the window. He took some solace in knowing where she'd be next week. According to the flyer the junior girl's class ran every Friday at 6:30 PM. Next week he wouldn't make the mistake of waiting. He'd go and grab her the second she was alone. Howard cursed again. He had planned his whole weekend with her while he was watching. Now what was he going to do?

His plans were ruined, and he was left only with a bitter rage that was not mixing well with his growing sexual frustration. He decided to drive to the Cross with the intention of finding a whore to take it all out on. He hadn't done that for a long time, not since ... *Shit*. Not since the night he'd abducted Kelly. And then he realised why. Planning and kidnapping the girls had given him a bigger thrill than the whores ever could. But tonight he needed something. Anything. He cursed for a third time, thinking about how much a whore would cost. *That little sugar wasn't gonna cost me a cent.*

Howard had considered abducting a street

walker, but where was the fun in that? They were already filthy and worn out. Good for fucking, but not much else. The fun in his victims came from their innocence. He took something beautiful and he changed it. It was art. There was no art in breaking something that was already broken. It was going to be a very long week waiting for the next dance class.

Chapter 22

Detective Ames was sitting at his dinner table, poking his fork at a piece of crumbed fish his wife should have left under the grill for five minutes longer. He didn't think it was worth the consequences to mention that. He was half listening to her talking, repeating gossip she had heard at the hair salon: Jane from the parents and friends committee at their daughter's high school was apparently fucking one of the teachers. Both were married, and not to each other, she had clarified in a hushed tone as if someone was nearby. She needn't have bothered. Their daughter wasn't going to hear anything from the living room where she'd had the good sense to take her dinner. The noise blaring from the TV would have covered the sound of Ames shooting himself.

His phone rang. Ames answered, though couldn't say anything at first, furiously trying to chew his food into a portion small enough to swallow.

'Detective Ames?'

Ames cleared his throat. 'Speaking.'

'Constable Davies, sir, I hope I'm not interrupting you.'

'You're not interrupting shit,' Ames said as he stood and started walking away from the table.

'We got ourselves a shooting sir. I think you're going to like this one.'

Ames did like it. And to think he'd only seen the sick son of a bitch the day before. Stepping into Hazelton's hallway shortly after 8:30 PM – because of Hazelton's high-profile, the GDs had come to his house only a half hour after the cut-off for his bail – the morbid pleasure of seeing a paedophile who had drowned in his own blood was quickly countered by the photos scattered around his body. The first girls he saw looked younger than his own daughter. Ames couldn't help but feel relieved that the photographer was dead.

'This doesn't exactly fit your profile of a trigger-happy boy killing people who annoy him does it?' asked Detective White, two days later when the forensic report had come back.

Ames took a sideways glance at his partner. He hated to admit it, but he was right. Someone didn't just stumble across Neville Hazelton. This had premeditation written all over it. Just when things were starting to make perfect sense, life, or rather the forensics squad, had thrown him a curve ball.

As always, there was a lot of information in the forensics report two days later. Ames found only a handful of take-home messages amongst the officialese. Neville had been dead for several hours by the time the police arrived. There were no signs of forced entry, the photographs were all Neville's – they matched eight of the victims who had come forward, though almost a dozen victims remained unidentified. And the weapon used belonged to the cowboy with all the anger issues that they had been looking for.

Thanks to the search by the police just a few days ago, Ames had a complete breakdown of what was in Neville's house. Or at least, everything that had been above the floorboards. The absence of Neville's shit-box of a car was the only thing that struck Ames as odd. Did the killer use it as a getaway vehicle? And if so, where was the vehicle he arrived in?

Ames was pondering the issue at his desk with

his partner over their morning instant coffee.

'Maybe he had an accomplice? Someone dropped him off, then he found his own way to leave?'

'Eh, that doesn't make sense to me,' replied Ames.

Ames thought about all the murders attributed to this pistol. Campbell, the drug dealer, killed from close range on the footpath. Meredith, shot in an alleyway. Bryant, killed walking in a car park. Vickery, also shot on the footpath from close range. Jordan, shot by a man walking across the street. He almost had a complete picture in his head, when his partner filled in the missing piece for him.

'All the phone calls we got after Jordan was murdered, they all mentioned they'd seen this guy walking around, right?'

'Right.'

'And we haven't found Hazelton's vehicle yet?'

'Uhuh.'

'Are you thinking this killer didn't even have his own car, and now he's taken this prick's because, well, because he needs a car?'

Ames pondered how a man manages to obtain

a silenced pistol and get six kills with it without even owning a car. Some people have interesting priorities. Yet it did fit the profile.

'Hell it's so simple, and stupid, and bizarre at the same time, that it fits this whole case just perfect like,' said Ames.

White considered it further. 'Right well anyway, that doesn't explain why this killing is so different from the rest. I mean, the others almost certainly weren't planned, what do you think changed?'

'That I'm not so sure about,' replied Ames. It was a curious situation. Ames wondered if the killer was one of Neville's victims, all grown up. Everybody on Earth would at least be able to understand that if not approve whole heartedly. Hell Ames would have been tempted to look the other way if that was the only thing going on here. But that didn't fit. This didn't look personal. One shot, one kill, no forced entry. If the guy's aim had of been a bit better, it might have looked like the work of a high-end contract killer.

'You were thinking this guy just kills whoever annoys him right?'

Ames stared at White but said nothing, waiting to see where his partner was going.

'... well, maybe he's still just doing that. I mean, nobody's going to miss this guy. Maybe he just read about the scumbag in the paper and it upset his appetite, so he decided to do something about it.'

'Yeah but that still doesn't explain why he's changed his profile, why he actually went out looking for the guy. I mean, how did he even find Hazelton? As far as we know the only place Hazelton went the day of his death was ...'

A thought hit Ames like a freight train that had run off its rails. 'Check all the cameras around the station when Hazelton reported for bail!'

'You think he followed the guy from here?'

'Makes sense doesn't it?' Ames bellowed back.

Twenty minutes later, Ames and White were looking at a grainy image of a man in a yellow hat, blue jumper and black pants standing across from the station. Ames couldn't help think that if they had a dollar for every pixel the man took up in the camera feed, they'd have about seventy-five cents, but he still knew it was their man, even if his clothing looked nothing like what they'd been told he always wore. A minute after Hazelton entered the station, Ames watched footage of himself trying to light his cigarette.

'Son of a bitch! He was only ten metres from me!'

'There's no way you could have known Brendan.'

Ames was too infuriated to let his partner's patronising remark get on his nerves.

'Well at least we know how he found him. Question is, where is he going to go from here?' asked White.

Ames shook his head. 'Fucked if I know. Killing over mild road rage first then taking down society's worst known paedophile. I can't fucking imagine where this guy is going to strike next. Shoot someone for short changing him or offing the district's drug kingpin.' Both seemed as likely to Ames as each other.

Ames peered closer at the screen and the grainy outline of Jason on the video feed as he turned and started following Hazelton. If nothing else, this guy was certainly a unique specimen. Maybe he'd write a book about him one day, Ames thought. He quickly laughed off the idea. He never wrote anything other than police reports and perfunctory replies to emails. Writing books was a hobby for people with way too much free time on their hands.

Chapter 23

Jason roamed the streets of Sydney for the fourth night in a row. Always on the lookout, always dressed differently and always in a different part of town. Last night he had made it all the way out to Coogee and back, damn near two hours each way. It wasn't about the destination, though, it was all about what you might find on the way. Tonight he was a bit closer to home; Surry Hills. Sure there was a better chance he'd find what he was looking for if he went just a few steps further into Kings Cross, but its reputation meant it was well patrolled by the police. After killing Hazelton he had taken the rest of the day off, save to find a good hiding spot for his new vehicle. He had presumed the police would be looking for it, and accordingly he parked a couple blocks from his apartment in front of an abandoned building. Close enough for when he needed it. Far enough away to not make him an immediate suspect if the police found it. Even if the car hadn't been hot, Jason still would have gone 'patrolling' on foot. He liked his long walks at night through the city. Just because he was looking for trouble didn't change that at all.

Killing Neville had gone better than he could ever have planned. But now that it was done, Jason was right back where he started. Hunting for the next person who needed to be removed from society. He had scoured the newspapers – it had worked last time after all – but there wasn't anyone who stood out. A thirty-three-year-old man, Richard Livingston, had been released on bail for drug importation, but there was no photo and no indication of which police station he reported to. Jason had searched on social media for the man, but he couldn't be sure which, if any of the three Richard Livingston's living in the city who had a Facebook profile, was the right one. None of them chose to share as much information about themselves as Thomas had. Maybe if Jason had a team working with him they could have put in the effort, scoped out several police stations and tried to match the people reporting for bail with the social media photos, but working by himself with his limited resources, he had written it off as a dead end. Everything about Neville had just seemed right. As soon as he read the article Jason had known what he needed to do. Maybe he'd just have to wait until something else made him feel the same way.

Patrolling the streets at night, Jason couldn't help but feel he was trying to force the situation – actively looking for anyone worth killing seemed unnatural – but he couldn't just sit at home and do nothing when so many crimes were being committed. Then again, it wasn't like he had anything better to do. Besides his gym sessions and a few shifts at the soup kitchen, Jason had nothing else on his agenda. He thought he might even notice something while volunteering like he had the first time with the drug dealer. But he hadn't noticed a thing, certainly not Margaret's apprehensiveness around him and the way she kept eyeing him suspiciously.

After his volunteer shifts ended, there was still time to go out on patrol. In fact, later at night was probably better. He reckoned there were bound to be more people up to no good later in the night, and fewer witnesses. Killing that asshole driver in broad daylight had been far too reckless. Not that the man didn't deserve it, but it had given the police more details about Jason than he had wanted, and forced him to change his style. It had taken some getting used to, but the new clothes were starting to grow on him. There was something kind of fun about choosing clothes that deliberately looked different from what you had worn yesterday. *This is how spies must feel,* he thought, *always disguising themselves.*

Jason had taken particular interest in this morning's headlines. As expected, the police had matched the firearm used to kill Neville with all the others. He was surprised to read that the police were still trying to determine how the killings were related. *Isn't it obvious?* Apparently not. Even an opinion piece covering the story raised speculation that given the latest killing, the previous victims may have been suspected paedophiles. This bothered Jason. While they had been deplorable people, he had no reason to believe anybody else he had shot had done anything to children. It wasn't the truth, and such misinformation bothered him just as much as him being labelled a madman for shooting Dean Jordan. Yet again, Jason had been tempted to make an anonymous phone call to the newspaper to set the record straight. He was still pondering doing so as he walked down the cold, dark street, lengthening his gait for a couple steps to avoid a series of beer bottles smashed on the footpath, when he noticed the approaching young man staring at him. Jason was used to stares. He met the man's gaze and returned it. The man didn't look too out of the ordinary. Dark blue pants and a grey jumper, face a little sleepy looking. Jason broke his stare a split second before the man smiled and spoke.

'Hey bro, know where I can score some weed?'

Jason looked at the man again. Well it wasn't much. Cutting off the source of the drugs would be a lot better, but one less user meant one less customer for organised crime. A small difference, but a difference all the same. He reached behind him, his fingers finding the butt of his pistol.

The man's eyes widened, but not out of fear. No. That expression was eagerness.

'Got something hey bro? Man it's been a hell of a day hey, just knocked off work, fucking double-shift, just wanna go and chill, find some peace, you know what I mean?' The man flashed Jason a tired but cheerful smile. He reached up with one hand and scratched his head, raising his jumper in the process and revealing the bottom of what looked like a high-visibility work shirt.

Jason hesitated. This didn't feel right. This didn't feel like anything at all. It wasn't what he was looking for. His fingers eased off the pistol.

'I, no, I don't have anything like that,' he said.

'No worries bro, you have a good night hey.' The man smiled and walked past him.

Jason turned his head and watched the man for a few seconds. For a junkie, the man had been awfully polite and well-dressed. Plus he surprisingly had a job. Well, maybe they weren't all bad. No that couldn't be right, Jason knew what drug users were like. Didn't he? He shook his head, confused. Fewer things seemed to make sense these days.

Jason looked at his watch. Another wasted night. Whatever it was he was looking for, he didn't think he was going to find it anywhere near here. A little frustrating, but certainly not the end of the world. He headed in the direction of home, wondering if he would ever find some peace himself.

Chapter 24

Detective Ames stared blankly at the multitude of papers spread out over his desk, making the most of the few minutes of silence he still had in the nearly deserted station before he headed home for the night. He was not looking forward to that conversation.

'I need to talk to you about something,' his wife Chloe had said this morning as he was getting dressed. The tone in her voice was concerned. Ames sighed.

'Look, if it's that important to you call a repairman or whoever today and get a quote, I'll think about it.' She'd been agitating about the railing on their back deck yesterday. It was falling apart she said. Embarrassing when entertaining guests she said. What if one of Jenny's friends leans on it and falls straight through she said.

'That would be one less teenager I have to deal with,' he had replied. The comment had not gone down well.

'No not that,' said Chloe, 'it's about Jenny.' Their daughter. Ames knew he wasn't going to like this.

'For the last couple weeks she's been telling me she's been hanging out with Maxine after school, but I ran into Kylie at the supermarket last night and she said Jenny's only been over to their place once or twice. I don't know where she's been going Brendan.'

'What time is she getting home?' Ames asked.

'Before five,' said Chloe, 'not long enough for me to really be concerned on its own, but Kylie said she's overheard Jenny and Max talking about a couple boys they met from the Lewisham school, I'm worried Brendan, we haven't even talked to her about sex yet.'

Ames leaned his head forward into one of his hands. Now there was a conversation he really didn't want to have. 'Surely they've taught her about that kind of stuff at school,' he said, 'she's thirteen already for Christ sake.'

'You don't have to talk to her about sex, can you first just find out where she's going? I was thinking you could run a trace on her phone's GPS.'

'Fuck Chloe you know I can't do shit like that. I have to put the request in to the IT clowns and justify it somehow. Even if I fudge some bullshit excuse they'll be raising their eyebrows when they see the phone is registered to someone with the same surname as me. And don't even think about telling me to have someone from the station follow her.'

'Well can't you just ask her about it then?' she replied.

'Why haven't you?'

'I thought it would sound better coming from you.'

Ames scoffed. 'Why, because I'm a detective?'

'No, Brendan, because you're her father.'

Ames put his head back into his hand for a second before he brushed it up through his hair, ruining the neat combing job finished only a few minutes ago. 'Alright, alright, I'll talk to her about it after work.'

Ames looked up at the clock on the wall. He had less than fifteen minutes of silence left before leaving would mean arriving home late. He looked back down at his desk. Yesterday's headline from *The Daily Telegraph*, 'Corporal Punishment Still at Large', glared up at him, seeming to accuse him of failure at work as well as home. He sighed. *Corporal Punishment*. The name was hardly original, but unlike Jack-knife Joker, at least it made sense. He was faintly aware of approaching footsteps from the hallway before a figure stepped into the doorframe.

'Brendo, we got someone at reception who might have an ID on Corporal Punishment.' *How quickly these names catch on*, Ames thought. Curious, but not overly hopeful, he nodded at the junior constable. The sound of detective White typing whatever the fuck he had been working from behind him stopped.

'Want me to come with?' White asked.

'Nah I'll have them bring you down if it's anything decent,' Ames replied as he stood up and made his way to reception. It was deserted save for the older woman seated opposite the front counter.

'Oh, you're the man I saw on TV,' said Margaret Pappas.

Ames smiled. Normally he didn't like being recognised, but he'd always had a thing about respect for the elderly, and the woman gave out a pleasant vibe. Even if her information wasn't helpful, he had a feeling she at least wasn't going to be painful to talk to.

'Brendan,' he said, extending his hand, 'how

can I help you?'

'I think Corporal Punishment is a young man who volunteers with me.'

Ames smiled. The name sounded particularly funny coming out of an old woman's mouth. 'Ok,' he said, 'what makes you think that?'

'Well I noticed that his description matched the killer. He always wore army boots and the same jacket and pants, but I wrote it off as a coincidence. He's just too nice and shy to hurt someone, he never even swears!'

Ames nodded, encouraging her to continue.

'But then I noticed he changed his style of clothes right after the description of the killer was released. And then I read the story in the paper last week, about all the victims, and I realised that the man who was murdered near where we work a couple years ago was the first one. I started to really suspect him then, but I just don't understand how or why he's doing it.'

'He may not understand why he's doing it himself. I'd really appreciate it if you could make a formal statement, right now.'

Forty-five minutes later, Detective's Ames and

White looked over their statement.

'It's him right?'

'Has to be,' replied Ames. Ames looked at the name again. Jason Ennis. He'd seen that name somewhere before. And now he was pretty sure where that was. Taking the case notes out of his desk drawer, he looked over the witness statements taken from the first murder.

'Son of a bitch. We even interviewed him,' said Ames.

'You did?'

'Nah, GDs took his statement there at the scene the next night. I don't remember seeing the guy around.'

'Well where's our first step from here?'

Ames looked at the volunteer details that Margaret had taken the liberty of bringing with her. Name and date of birth, but a PO Box given for his address.

Switching the monitor for his computer back on, Ames punched in Jason's details. Bingo. There was his driver's licence, and a residential address. Not a bad looking kid, thought Ames, if he ditched his slight scowl in his licence photo for a smile he could have been some kind of model.

'Bastards only got his learner's permit,' said White, leaning over Ames' shoulder.

'Hmmph. Explains him being on foot all the time,' said Ames, 'guess you were right about him taking that sick bastard's car just cause he needed one.'

White glowed with recognition. As far as compliments went, that was about as close as his partner had ever come to giving him one.

'So are we gonna get a squad and pick this guy up?' asked White, motioning with his hand at the address linked to Jason's licence on the screen.

Ames shook his head. 'First we'll discreetly make sure he still lives there. Find out who owns the apartment block. We'll check the leases, then we'll look at putting twenty-four-hour surveillance on the joint. Even if he still rents it, he may not live there, could just be a safe-house. This guy is dangerous. We're going to have to take him hard and fast when we move in. We're not going to go off half-cocked on this one.' Ames paused for a second, then added. 'Call the whole team. I want everyone back in here for a briefing tonight.'

Ames leaned back in his chair. He looked at his watch. 6:45 PM. *Shit.* He'd forgotten to tell his wife that he wasn't going to be home on time. He'd already put in almost two hours overtime taking the statement and putting the pieces together, but as he found his wife's number in his phone and prepared himself for the pissing and moaning he was about to listen to, he had a feeling he'd be putting in a lot more overtime yet.

Chapter 25

The last four days had gone even slower for Jason, and he still had nothing to show for it. Scouring the newspapers for clues for a new target certainly hadn't helped either. Every day another opinion piece on his work, every day seeing them not understand. He didn't mind working in the shadows, uncredited, in fact he preferred it. Now that his work was getting attention, he was struggling with the criticism. After some sleepless nights – which had given him the chance for extra patrols – he'd resolved to stop reading the news websites. They were just making him upset, and he had enough problems to worry about.

Jason checked his watch. 6:53 PM. It was dark outside, but it was probably too early to find anyone up to no good. Sure it was a Friday, but the city's drunken scum wouldn't even be getting started yet. Jason was eager to get back to work, hoping to make up for the six-hour patrols he had put in the previous two nights with nothing to show. He had a good feeling. There was bound to be more action at the beginning of the weekend. Somewhere, crimes would be committed. Jason hoped to find at least one. Maybe he'd catch a pair of criminals in the act. He smiled at the thought. He'd never killed two people in one day. It wasn't a game of course, this was serious work, but he couldn't help but feel excited by the thought of getting a higher score, maybe even taking down a whole group of people.

Jason patted his many pockets. Phone, *burner phone,* car keys, tracking bug, mini med-kit, notepad, pen, folding knife, pistol. And, of course, his armour. Everything he needed to leave home. Stepping outside his apartment block he gazed up at the sky. It was a cool, crisp night. A slight chill went up his neck as a gush of wind blew past, carrying a flurry of leaves and light garbage up the path in front of him. Jason sighed. This city was filthy in more ways than one. He looked to his left and right. He never really planned where he went, other than to avoid visiting the same area twice in a row. Since the police were looking for someone who matched his description, it was important to not have a pattern.

Jason thought he'd check on his car on the way out of the neighbourhood. He'd looked at it this morning on the way to the gym, but it didn't hurt to check again since he was heading in that direction anyway. Finding it exactly where he had left it eight days ago, Jason continued his walk. He headed in the direction of his old workplace in Marrickville, though he planned to keep going further, to see what he'd find. He hadn't gone that way at all recently. Jason smiled. Sometimes change was as good as a holiday.

* * *

Howard looked at the clock in his van. 7:26 PM. It had been a long week. He'd spent every night thinking about that sweet little girl and all the things he was going to do to her. *Just a few more minutes and she'll be out.* The last half hour as he waited in the car park behind the studio – the very same spot he'd been in last time – had been the longest of the week. His knees bounced up and down in anticipation as his knuckles turned white from gripping the steering wheel. He hadn't even touched her and already he felt twice as excited as he had been with the last two. Younger had been a good choice. How completely innocent she was. Howard relished the thought that he would be the first and last man to have her. He had been looking at his photos all week in anticipation. Those photos. Just because they were younger didn't necessarily mean they were pure. Some of the youngest ones in his pictures were the filthiest of all of them. But no matter. She'd at least be purer than the other two. Her innocence and the taboo of her age was a tantalising combination. Maybe he'd take some photos of her and add them to his collection, he thought, suddenly lamenting that he'd never considered taking photos of the last two. No matter, there were plenty more where they came from, and now he'd make up for the last two with her.

The door to the dance studio swung open and a handful of young girls exited. A middle-aged woman wearing a pantsuit exited the car three spots down from him and collected two of them. She spotted Howard on the way back to her car and had the time to frown at him – he didn't notice – before bundling her kids into the car. She knew all the parents of the kids in the class, at least by recognition if not personally, and he wasn't one of them. In a hurry to pick up her son from football practice, she decided to give him the benefit of the doubt. He was probably some kind of tradesman. Her car pulled out and was promptly followed by three others.

* * *

Sonia and her best friend Karen stood alone outside the dance studio.

'Looks like my mum isn't the only one running late this week,' Sonia said.

Karen laughed. 'Maybe yours is having a bad influence on mine, oh nope, here she is,' said Karen as her mother pulled up. 'Text me when you get home,' she said as she headed towards the vehicle.

'Hi Sonia,' said Karen's mother Celine, the electric mirror on the passenger side moving down as the SUV pulled up.

'Hey again missus B,'replied Sonia.

Celine Bowers gave Sonia a compassionate look. She felt bad leaving the girl there on her own, but she knew how much Vanessa looked forward to picking up her only child after work. 'You want me to wait with you till your mum gets here?' she offered.

'Mum! Don't be such a dork!' Karen protested as she watched her best friend blush.

'Ah, no it's OK, I'm sure she'll be here in a

minute, thanks though,' said Sonia, weakly trying to laugh off the unwanted offer.

'Ok, well we'll see you Monday after school.'

Sonia smiled.

'Text me,' Karen mouthed as the SUV pulled off. Sonia nodded eagerly in reply.

* * *

Howard watched the vehicle pull away. His heart skipped a beat when he thought it was going to pick up both of the girls, but everything was going as planned. Now that the girl was alone he would have just over fifteen minutes to get the job done, just like last week. It was more than he needed. Howard reached for his tyre iron then reconsidered. This one was just a child; he wouldn't have to knock her out. He reached for his tradesman's knife instead. He thought it was more intimidating, and all he had to do was scare her into the back of the van, tape her up and drive off. Concealing the knife behind his back, Howard stepped out of the van and walked straight towards her. Engrossed in her phone, she didn't even look up until he was practically on top of her.

* * *

Vanessa Marshall rounded the corner towards the

car park. She was making good time this week. At least by her standards anyway. Still expecting to hear an earful about being five minutes late, she hoped Sonnie would at least want to eat and watch their show together before the girl disappeared into the void of her computer's LCD screen for the rest of the night. Kids these days. See each other all day then still have to text and FaceTime each other all night. She shook her head and smiled. She was glad to not have had computers and mobile phones when she was her daughter's age. She didn't think all this high-tech stuff was good for kids, but neither was being teased for being the only kid in school who wasn't allowed to have a phone. What could you do?

Pulling into the car park Vanessa drove up towards the dance studio. Her jaw dropped and her foot slammed on the brake as she saw something that nothing in life could have prepared her for.

* * *

Sonia stood frozen. Her ears heard the words that had come out of the man's mouth, but they just weren't processing. The knife in front of her face had drawn all her attention as if she was a gnat and it was a stadium light. She had a few seconds to think about what it could do to her before he grabbed her shoulder with his other hand and started pulling her.

'I said get in the van or I'll slit your little fuckin' throat open.'

Somehow Sonia managed to put one foot in front of the other, each felt like it was encased in concrete and she was wading through molasses. If he hadn't been pulling her so forcefully, Sonia didn't think she would have been able to walk at all. The sound of car brakes to her right got her attention. She turned.

'MUM!'

'Sonia!'

'Fuck!' said Howard.

Why the fuck was she here so early? Howard felt the hairs on the back of his neck stand up. This wasn't good. He was losing control of the situation and he needed to tighten his grip on it, and fast, but he didn't know how. Afraid, he found himself just as stuck to the ground as Sonia had been only a few seconds ago. He might have stayed there indefinitely if Vanessa Marshall hadn't forced his hand.

Throwing open her car door, Vanessa grabbed her seat and tried to launch her body out of the car.

Momentarily confused by why she wasn't going anywhere, she realised her seatbelt was still fastened. Still riding the adrenaline rush after having seen her only child being man handled by a stranger, Vanessa unclipped the belt and ran towards him.

'Get your hands off my daughter!'

The knife obscured from Vanessa's vision by his body, Howard suddenly found a reckoning force pulling against his left hand.

'Mum! Help me!' Tears rolled down Sonia's face as she found the strength that had abandoned her only a minute before. She pulled against the man's grip as she began slapping his face.

* * *

Annie May heard the yelling over the dance track still playing in her studio. She always left the music on after the classes ended, while she did whatever paperwork and cleaning needed doing. Years ago she hired one of the older girls to clean the tiny studio, but times were tougher than they used to be. A businesswoman would have closed the studio a couple years ago, but Annie wasn't a businesswoman. She was a dancer. Had been quite the dancer back in her day. Nearly two decades traveling between theatres, working with the best dancers and producers in the industry, waking up in new cities, enough lovers and parties for several lifetimes. But ageing was a motherfucker. Year after year, a little less agile, a little less pretty, and before she knew it, she couldn't compete with the next generation on any level. They weren't going to keep her in the A league as an instructor. Annie was a competent dance instructor, but she wasn't world class. And she knew it. So she had come back home. A couple of years of self-pity had passed before she realised she was still more than good enough to instruct at a local level. And the job had been more rewarding than she could have imagined. She hadn't exactly found the next Maddie Ziegler in this neighbourhood, but she enjoyed seeing the girls improve and enjoy themselves while they did it. Never having found the right, or wrong partner to start her only family with, and being far too old now anyway, Annie loved her students as if they were her own.

She recognised the voice the second she heard its vociferous cry. That was Sonia. Not a particularly promising student, but a pleasure to teach all the same. And she was in trouble. Annie dropped the broom and rushed to the door.

* * *

Jason heard the scream over the sound of the traffic on the main road. Half-way through crossing a side street, and still with only a vague idea of where he was heading after walking for over half an hour, he stopped mid-road and oriented in the direction he thought the cry had come from. '–hands off my daughter!' The distinct yet distant voice broke through the sound of a car horn blaring in the opposite direction. Jason turned to the line of cars waiting for the light ahead. A man in the car idling a couple meters from him was tapping his hand on his steering wheel to the tune of his radio. Nobody else had heard the cry. 'Mum! Help me!' a second, younger voice cried out. Jason turned and ran down the alleyway in the direction of the scream. The sound was coming from somewhere on his left. After about twenty metres the high brick wall on the side came to an end for an entrance to a car park behind all the shops on the main street. Turning into it, Jason was just in time to watch Howard thrust his knife into Vanessa Marshall's neck.

'MUM!' Sonia half-screamed half-sobbed.

Having solved his first problem, Howard pulled his knife out and the woman slumped to the asphalt. The young girl's frenetic movements were beginning to take a toll on both his strength and patience. Plus he wasn't going to forgive her for slapping him like he was some kind of dog. Ramming his free fist into her stomach, Howard solved his second problem and put her in her place at the same time. All he had to do now was pick the girl up and put –

'Put her down!'

Howard turned towards the dance studio entrance. The sight of a woman in her fifties decked out in a tracksuit and giving him a death stare might have been comical under any other circumstances. Howard thought the number of wrinkles in her face contrasted oddly with how young her bright curly blonde hair looked. *All the hair dye in the world ain't gonna mask how old you are lady.* Another teasing slut, just like all the others. The kind of whore that looked downright fuckable from behind, until his van crawled past and he got a look at her from the front. She started to walk towards him with her arm outstretched and pointing. *Is this bitch for real?* Not feeling particularly intimidated despite the old woman's apparent fearlessness, Howard continued to drag Sonia's now limp body, by the hair, to the back of his van. If the old woman came close he would just dispose of her like he had the mother and then -

'Hey!' Jason instantly regretted yelling out. He had lost the element of surprise. Seeing the young girl being struck, all the memories of his childhood came rushing back to him. His father. The beatings. The cutting. The burning. The scars. The hate. Curling his hands into fists, Jason yelled out and began sprinting to the girl. He was a good fifty metres away at the entrance of the car park. Fuelled by a lifetime of hate, Jason ran on autopilot, completely forgetting he had a handgun. He was going to make this abusive girl's father die using just his bare hands.

'Are you shitting me?' Howard yelled as he witnessed the new, considerably more threatening opponent emerge. Having just reached the rear of his van, he opened the hatch. Placing one hand around the band of the girl's pants and still holding her hair with the other, he threw her unceremoniously into the back. He had time to see her body thud against the hard metal floor and her curl into the foetal position, still incapacitated from his punch, before he slammed the hatch shut. Coming around the side of his van, he stopped dead in his tracks at the sight of the old woman.

Having leg muscles easily several times as strong as the average woman her age, and completely aware of it, Annie wasted no time in planting her foot in-between Howard's legs. She only had a second to enjoy the sound of him cry out as he dropped the knife and started to sink to his knees. Having expected the attack to the groin to be more devastating, Annie hadn't been prepared for his vicious counter-attack. Still on his feet in a crouched position, Howard lurched forward, grabbed her by the shoulders, pivoted, and threw her with every ounce of force he could muster. Trying to catch her step, Annie succeeded only in keeping herself upright long enough for her to be thrown across the empty car spot next to the van and face first into her own car, leaving a soccer ball shaped dent in the ancient panelling. Badly concussed and lying prone on the ground, Annie could only watch the rest of the events unfold out of her eye that wasn't swollen shut.

Having taken care of yet another unexpected problem on this fuck-up of a night, Howard stumbled forward towards the driver's side door. The woman had hurt him worse than he had been hurt in years, but he was still on his feet. *Take more 'n that to take me down!* Howard spat on the ground, feeling like he was going to cough out several organs in the process. He heard the footsteps of his other opponent closing in. Howard knew he was only going to get one shot at this. He might have had the strength left to dispose of an old woman, but he was in no position to take on a younger man. He opened the driver's side door and reached inside. He was going to have to time this perfectly.

Seeing the older woman's head hit the car door fuelled Jason's rage even further. Running faster than he would have thought possible, he closed the final ground between him and the van. Swinging around the back corner of it at full speed, he never saw it coming. Everything went grey for a second as he hit the ground.

Howard smiled. *Bullseye.* He was impressed

with himself for throwing the tyre iron before his target had even come into view. Howard looked at the man then again at the old woman. Neither looked like they'd be making any more trouble for him tonight.

Not wanting any more surprises than he had already gotten, Howard hobbled into the driver's seat, his movements slow and painful thanks to the throbbing ache between his legs and a sinking feeling that gave him the impression his stomach was going to fall out his navel any second now. He heard the moans from the back of his van.

'Shut the fuck up!' he said, turning his head in Sonia's direction. The sobbing only increased.

Howard turned over the ignition and started to pull the van out of the car park. This had gone far from the simple operation he had planned, but he had what he had come for and that was all that mattered.

Red light filled Jason's vision. It took a few moments for him to realise what he was looking at. *Tail light.* The van moved forward. *The girl!* Jason tried to sit up, the effort felt like he was trying to climb a mountain made of feathers. His head was spinning. His vision was blurred. He still didn't know exactly what had happened to him, but he knew he was injured. There was a warm, sticky feeling as the blood ran down his cheek. He touched his forehead. Whatever had hit him had connected just above his ballistic glasses and ripped a hole in his hat.

Jason tried to focus on the van. It was getting away. Having reached the sitting position, he tried to upgrade his status to standing. Realising he wasn't going to accomplish the feat in time, he fumbled for his pistol. He was still trying to coax it out of its holster when he realised he couldn't use it. His aim was compromised, he might hit the girl. He looked around him. A knife and a tyre iron lay on the ground. Jason guessed the tyre iron was what had hit him. Finding it just out of reach of his fingers, Jason started to lean towards it when he realised he wouldn't be able to accomplish much with the item. Throwing it would do no more than dent the van's metal surfa–

A moment of crystal clarity shattered through the opaque glass of his confusion. Reaching into his top jacket pocket he removed his tracking device. His magnetic tracking device. The van was about ten metres away now and heading towards the exit. He was going to have to time this perfectly. Aiming for where he thought the van would be when the bug reached the end of its trajectory, Jason pulled his arm back and lobbed it high. A straight throw would have been easier, but would almost certainly have bounced off, regardless of the magnet. Jason squinted as he tried to follow the small metal object as it reached its apex. The aim looked good. The van's speed didn't change. It was going to at least hit it. Jason watched the bug briefly connect with the top of the van. His heart sank when he saw it bounce on the roof. He saw it hit the roof a second time before he lost sight of it. No longer needing to maintain the effort to sit up, Jason slumped back down. His head resting awkwardly on the ground, he pulled his burner phone out of his inner jacket pocket and tried to focus on it. Loading up his tracker app, he held his breath as the program searched for a satellite connection. The red dot appeared. It was moving. Fast. Jason breathed a sigh of relief. He'd be able to find the girl and her abusive deranged sadistic psychopathic criminal of a father, but he needed to move now. Digging deep he tried to stand again, pausing as he got one foot flat on the ground while he focused his will on the other.

'You … you okay?'

Startled, Jason turned around. He'd forgotten about the woman behind him. She was sitting up now, propped against a car. She looked badly beaten, but he assessed her and decided she didn't need immediate attention. The girl on the other hand, did.

'I've taken worse,' he replied, before he started to hobble off.

'Wait …' the voice behind him started.

'Can't wait, she needs me.'

'What? Who are you?'

Confused, Annie watched the young man head down the car park. Her own concussion clearing, she started to stand. She took one last look at the other would-be good Samaritan before she went to help Vanessa.

Reaching her body, Annie didn't need to take her pulse to know she was dead. She'd seen that glassy look in her own brother's eyes after his heart attack. Starting to cry for the loss of a woman she hadn't exactly been friends with, but had known was a good mother, Annie noticed the bulge in the woman's pocket. Annie's phone was back inside on the counter. She grabbed Vanessa's instead. Her finger trembled as she dialled 000.

* * *

Jason left the car park and turned into a side street, the opposite direction to where he had come in. He put half a block between himself and the crime scene before he realised he couldn't go anywhere like this without drawing attention to himself. Blood was running into his right eye and he still didn't know how bad the wound was. Taking refuge behind a dumpster, he took off his hat and felt the damage. The gash felt warm, and about an inch wide. He took the mini med-kit out of his pants side pocket. He'd been carrying it for over six years and never needed anything other than a Band-Aid and gloves out of it before tonight.

Finding the pre-cut steri strips, Jason closed the wound with half a dozen of them. If he had a mirror it probably would've only taken three, but by touch with his fingers covered in blood it was guess work. He took the sole bandage out of the kit and wrapped it around his head before placing his hat back on.

Figuring the wound to be well enough patched to get home without too much trouble, he took the alcohol wipes out of the kit and cleaned all the blood off his face, neck and hands. Once he was confident he could walk the streets without getting any more stares than usual, Jason considered his bigger problem. The tracking bug was still moving fast from his location. That woman he had left behind would no doubt call the police, not that that would accomplish anything. Based on how long he'd seen them take to respond to calls in the past the girl might be half beaten to death before they'd even started taking statements. And if he gave them the tracking bug information they'd just go arrest this monster, and he couldn't have the son of a bitch getting off that easy. Plus he knew he was still wanted by the police himself. Getting them involved wasn't even worth considering. He knew what he had to do. Rage and instinct told him to follow on foot; logic reminded him that plan had already backfired once, and that he needed the vehicle and the rest of his armour. He continued down the alleyway. Dulwich Hill train station was not too far from here, not a direct route to Newtown, but he could get off at Erskineville and that was close enough. It wasn't a perfect solution, the train station had security cameras and was bound to have a handful of witnesses, but it was the best option available. Walking would take too long, especially in his condition, and a taxi driver would almost certainly remember such an odd and injured passenger.

His head felt like it had gone fifteen rounds with Joe Frazier. Clutching at it with one hand and walking down the main road as fast as he could manage, Jason fumbled for his med-kit again and fingered for the two paracetamol tablets he kept in there. Placing them in his mouth, he waited a few seconds to try and produce enough saliva to swallow them. It felt like he was gulping down poison flavoured chalk. It was the second time he'd resorted to painkillers in a month, a fact he was not happy about. He felt like it was starting to become a habit, and Jason didn't need an addiction. He'd seen what happened to people who had those.

Checking his tracker app for the third time in the last fifteen minutes, Jason saw the marker still moving as he entered the desolate train station. The

7:55 PM train towards the city was just pulling up when he got there. *Finally some good luck.* It was a twenty-minute ride to Erskineville, and then a ten-minute walk from the station to his apartment. Jason guessed he could be suited up and ready to deploy in well under an hour.

The automated doors whirred open. Jason stepped in and went straight to a seat, taking as little notice of the other two people in the carriage as they did of him. Sitting down seemed to only give the pain a chance to catch up with him. If the drugs were alleviating it he couldn't tell, but he wouldn't have taken any more even if he had them. He felt weak for taking any already. He didn't want his judgement or reflexes to be impaired, and anyway, pain could be a useful weapon, a lesson he'd been taught a long time ago.

Chapter 26

Ames stood at the head of the briefing room and watched the final member of his team, the only detective even younger than White, come through the door. Ames ostentatiously looked at his watch then at the team member. On such short notice, Adams had made good time, but he was still last in. Adams apologized; Ames turned to address the small crowd without acknowledging him further.

'Right. Now that we're all here I'll get straight to the point. As you were told over the phone, we're fairly certain we've found 'Corporal Punishment'.' Ames made inverted commas with his fingers as he said the tabloid name.

'Jason Ennis. Twenty-five-years-old. No record, but he was the victim of domestic violence as a child. We'll go over that later. Volunteers at a local soup kitchen in Redfern opposite where the first victim, Campbell, was killed. We got a tip-off from his manager there. The description she gave matches the one we already have from the Jordan shooting. She says he always wore the same military styled clothes until we put out the description of him in the newspaper, but he's been dressing a little more conservatively since then. He was recently laid off from a job at a wholesale food joint, it closed up for good a few weeks later though, we're still trying to track down his former boss and co-workers. The soup kitchen manager says she doesn't really know much about him even though they've volunteered together for over three years. Apparently he fits the quiet weirdo mould. Keeps to himself etcetera.'

Ames looked out at several people nodding at him in the audience. Two of the detectives were taking notes, the rest just watched.

'We pulled his address via his licence, or his learner's permit rather,' Ames continued. One of the detectives gave a short laugh. 'We got a hold of the real estate company already.' The agent had recalled Jason immediately. Jason had been there for years and was the only person in the derelict apartment block who was never late paying rent. 'The address is valid, but we have no idea where this guy is right now. For all we know he could be hiding under his bed. We've already got a tap on his phone, but he doesn't have GPS, and a preliminary look shows he barely uses the phone anyway.'

'Whack job probably doesn't have any friends,' a detective remarked. Ames tolerated the interruption.

'Anyway that's what we've got so far. We're going to set up a twenty-four-hour watch on his apartment. Thompson and Schmidt, I want you to take the first watch, we'll arrange to get a surveillance van and you'll go straight from here. Brooks and Oaten, go home after the briefing and get some rest, you'll relieve their shift in eight hours and so on until we make a move, probably in a few days. This is the department's top priority men,' Ames said, despite a female detective being present in the room, 'we'll make a move soon enough, but until then, you're all going to be living out of the station. I'm certain this is our guy, but I want everything on him before we take him down. I want to know where this son of a bitch eats, shops, takes a fucking shit. I don't have to remind you that this guy is armed and extremely dangerous. When we go for the take down naturally we'll have a full tac team assembled. But we're not making a move until we know his routine and know we can minimise the fallout from a shoot-out as much as possible. Any questions?'

Taylor, one of the older detectives, put his hand up.

'Shoot,' said Ames.

'Before we take this guy down, mind if I post him the address of a couple scumbags on bail?'

'Yeah, I got some people in mind too,' said another.

'My ex-wife gets terrible road rage. I can give him her address, see if he'll take care of that for me?'

A sea of chuckles undulated through the room.

'Alright knock it off,' said Ames through a thin smile. 'Hell if he was only killing people like Hazelton I'd be happy to take my long service leave and hold off the search until I get back, but I think we all know this one is unstable. This guy isn't just a ticking bomb, he's a stick of gelignite being kicked down the sidewalk.'

The door to the meeting room burst open, revealing a heavy-set sergeant with a handlebar moustache. 'Been trying to call you Ames,' the sergeant said.

'I'm in the middle of something if you haven't noticed,' Ames replied.

'This is more important,' snapped the sergeant, 'we just got a witnessed kidnapping and murder. Thirteen-year-old girl. Mother stabbed to death. White van. They think it's the Joker.'

Ames didn't even register his dislike for the nickname. 'Where?' he asked.

The sergeant gave him the address of the studio in Dulwich Hill. 'Witness is still talking to the first constable on scene,' he continued. 'She got a good description of him, and a partial number plate. She stepped in and tried to stop him, got herself badly beaten in the process, so did someone else apparently, but he's nowhere to be found.'

Ames was usually quite good at processing new and dramatic information. Getting so much info on both the town's serial killers in one night, however, was like throwing the contents of an old tool box among the cogs in his brain. He looked like he was staring right through the sergeant.

'What are we doing boss?' Detective White interrupted the silence. In a way, Ames couldn't believe his luck. He had his entire team already assembled for one game. So what if he was going to make them play another.

'Right. Everybody on this now. Let's get to the crime scene. I want to talk to that witness.'

'What about Jason?' asked Taylor.

'Forget about him for now. We know where he lives. He's been on the loose for three years, another night won't hurt. The girls the other one kidnaps only stay alive for a couple days after he takes them.'

Ames looked at the sea of faces staring back at him. 'Well what the fuck are you waiting for? Move already!' The crowd quickly dispersed.

'And get our tac team assembled to respond asap!' Ames yelled out to nobody in particular. *We might be needing them a whole lot sooner than I thought.*

Chapter 27

'What happened next?' Half squatting down to make his height match Annie's, detective Ames waited for her to continue. Her face, like the rest of the car park, was bathed in alternating blue and red lights from half a dozen police cars and the two ambulances now filling the area. The paramedics from one ambulance had just finished loading Vanessa Marshall's body into a black canvas bag. Annie May was sitting on the back step of the other with a shelter blanket wrapped around her body and a bandage around her head. She took a slow draw on her cigarette. She had quit four years ago, but the offer from the detective as he lit up his own had proved far too tempting.

'It was a bit of a blur after he threw me down. I didn't know what was going on, then all of a sudden there was a young man on the ground a couple metres from me. That piece of shit hit him in the head with something.'

'The tyre iron?' Ames suggested, having already surveyed the crime scene.

'Yeah I guess so.' Annie exhaled a cloud of

smoke.

'And where did this second man come from?'

'I don't know. All of a sudden he was just down on the ground.'

'Had you seen him before?'

'No. Never saw either of them before tonight. I never forget a face.'

Ames nodded. 'Then what happened?'

'That asshole got in his van and just drove off.' She took another draw on her cigarette. A short one this time. The way her hand was shaking it didn't look like she could hold it much longer.

'I know this is difficult, but can you tell me what happened to the other man?'

'He threw something at the van as it left, a rock I think.'

'A rock?' Ames raised an eyebrow.

'Maybe, whatever it was it was small. Then he got up and left the same way the other guy did.'

'In a car?'

'No,' Annie shook her head, 'on foot. He was bleeding bad. I tried to call out to him but he just left.'

'Did he say anything?'

Annie buried her face in her free hand. 'Something about saving Sonia. I don't know. It didn't make any sense. None of this makes any sense. Oh god ... Sonia.' The remains of the cigarette fell to the ground, the tip glowed brighter as the wind rolled it away.

Ames knew it was important to question a subject as soon as possible, even though she'd already been through this with the first constable on scene. As Annie sobbed into her hands, Ames also knew he wasn't going to get any more out of her now. But that was fine. She'd done more than enough for the time being. Ames gestured to one of the uniformed female officers in the now crowded car park, then motioned at Annie.

'Thank you for all your help Ms May.' Annie didn't look up. Her nod was barely perceptible. The female officer sat next to her and placed her arm around her shoulder as Ames walked away. Detective White joined him.

'What do you make of this other injured Samaritan?'

Ames shrugged. 'They already searched the surrounding area, the literal blood trail stops at a dumpster around the corner. He probably just went to nurse his wounds. Could even be at a hospital. I'm sure we'll hear from him before too long.'

Detective Adams came rushing over, holding his phone in his hand.

'Boss we finally got a match on the partial number plate that lady gave us. She only got the first four digits, we cross referenced that with all the white vans in the city ...'

Ames stared at the young detective and made a circular motion with his hand.

'... anyway there was only one match. It's registered to an address in Villawood, about forty minutes away.'

'Out-fucking-standing,' said Ames, 'what's the word on our tactical response unit?'

'Still two hours out.'

Ames considered the situation. The history told them the girl would still be alive for a couple days, if the bastard was still playing by the same rules. Except he wasn't. The last two victims had been adults. Barely, but adults all the same. *I wonder what Dr Edwards will have to say about this,* thought Ames, *victims will fit the same profile my ass.* This girl was only a child. His own daughter's age. Ames only had to think about his own daughter being carried off in a van before he knew what he had to do.

'We've got an address. We're not waiting for those black pyjama clowns, there's more than enough muscle here. Tell the team we're moving out in two minutes.'

Adams nodded and hurried off.

'Brendan ...' Detective White began.

'Look Mick, we've got no reason to believe this one's armed with anything better than a fucking jack-knife,' said Ames. His mouth grated over the word 'jack-knife' as if saying it produced a foul taste. 'We know where he lives, and I don't want this girl's rape, or death, on my conscience just because we were sitting around with our thumbs up our asses waiting for officers with bigger guns and better armour. We're moving now.'

'Alright,' White acquiesced, 'but can't we at least get some of the locals on the scene first? Villawood's a stone's throw from Fairfield, a couple cruisers from that station would get there in a few minutes.'

'Yeah and in the process they'll probably let

this scumbag know we're on to him before he's properly surrounded.' Ames paused, thinking for a few seconds before he spoke again. 'Call ahead, get whatever they've still got on at this hour to wait a couple blocks from the house, we could use the support once we get there, but that's about all the GDs will be good for.'

White nodded and pulled out his phone.

Hands on his hips, Ames took a deep breath. He knew if this outing ended in the loss of innocent life, having refused to wait for tactical support, he could kiss his career goodbye. But the girl was more important than a job that drove him fucking insane anyway. He walked to his unmarked police car and popped the boot. Rummaging through its disparaging contents he found what he was looking for, underneath his box of fishing lures. He briefly lamented that he hadn't had the time to go fishing since he took over as lead homicide detective. He picked up the bullet-resistant vest. They didn't have any reason to believe this 'Joker' was armed with anything that didn't fit into the league that knives and tyre irons fell into. But that was no reason not to take at least some precautions. Taking off his suit jacket he strapped the heavy vest to his torso. He ignored a memory of it fitting around his waist a little easier the last time he wore it. But he didn't ignore that certain rush he felt just putting it on. It was bulky and cumbersome, but it did give you a certain feeling of invulnerability.

* * *

Jason picked up the station wagon on the way from the train station to his apartment and parked it across the road. It took him twenty minutes to redress his head wound and put on his full outer armour over his black tactical pants and old jacket. There was no point in wearing indistinct clothing under his armour. Taking a last look at himself in the mirror, Jason worried about the short trip from his apartment to the car across the road, but there was no way around it. He needed to be fully prepped and ready to go when he got to the location where the tracker bug had been idling for the last three minutes. He didn't know what he would find there. It was no good getting there, seeing a situation and needing to put his armour on in the street. The girl was more important than drawing attention to himself and further compromising his identity. If he saw any of his neighbours on the way down or people on the street, he'd tell them he was on the way to a fancy-dress party, and if they didn't buy that, then fuck it. He picked up his damaged hat and put it on, and placed the helmet and other items under his arm before heading out the door.

* * *

'Forty-five minutes, did you hear me? Everybody in position by then. No sirens. Try not to draw any attention to yourself. Sit tight. We'll all move in on my command.'

Ames bellowed his orders into the cold night in the crowded car park. Forensics were still working their magic, and one uniform car remained to guard the scene and keep the dogs from the media out when they got here. He was amazed they weren't on the scene yet. 'Any questions? No? Let's move people. Try and keep it together in one convoy. The other units are inbound. We'll meet them there.'

Ames got into his vehicle. White rode shotgun.

'You all good boss?'

Ames took a deep breath. Normally he'd snap at a comment like that. But no, he wasn't all good. He was afraid. He had grown used to the comfort of his desk and observing the grisly remains of crime. Leading a team into a killer's den was a younger man's game. *Fuck it*, thought Ames. 'Yeah, yeah I'm good,' he said to White.

White nodded. He knew when his partner was lying. If anything, White was relieved that he wasn't the only one who looked like he needed to throw up before they headed out. He'd never come close to losing his lunch over a dead body, but the process of preparing for a battle of sorts had created a sense of dread that he'd hoped four years peacetime in the army might have countered.

* * *

Howard had been laughing for a good minute before he even realised what he was doing. He had gotten away with it. Again. He'd taken down three unexpected opponents, and still got what he had come for. If it wasn't for the subsiding ache he still felt in his scrotum, he would have felt invincible.

Rounding the last corner before home faster than he needed to, he heard the girl slide across the back of his van and thud against the closed side door. Her sobbing was replaced by a brief yelp. Howard laughed again.

'You're going to have something to really cry about soon.'

No response. Not yet anyway. She'd start begging soon enough though. The last one had, to begin with anyway, before he taped her mouth. It had been particularly satisfying to hear her plead, but he couldn't have them screaming. Perhaps he'd find a way around that this time. Pulling into his driveway, Howard hit the control on his dash for the garage door. A minute later when it closed, he cautiously opened the side door to his van. He wasn't going to cop a surprise attack twice in one night. He needn't have bothered. She was sobbing in the corner. Stepping into the van, Howard seized her arms and started to drag her out. She screamed and struggled against him. Howard smiled. Good. There was plenty of fight left in her. But screams like that would attract the neighbour's attention. He dragged her to his workbench, turned her over and pinned her to the ground with his knee. When she refused to stop struggling he grabbed her hair and drove her forehead into the concrete. Not hard enough to cause any lasting damage, but hard enough to convince her to stop fucking with him while he got this part over with. She could struggle all she wanted later, but right now he needed her to shut up. He pulled her head up and duct taped her mouth. Opening the side door to his basement, Howard dragged her by the shoulders to the mattress, pulled off her jumper and cable tied her hands to the bed frame. He grabbed her legs, intending to tie those to his ropes. She kicked out at him, striking him in the shoulder. He laughed, trying several times to grab at her before deciding it wasn't worth the effort. She wasn't going anywhere. He'd finish the job later, or maybe not, maybe taking her would be more exhilarating if she was fighting him off with her legs while he did it instead of just with her eyes like the last two. He shrugged, went back to his van and took his deck of cards off the dash. Taking out the next card – he'd ordered them back when he started with Kelly – he licked the back of it and stuck it to her forehead. The three of hearts stared back at him above her swollen, pleading eyes.

'Let's play Indian poker. Guess what card you've got?' he asked with a sardonic smile. She started to cry again. A wave of exhaustion overcame him. He'd already expended more energy that he had planned, and he was planning on expending a lot more later. But right now, all he wanted to do was go upstairs, sit down and crack a beer.

Chapter 28

Eight police cars, five unmarked and three cruisers, took up position near the target van's registered address in Villawood. All far enough away from the house not to be spotted from the windows. Ames didn't want this prick to have any possible warning that his time was up. He looked at his wrist watch. The second hand seemed to hold at 8:59 and 46 seconds for just a moment longer than it should have before it recommenced its steady, unending circumference. Everyone was in position by 9 PM, just like he had ordered.

He checked in with all the other units. Everyone was good to go. 'You know the plan,' he said over the radio, 'let's move.' Ames sped his own vehicle up the driveway of the house, and the other cars pulled up, two on the front lawn, the others completely surrounding the property on the street. A ninth car remained in position in the street parallel to theirs, in case their target managed to jump his back fence and make a run for it in the confusion.

Ames opened his car door, stepped out, drew

his sidearm, cocked it and made a quick yet quiet approach to the front door. A real commander leads from the front, Ames thought, as he climbed the front steps. Ames wasn't sure if he felt like a leader, he just felt like he was doing his job. White, two other detectives and two uniformed officers were right behind him. A dozen other officers crept into positions on the front lawn, moving with the grace of a well-disciplined sports team. As per the game plan, a half dozen officers made their way through the side gate and took up positions covering the rear. There was no sign of the van, though it was almost certainly in the garage.

The plan was simple. Surround the house. Knock on the front door. There wasn't enough time to obtain a search warrant, but that shouldn't be a problem. When the perp opened the door he'd either co-operate, realising the game was up, or he'd resist, giving them probable cause to step inside and make the arrest. Ames took a deep breath. He could hear the faint sounds of a television from inside. The lights were all off, but someone seemed to be home. *Now or never.*

* * *

Sitting in his favourite chair, he took a swig from his beer as the TV broadcast a delayed football match. His peace was interrupted by a short series of knocks at the front door. *Who the fuck could that be?* He pressed the info button on his remote. His TV displayed the time, amongst other information in reply. *Whoever it is, at this hour, it better be fucking good.* He stood up, still holding his beer, and shuffled his way to the front door, flipping on his porch light a second before he opened it.

'Justin Reed?' said one of the six men crowded into the tiny space between his front steps and the door. Justin's eyes squinted at the bright light, accentuating the many wrinkles on his forehead. His first thought as the shapes came into focus was that the men looked like they were trapped in a sardine can, boxed in by the wall, the metal railing behind them, and him. Then his eyes noticed the lead man's handgun – he was holding it with both hands yet pointing it angled at the ground – and moved straight from it to the bright white letters on his jet-black body armour. POLICE. He looked at the stern expression on the man's face, and the identical expressions on the men around him. His eyes not entirely adjusted to the porch light, Justin thought he could see more people spread out over his front lawn. His jaw dropped.

'Mr Reed,' the lead man said in reply to Justin's silence, 'my name is Detective Brendan Ames. I need you to keep your hands where we can see them. We'd like to talk to you about the murder of Vanessa Marshall and the abduction of Sonia Marshall.'

Justin had had a few seconds to take in the presence of the police on his doorstep, but after hearing the words he felt even more confused than when he had opened the door.

'This is a joke right?'

'Mr Reed, do you own a white van,' began Ames, proceeding to recite the van's registration number.

'Uh yeah, I own that, or rather my business does anyway.'

'Where is that vehicle now?'

'One of my employees keeps it. Look, what's going on here?'

'Mr Reed, we believe that vehicle was used in a serious crime tonight. We need to come in and talk to you about that.' Ames took a step forward, the only one the porch would allow him to take before he was practically in Justin's face. Justin instinctively took a step back.

'Uh, ok, come in I guess.'

* * *

It took the officers under two minutes to establish that nobody else was in the house or on the property. Ames looked at the old man leaning against the kitchen counter, his beer belly swelling out from underneath his singlet top. It reminded him of a case a couple years ago where they'd found a man with his skull split open, his swollen brains eagerly trying to escape through the jagged crack. For what must have been the thousandth time, Ames thought he needed a new career.

'So where is this van Mr Reed?'

'Call me Justin. It's with one of my employees, I only have three, it's a small company. Anyway that's the oldest van, doesn't even have the company logo on it. I gave it to Howard. Howard Silverman. He's a total ass. The only reason I haven't fired him is because I was such good friends with his father.' Justin took off his glasses and wiped the sweat off his brow.

'And can you tell me where this man lives?'

'Yeah, I mean, I don't know the house number off the top of my head, it's in Riverwood, I'll have it written down here somewhere.'

'I'm going to need you to get that for me Justin, right now.'

'Right, yeah, uh, it'll be in my study.'

Justin Reed turned to leave the kitchen. Detective Ames nodded to a pair of detectives who promptly followed him. He turned to White. 'Have base run a check on that name, see what we come up with.'

Justin returned with Howard's address. Ames asked him for Howard's description as he read over it. A minute later, base called White with the address belonging to the only person named Howard Silverman in this city, according to driver's licence records. It was a match.

'Well,' said White, 'are we rolling out again?'

'Yeah, yeah I guess we are,' Ames snapped. He turned to Justin and tried to regain some composure. 'Thanks for the help, I'm going to have to ask you to accompany one of my officers back to the station so you can make a statement.' *And so we can keep an eye on you while we sort out this new lead, can't be absolutely certain you're still not involved in some way.*

'Yeah, yeah I understand. I hope you get the snivelling little prick.'

Ames addressed his team on the front lawn of the house. The neighbours next door were standing on their front balcony, no doubt wondering what the hell was happening in their quiet street.

'Right, same plan, new address. Except our tac team is only half an hour out now. We'll hold the perimeter until they arrive. They'll move in and work their magic. Any questions?' For the second time tonight, his team had none.

'Then let's move out, again,' said Ames. 'Fuck me,' he added somewhat quieter once the crowd of officers started to disperse back to their vehicles.

'Can this night get any weirder?' asked White.

'Don't fucking jinx it!' replied Ames, as he led the way back to their car.

Chapter 29

Jason pulled the station wagon up opposite the house in Riverwood his tracking bug radiated from. Taking his hand off the steering wheel to pull up the park brake, he realised it was shaking. He didn't understand why. There had been more than a few nerves when he waited for Peter, and he'd noticed his heart rate increase when he had gone into Thomas' house. It had happened the first time he'd shot someone too. But there'd been no nerves at all with the others. Never anything like this. Jason remembered being this nervous before, a very long time ago. Vague flashes of his father pinning him down and a cigarette hovering over him went through his consciousness. Jason gritted his teeth, squinted his eyes and jerked his head to the left. *Just leave, fucking, just fucking leave me alone Dad!* 'Arrghh!' he cried. He grabbed his helmet and its contents, threw open the car door, stepped out into the road and slammed it behind him. He took off his hat and hurled it to the side as he stormed across the road. Struggling to get his balaclava on, he realised the bandage was in the way. He pulled it off and let it fall on the front lawn. His wound had stopped bleeding anyway. He placed his clear ballistic glasses and helmet over his balaclava. The chin strap was firm. Secure. Jason's whole body felt secure under the armour. Safe. He was safe. *He can't, fucking, hurt me now, and he won't hurt her anymore either!* Climbing the stairs to the house, Jason pulled out his pistol. He didn't understand why, but he felt like he'd been waiting his whole life for this one moment.

* * *

Howard came down the stairs, the kitchen knife in his hand. He looked at his victim, twisting and turning in desperation as she saw him and what he was carrying. The playing card had fallen onto the mattress in the process.

'Lost your card did you? No matter, I'll put it back on you later,' he said, flashing her a cold smile. He'd decided he was going to staple it to her forehead once he was finished with her, but she wouldn't guess the hidden meaning. Howard chuckled at his wit as he got close to her. He ran the knife down Sonia's face. Only her eyes moved, widening as the rest of her tried to resist any movement that would have made the cut worse. But Howard only pressed the knife firm enough for her to feel its potential, its power, *his power,* not enough to break the skin. No. He wasn't going to cut her skin, not for a while. Not until he had drawn out all the fear he could without injuring her. It was important to not rush things. He was going to ration as much misery out of this one as he could. He moved the knife down until it reached her singlet top. Holding the inch of material that curved around her shoulder, he used the knife to saw through it. The bluntness of the kitchen blade struggled for a couple seconds against the inside stitching before it yielded. He pulled down the severed part of her top, revealing one cup of her tiny bra underneath. *Adorable.* She squirmed as he ran his index finger against the curve of the nylon material. It felt so plush. Howard felt a fire ignite inside himself, an exhilaration unmatched by the last two. And he was only getting started.

He needed more foreplay. Some begging would set the mood. He grabbed the side of the duct tape and leaned in till his face was only an inch from hers. 'If you scream, I'll kill you. Do you understand?' She nodded repeatedly. He peeled off the tape.

'Please … don't,' she sobbed. Tears rolled off both sides of her face. There were tiny damp spots on the mattress below both her ears. 'What do you want from me?' she pleaded.

'Everything,' Howard replied, 'I want it all.'

Sonia cried harder at first, then coughed as the mucus from her nose ran back into her mouth. She closed her red raw eyes.

'I want my mum!'

Howard laughed like he was possessed. 'You don't have a mother anymore.' The sound of his laughter drowned out her crying.

Crack–thud–smash.

Howard jerked his head, looking up the basement stairs. His heart raced. He could only guess what the first two of the sounds were, but the last one was un-mistakenly the sound of shattering glass. Howard could picture the vase on the cabinet next to his front door in pieces all over the wooden floorboards. Someone had just broken into his house. His home. He tightened his grip around the kitchen blade.

Crack–thud.

Still upstairs. To the right now. Someone was moving through the house. *The police?* No, Howard reassured himself. If the police were onto him there'd be more of them. Howard could only hear the sounds of one person upstairs. *A burglar?* That seemed more likely. It was late at night, the upstairs lights were all off and his van was concealed in the adjacent garage. There were no signs anyone was home. But Howard was here. And he was ready. A rush of excitement consumed his fear. This was the night that just kept on giving. He'd taken down three people already, and now he'd have the satisfaction of a fourth, who'd done him the favour of coming directly to him. Convenient.

Crack–thud.

Howard heard Sonia draw breath to scream, and quickly closed his hand over her mouth. He held the knife above her eye; the implied message was clear. He took off his hand and she didn't move a muscle as he put the duct tape back on her.

Crack–thud.

Howard looked at his kitchen knife. It was only a matter of time before the intruder came down, and he had a better weapon in the garage next door. A much better weapon. Something that had been his father's. And he was going to let the intruder feel the power of it. Both barrels. Leaving Sonia on the mattress, Howard went into the garage, found what he was looking for in one of the lockers against the wall, and waited.

Crack–thud.

Jason kicked open the fourth door and the inside handle smashed against the wall. The laundry. Furious to find nobody there, Jason stormed to the next room. Pistol raised and aimed in front of him. Hand over hand, thumb over thumb. He entered through the open walkway into the kitchen. Empty. Hallway: clear. Bedrooms: clear. Bathroom: clear. Laundry: clear. Kitchen: clear. There were only two doors left. One went to the backyard; he'd check that last. Maybe that sick, child torturing son of a bitch was in the tool-shed he could see out there, but it was more likely he was in the garage. He could only assume that was where the last door led. He planted his left foot on the ground and lifted his right. He'd lost the element of surprise when he kicked the front door in, but he hadn't needed it to begin with. On the paperwork that had come with his bullet-resistant vest, the manufacturer had included the following advice: *Please note: amour should never be a substitute for caution.* Jason thought that was good advice. In theory at least. Fuelled with a lifetime of rage, the confidence that came with killing eight people, holding a gun, and literally decked from head to toe in the best armour money could buy, Jason felt no need for finesse. Abusive fathers could run, but they couldn't hide.

Crack–thud.

Jason looked down the staircase in front of him. The light from the sixty-watt globe downstairs barely permeated up to his position. With his pistol angled down the forty-five-degree slope, he began his descent. Six steps down the bed frame came into sight. Seven steps down he could see her leg. Recognising the white striped pattern that ran up the side of her dance pants, Jason took the remaining six steps in two bounds. Slightly losing his footing at the bottom as he turned under his momentum, his shoulder hit the brick wall. He barely felt a thing through the armour. The basement came into his view. The bed. The girl. Her mouth taped. Her wrists spread out and tied. Her shirt cut. Her face streaked with tears. Her eyes begging him for help. All alone. Afraid. Helpless. Jason supposed she was wondering what she had done wrong. What she possibly could have done to upset her father so much. Jason knew exactly how she felt. He only hoped he'd gotten here in time to save her before the scars started.

Overwhelmed with emotion, Jason took two steps forward. 'It's okay,' he began, 'I know what he's going to do and I'm here to stop h–'

'Hey asshole!'

Jason turned though not fast enough. His focus had been on the girl; he hadn't even seen the doorway at the opposite end of the room.

Stepping through the doorway, Howard lined up the bead at the end of his shotgun with, *with what? The police?* No. SWAT agents didn't go out alone. *Some kind of jacked-up super burglar?* Whatever. This masked jackass had picked the wrong house. He pulled the trigger twice in quick succession. Ka-boom ka-boom. Sonia screamed into the tape against her mouth as two lots of fifty pellets rode the express train from Howard's double-barrel twelve-gauge to Jason's body. The first found a tight grouping dead centre in Jason's heavily armoured chest. The force knocked him back a step, before the second grouping took him in the head. He fell backwards. A sharp crack echoed through the basement as his helmet slammed into the cold, damp concrete.

Howard grinned. He'd aimed for the bastard's chest. The recoil from the first shot had unintentionally elevated the barrels so that the second had hit him in the head. Perfect. This night just got better and better.

Howard let his shotgun, both its barrels spent, hang loose in his right hand. With his left he pulled out the kitchen knife from where he had tucked it in his belt. If he was really lucky, the intruder would still be alive, and they'd be able to have some real fun. The girl could watch. She'd have a front row ticket to what would happen to her once he'd used her up. Howard felt there was something beautiful in that, poetic even. He walked towards Jason's body.

My eyes. What's wrong with my eyes? Head angled towards the ceiling, all Jason could see was a spider web of blurry white and grey cracks. It took him a moment to realise his ballistic glasses were shattered. They'd done their job stopping a half dozen shotgun pellets. Another half dozen had hit him below them. He felt like a power drill had bored several holes into him, and he was mildly concussed from where his skull had hit the inside of his helmet. He struggled to get his left hand up to remove his glasses. Through the ringing sound in his ears, he perceived a noise in front of him. Or rather, the abrupt lack of noise as someone stopped dead in their tracks. His vision returned as he threw off his ballistic glasses, his second ruined pair this month. He saw the man in front of him staring down at his hand, no, his pistol. There was a look of fear in his face. It was clear he had expected Jason to be more injured, and less armed. Howard dropped the spent shotgun just as Jason started aiming his hand. He lunged at Jason, the knife aimed at his neck. Jason knew he couldn't move his body out of the way in time. He brought his left arm up in a defensive move as he pointed his pistol at the moving target. He fired, a fraction too high in his haste and disorientation. The bullet buried itself in the ceiling as Howard's knife came plunging down. His arm in front of his face, Jason saw the knife come through his forearm and stop a couple inches in front of his eye a moment before he felt it. Screaming more in frustration than in pain, Jason angled his pistol towards Howard's ribs as Howard lent his body onto the embedded blade. It had crept through another inch when Jason pulled the trigger. His view mostly obscured by his forearm, Jason didn't see the bullet hit home, but he felt the pressure drop off the knife in his arm immediately. A second later, Howard rolled off to Jason's side, clutching at his mid-section. Knife still embedded, Jason gripped Howard's neck with his left hand. The muscle contraction needed to clench his fist tore against the knife blade, but the extra pain only gave Jason the final push that he didn't need. Kneeling up over Howard's body, he turned the pistol around and raised it high.

'No, no wait. Wait!' Howard begged, one hand leaving the gushing wound in his ribs, now outstretched to shield his face.

Jason brought the butt of the pistol down into his skull. Again. And again. And again. Before he knew it, he was mashing fragments of skull and grey gloop into the concrete. Only the distraught noises of the girl made him stop.

Jason turned towards her. He dropped the gun

and it bounced under the bed.

'It's ok,' Jason said. The words hurt as the torn muscles in his face moved, 'he can't hurt us anymore.'

Sonia nodded. She'd seen police officers who looked just like him on TV. 'Help … me … please.'

Now that the fight was over, everything suddenly felt heavy. He unclipped his helmet. There was a large, shallow and uneven dent in the top left-hand side where the majority of the pellets had hit, and a series of small pock marks radiating out from that. As he peeled off his balaclava, he felt the sharp sting where two pellets had snuck inside the front of his helmet and hit his ear, momentarily distracting him from the agony in his left cheek bone.

He surveyed his forearm. He knew the theory. Kevlar was good at stopping small arms fire and slash attacks. Pound for pound, however, it wasn't much better at stopping stabbing attacks than denim. And here was the proof. Gripping the handle with his other hand, Jason pulled. The knife hurt more on the way out than it did on the way in, but he gritted his teeth and bore the pain. He pulled the Velcro tabs on his forearm armour off and let it fall to the ground. The absence of the weight brought instantaneous relief. A slow but steady flow of blood followed. Observing the wound, it appeared the knife had gone clean through the middle of the two bones in his forearm. Lucky. If being stabbed could ever be considered lucky.

Still holding the knife in his hand, he approached the girl's wrist. She didn't flinch. He cut through the first cable tie and she curled her liberated arm into her chest. He cut her other bond and dropped the knife. She tried to sit up.

'I, I can't, I don't know … what's happening?'

'Adrenaline,' he said gently, 'it will pass.'

She nodded, looking at him with a mixture of emotions. Appreciation. Curiosity. Something else she couldn't quite place. Jason returned her gaze. Despite the pain in his face, he managed to smile. 'I'm Jason.'

'Sonia,' she replied, out of force of habit. The rest of her life was ahead of her, but she'd never experience an odder circumstance under which to introduce herself.

'Here, I've got you now.' He reached out one hand around her back and the other around her knees. The hole in his arm screamed against the weight of her small body, but he ignored it. Sonia wrapped her arms around him and buried her face into his shoulder armour.

Climbing the basement stairs, Jason didn't know exactly where he was going to take the girl. Away from here. That was good enough for now. A faint voice in the back of his head told him he had left his pistol behind, but he didn't care. For the first time since he had found it, he felt like he didn't need it anymore. He left it in the basement, along with something else he'd been carrying around for a whole lot longer. Just like when he had killed Peter, he felt like a mission was over, only this time, there was no aching feeling that there was something unresolved. It was done. He was done. He didn't want to go out and find anybody else to punish. He just wanted to go home and sit down. And to take care of the girl. Jason smiled warmly at the young girl in his arms. He'd always wanted a sister. Someone he could love, look after and protect.

Chapter 30

Ames and his team pulled up several minutes too late to hear the gunshots themselves. The street was deserted when they brought their cars to a halt outside what Ames hoped was the right fucking house. From his position Ames saw that the lights were on, and the front door was ajar. *Weird.* And was that a blood-stained bandage on the front lawn? Combined with their intel it was more than enough to give them probable cause to storm the home. But Ames knew that if things had gone pear shaped at the last address he would have had a hard time justifying to the coroner's court why he had moved in without a tactical response unit that was only two hours out. He'd be crucified for moving in without one five minutes away. Besides, those guys were so heavily armoured they were practically invincible. Let them do the hard work.

Radioing in with the tac team on the way, they had confirmed they were inbound and five minutes out. Ames had hoped they would have gotten there before him, but he wouldn't have to hold the fort for long. His pistol drawn and held by his side, Ames let out a long breath. The white steam poured from his mouth and melted into the black night as he stood there at the edge of the front lawn. The deafening quiet was interrupted by sounds coming from just inside the house. Sixteen police officers held their breath and concentrated their attention on what sounded like footsteps on glass. Ames attention piqued as the front door swung inwards.

'Movement,' said one of the officers in a low voice. *No shit*, thought Ames as they crept forward and fanned out along the lawn. A dark figure emerged from the doorway. The light coming from behind the door accentuated the figure's black silhouette. The distinct shape of a person in the man's arms, however, was impossible to miss. As if they shared a collective mind, the officers moved forward as one and the man found himself basked in the blinding light of a dozen torches. He stopped.

'Freeze!' bellowed Ames at the already stationary target. His attention, however, was focused on the girl. She was shielding her face from the beams of light with her hand. Ames didn't need to see her face to know it was Sonia, and that she was okay. Raising his eyes he looked at the man carrying her. The first thing that struck him was that it was clearly not Silverman. Despite the wounds that had streaked it with coats of blood the face indicated the guy was in his early twenties. The man was wearing combat boots and tactical clothes covered by full body armour. If he had of been wearing a helmet, he could have been …

White was apparently having the same thought. Looking at the man ten metres away, he cocked his head to the side in Ames' direction. 'Is that … is that one of ours?'

Ames narrowed his eyes. Tactical response weren't supposed to be here yet. He shook his head from side to side with an even slowness that made the movement look mechanical. 'I, I don't know what that is.'

A trickle of blood rolled from the man's forearm, and Ames took notice of the thin wound on it. Judging from the blood flow, it was a deep one. The man's face, which looked like it was half concealed in red war paint, had seen better days as well. A wound on the left side of his forehead looked coagulated, unlike the holes oozing blood further down, the thin blood trails looked like his face was rusting from a half dozen water leaks. His face. Ames squinted. He thought about the good Samaritan that had been struck in the head trying save the girl. The one that had disappeared. A thought came to him that seemed so bizarre, he hesitated for several seconds before he said it out loud.

'Jay … son?'

The figure's face prickled with recognition and confusion. *That is his name, and he doesn't understand how I know it.* Ames' jaw dropped open. *Dear. Sweet. Merciful. Fucking. Christ.*

'Brendan, is that …' White's voice trailed off.

Ames moved his head up and down.

'How?'

'I don't know Mick, I don't fucking know.'

'What are we doing boss?' asked one of the other officers.

Ames shook off the feeling that he was in Wonderland. This was the real world, and apparently outlandish shit happened here as well. But he'd have the time to figure out what the fuck had happened later.

'Jason Ennis, put the girl down and lie face

down on the ground,' ordered Ames.

Responding to Ames' cold, demanding voice, Sonia wrapped her arms around Jason tighter.

'No,' Jason said flatly.

Ames blinked. He'd been preparing himself for a fight, or for the man to drop the girl and run. Or for a piano to fall out of the sky, Ames didn't think anything would surprise him for the rest of his life. But passive refusal? He didn't know what to say to that. He resisted his first impulse, which was to say 'please'.

Jason broke the silence. 'She's afraid, she doesn't want me to put her down.'

Ames was taken back. The man's concern was genuine. But that didn't change the situation. It didn't work like that. 'Son, you're going to have to put her down.'

'No, I don't,' Jason replied.

Ames didn't know what to do. He looked at Jason, who was facing the girl who was now looking back at him. In spite of the armour, in spite of the blood all over his face, the way he smiled at her. There was no malice there. No anger. No lust. He smiled at her the way a toddler smiles at his parents.

Or siblings. Ames suddenly found it very hard to picture Jason Ennis being angry at all, let alone murdering six people. And the girl, she wasn't afraid. Not of Jason anyway. He looked very protective. Ames felt confident he wasn't going to do anything to put the girl in danger. Did they know each other? It wouldn't have made the night any stranger.

'Where's Silverman?' Ames asked, fishing for some kind of rapport, and besides, they still needed to deal with that prick.

Jason didn't know what the man's name had been, but the officer could only be asking about one person. 'In the basement. Dead,' he replied.

'Anyone else in there?'

'No.'

Something made Ames take Jason's word for it as if it had come from one of his own officers. Realising he wasn't going anywhere, and not wanting to waste the energy standing since he was aware he was losing a reasonable amount of blood, Jason sat down with Sonia in his arms. A dozen pistols followed his movement. Ames motioned his hands up and down at the team. 'Take it easy,' he said to them.

'Boss, what are we doing here?' asked one of the other officers.

'Thompson and Schmidt, stay here with me and White. The rest of you, search the house, and maintain the perimeter,' said Ames.

Aware that his partner and two other detectives were still covering him, Ames holstered his own weapon, walked up and squatted down a metre away from the odd pair.

'You can't stay there all-night son. You want to help her?'

Jason nodded.

'She needs medical treatment,' Ames looked at Jason's face, 'and so do you.'

Jason nodded again. The argument was logical. 'You should call us an ambulance,' he said.

Ames made eye contact with White, who along with Thompson and Schmidt, had formed a semicircle around him, Jason and Sonia. White nodded, took one hand off his pistol and reached for his radio.

'You'll let her go when the paramedics arrive?' asked Ames.

Jason nodded. The medics had training that he did not. She'd be safe with them.

'Ok son. Just don't make any sudden movements.'

Jason nodded again. Ames stood up and stepped back.

'We're just gonna leave him there?' whispered White once he was closer.

'For now. She's calm, he's calm, he looks unarmed, the last thing we need is this situation unnecessarily escalated.' Lowering his voice he added, 'and did you see the look in his eyes? Like a tiger looking after one of its cubs.' *Content now, but with primal evolutionary rage lurking just below the surface.* A silence fell over the scene on the front lawn. Two of the officers who had entered the house returned a couple minutes later. Walking towards Ames, they eyed Jason curiously, probably trying to imagine why he wasn't bound in chains.

'What have we got inside?' asked Ames.

'Fucking bloodbath in the basement. Empty shotgun, loaded pistol. Bullet proof helmet that looks like it took a round. Guy missing most of his face. Can't exactly ID him but he was carrying Silverman's wallet.'

Ames nodded.

'What the hell happened here boss?' asked the officer.

'Can't fucking wait to find out,' replied Ames.

A minute later the ambulance arrived. The tactical response unit pulled up at the same time from the opposite end of the street.

Chapter 31

Jason calmly relented and let the paramedics take Sonia from him, as Ames had somehow known he would. She had held her rescuer's hand as long as she could as they carried her from him to the stretcher. Jason had refused treatment until the medics had assured him the girl was okay. Under heavy police escort, he was taken to the nearest hospital and went straight in for surgery. The tyre iron had caused a hairline skull fracture and jagged tissue damage, the knife had punched straight through the meat. The shotgun pellets had torn through some muscle and bone, but they wouldn't cause any permanent damage. When he woke the following day, handcuffed to the hospital bed and with a police officer seated directed opposite him, the doctor had told him he would make a full recovery. Other than the scars.

The small scars from the shotgun pellets didn't look much different from the ones his father had given him with the cigarettes, but it wasn't about what they looked like. It was about what they reminded him of. The ones on his chest reminded him of his father. But the ones on his face and forearm reminded him of her. How he had taken them for her. How she was still unmarked.

Two weeks later, when he was mostly healed and capable of being interviewed, they took him from the hospital to be processed at the police station. Ames had managed to put most of the pieces together by then. The tracking bug found on Howard's van, the smart phone found in Neville's car. How Jason had managed to find Howard in the car park was another story though. They'd done a full search of Jason's apartment. It hadn't taken long. Breaking into Jason's trunk, Ames had found his university degree, his appreciation certificates for years of volunteering, his sketches. They were good enough to be in a gallery, thought Ames. Having read Jason's child services file, Ames wondered what Jason might have accomplished if his childhood hadn't been so traumatic. Sure, it was no excuse to declare yourself the town's executioner. Plenty of abused children were able to lead productive lives. But plenty more ended up addicted to drugs. Abusing children themselves. Suiciding. Looking at them as children, you could never tell who would recover. Who would make something for themselves. Who were too far gone. Who would turn into a confused killer with a deluded sense of achieving justice for others when he hadn't gotten any for himself.

Ames had picked up the bundle of cash at the bottom of the trunk. Thumbing through the end of it, he guessed it must have been ten grand.

'Proceeds of crime?' asked White. The police had the authority to confiscate such money.

'Eh I don't see how being a crazed vigilante earns you this kind of cash. Maybe he just doesn't like banks. Let him keep it. He's probably going to need it for his legal defence.'

Jason didn't need a cent for his legal defence.

'Who are you?' he asked the well-dressed young man on the other side of the plexiglass in the box room the police officer had just brought him to from his holding cell. The pain in the barely healed facial muscles gave him a dull reminder of his injury as he spoke.

'The duty solicitor,' the man replied.

'What does that mean?'

'I'm from legal aid, and I'm on duty for anyone who is being charged today.'

Jason nodded. 'What are they charging me with?'

'Six counts of murder, and possession of an unlicensed firearm. Naturally with charges this serious we can't even think about applying for bail.'

Jason waved aside any considerations about applying for bail, that wasn't the part of that sentence that had got his attention. 'Six?'

The solicitor looked at Jason's confused expression, then looked at his paperwork.

'Six of the seven people that forensics have linked to the firearm they found at the property where you were arrested. They're willing to count the last one, one Howard Silverman, as self-defence, but they're going to talk to you about it first. They also want to talk to you about the murder of,' the solicitor looked over his paperwork again, '... Thomas Williams. They've uncovered you used to work with a friend of his. Probably just seems like too much of a coincidence given your current arrest. I don't think they have anything solid, making their interest in that disappear will be the easy part.'

'But I did kill him as well,' said Jason.

The solicitor looked up from his notes. For a man who had apparently just admitted to killing eight people, the voice seemed surprisingly calm. 'Mr Ennis, are you telling me you committed all these crimes?'

'Yes. I also stole a car and drove without a licence. Why haven't they charged me with that?'

The solicitor chuckled. 'Mate I think they're just going to focus on the big stuff.'

Jason nodded. 'Well that's good.'

The solicitor eyed his curious new client. 'The other charges are going to be very difficult to fight. We'll have to start–'

'But I don't want to fight them.'

'Huh?'

'I did it. I'm not a liar.'

The solicitor adjusted his tie. 'These crimes are very serious. We can try for a Section 23, a mental health defence, if you want. Either way if you confess I don't think you'll ever get out of prison, or a mental health asylum. Same difference really. Do you understand?'

Jason understood. The prospect of going to

prison at all, let alone for a lifetime, would have made him put his pistol in his mouth a few days ago. Today, somehow, he didn't seem to care. He felt like he'd made a certain peace with himself. He had something now that nobody, not even the law, could take from him.

* * *

'Are you ready to start the interview Jason?' asked Detective Ames.

'Yes,' said Jason with a smile. He'd never been in a police interview room before. It was very exciting.

Ames hit the record button on the oversized digital centrepiece on the table. He monotonously stated the date, time, where they were and who was in the room. Himself. Detective Michael White. And Jason.

'Jason can you start by telling me what happened on the night of February the 15th this year at the soup kitchen you volunteer at?'

'I killed him. And I killed all the others as well. And Thomas. I don't want to waste your time. I confess.'

Ames smiled. 'Well I appreciate your

consideration but we're still going to have to go through all the details anyway.'

'Oh, ok,' said Jason, returning a smile of his own.

Ames looked at his paperwork. 'Why don't we go back to the first one Jason. Do you know who Corey Campbell is?'

Jason recognised the name from the newspaper. They'd always told him he had a good memory. 'Yes, but he wasn't the first.'

Ames' calm from Jason's complete cooperation felt like it was jolted by an electric shock. He slowed his voice and leant across the table. 'How many more are there Jason?'

'Just one before that.'

Ames breathed a sigh of relief. He wouldn't have been surprised if Jason had of said thirty. Still, this interview was going to take a very long time.

Three and a half hours later they broke for lunch. They'd covered Peter Jones – Ames believed Jason's version of what the man had done and didn't really want to charge him with the murder, but he had a job to do, and anyway, it wasn't going to make much difference to the man's sentence. Nothing about Campbell, the meth dealer, had surprised him either. Hearing Jason's story about Gary Meredith assaulting a woman filled in one of the blanks he still had. He wondered why the woman had never come forward.

When he asked about Alex Bryant, and then about Dean Jordan, Jason had, for the first time, seemed a bit embarrassed about it. He stared at his feet when Ames had asked why he had killed them.

'I just don't like jerks,' Jason said.

Ames chuckled. 'Yeah well neither do I,' he said. Jason beamed in response.

By the conclusion of the interview, Ames couldn't help but like Jason. He was dangerous, unstable, he needed to be behind bars but he certainly wasn't the typical kind of person he arrested. He was well-spoken, and had a particular childish charm to him. As he left, Jason stuck out his hand. Ames shook it.

'I can certainly understand most of what you did Jason, but you know I have a job to do.'

'I don't have a problem with you,' Jason replied, 'if you ever want to know anything else, just ask.'

Ames nodded. 'Goodbye Jason.' A constable led Jason back to his holding cell.

'So … what now?' asked Detective White.

'Well that was certainly interesting. Look up this Peter Jones, it rings a bell but it wasn't my case. Anyway we'll add that to his murder tally. I'm going to call self-defence on Silverman though.' Ames leant back in his chair, holding his pen against his lips.

'His family might have a problem with that,' replied White.

'Huh?' said Ames, who had been deep in thought. 'Jason doesn't have a next of kin. I looked it up. His mother hung herself a year ago. I don't think he knows.'

'No no, I mean Silverman. His family might have a problem with taking another serial killer's word of events as fact on what happened in that basement. At the end of the day, it was still at least a home invasion.'

Ames shook his head. 'I wouldn't worry about that, Silverman doesn't appear to have a next of kin either.'

Ames put his pen down on his clipboard. He could file all the paperwork tomorrow. All of a sudden, he really wanted to go home. He'd only seen them this morning, but he felt like he needed the company of his nagging wife and brat of a teenage daughter.

Chapter 32

'Got any patches bruh?' the man whispered.

Jason stared at his new cellmate, as the sound of the guard closing the heavy iron door reverberated behind him and throughout the prison wing. Jason's sentencing wasn't going to be for months. 'The grinding wheels of justice turn slowly,' Detective Ames told him when he explained they were moving Jason from the police holding cell to the remand section of Long Bay Correctional Centre, where all un-sentenced prisoners awaited their day in court. Jason had gone through inmate processing at reception. The guard had asked him a couple dozen questions. 'Are you on methadone? Can you read?' Half way through the questions, Jason realised he wasn't going to have much in common with the other inmates. He traded his combat boots, tactical pants and jacket for the standard green prison tracksuit pants, singlet and shirt. The guard sealed Jason's clothes into a canvas bag. 'You'll get the clothes back upon release,' he recited. Jason knew he'd never see the clothes again, but he didn't mind.

The police had confiscated his armour before he went into surgery. He had felt weird without it in the hospital at first, but strange enough, he didn't feel unsafe. After a couple days, he realised he had been relieved of both a physical and psychological weight from his shoulders.

'Patches of what?' Jason said in reply to his cellmate.

It was now his cellmate's turn to stare at Jason like what he had said made no sense.

'Nicotine patches bruh, what do you think?'

'No I don't have any, I don't smoke.' Come to think of it, the guards had seemed surprised when he told them he was a non-smoker.

'Fuck bruh you shoulda told them you smoked.'

'Why?'

'So they'd give you nicotine patches.'

'Why would I want nicotine patches?'

'So you could give' em to me bruh!'

Jason was confused. 'Why don't you have any?'

'Fuck bruh smoked almost all of 'em in two days, down to me last three strips!'

'You … smoked them?'

'Cunts banned tobacco last year. Have ta smoke nicotine patches now.'

Have to? thought Jason.

'Fuck bruh talking 'bout it makes me feel like one now heh.'

Jason watched in fascination as his cellmate cut a thin strip from the remains of an already butchered nicotine patch, stuck it on a page from the bible and sprinkled a brown grainy substance that looked kind of like tobacco over it.

'What is that?' Jason asked pointing.

'Tea leaves, smoke won't stay lit without 'em.' He cut out a square of paper from the bible with a razor blade, rolled up his cigarette and went over to the wall. Two bits of aluminium foil stuck out from each slit in the power socket. The man picked up a small plastic container, squirted a mini tube of green shaving gel into it, then pushed the container up until the liquid touched the foil. He turned on the power, held some rolled up toilet paper next to the container, then adjusted the angle of the container until sparks shot out of the socket. The toilet paper caught alight, and the man lit his cigarette from it.

Jason didn't know whether to be appalled or

impressed. He considered what he had just seen, and thought back to his unfinished science degree. He could admire the simplicity of it on a scientific level. The positive charge carried through the liquid to the negative side to complete the circuit. The heat and sparks were the by-product of the current trying to jump through the air into the solution once the circuit was broken. He wasn't sure his cellmate understood the theory of what he had just done though.

The man took a long drag and a fifth of the thin cigarette turned to ash. He exhaled. The smell was horrid, but at least Jason now understood where the stench that filled the prison wing came from. He held out the cigarette to Jason. Jason looked at the man's outstretched arm. The dark brown stain between his index and middle finger, the small open sores up his arm, the outline of a naked woman tattooed on his shoulder. Judging by the quality it looked like the tattoo had been done with a sharpened stick. Considering what he had just witnessed, Jason didn't think that was too unlikely.

'Wanna hit cuz? Get that V8 into ya!'

Jason was about to ask what the significance of the term V8 was, when he realised he didn't actually want to know. 'No thank you.'

'Well fuck ya then,' the man said, putting the smoke back between his lips. Jason was confused at the man's sudden change in demeanour. He wondered if the man's remaining half dozen teeth had turn greenish-brown before or after he had started smoking V8's.

'Why don't you just use the nicotine patch?'

'Huh?' The man asked in between drags, clearly puzzled.

'If you want to get nicotine, why don't you just put the patch on and use it properly?'

The man looked pensive. It occurred to Jason he'd probably never considered that before.

'Fuck bruh where's the fun in that?' The man chuckled, holding his thumb and forefinger together like a pair of pincers, trying to get the last possible half-drag out, the embers now so close to the man's nails Jason was expecting him to flinch from the heat. He flicked away the remains then exhaled one last cloud of poison.

'So what are you in for?' Jason asked, still standing in the doorway as the man sat down on the lower of the bunk beds. The man's expression changed to one of mistrust. Jason could tell the man didn't like the question, though he couldn't understand why. Just as the silence was starting to become unbearable, the man shrugged and laid back, as if he'd decided to give Jason the benefit of whatever doubt had come over him.

'Suspicion a' manslaughter. Plus the cunts caught me with a shotgun and an ounce a Frankie when they arrested me. I'm fucked on those charges but gonna fight the manslaughter, I reckon' I got a good chance'a beatin' it.'

'Frankie?' Jason questioned, 'I'm not familiar with that term.'

'Ya not … familiar with …' The man laughed, as if there was something funny with the statement, before shaking his head. 'Fantasy bruh, Gee-aitch-bee, Jesus. So what 'bout you? What are you in for eh? Fraud?' The man started laughing again.

Jason considered the man. He was a danger to society. That was evident. Somebody had to do something about the problem, and he was happy to take that responsibility upon himself.

A quick punch to the throat and the fight was over before it began. Jason wrapped his hands around the man's neck. As he choked the life out of him, Jason felt no more or less at peace with himself than he had five minutes ago. He was finally free of the demons of his childhood – and didn't need to go looking for trouble anymore – but that didn't mean this piece of shit in front of him had any right to live. His heart hadn't raised a beat when the reality of what he'd done finally dawned on him. He didn't need any equipment or anything to protect him. He was completely unarmed, and unarmoured, and still he'd managed to dispose of this bastard with his bare hands. If Jason had believed in god, he would have dropped to his knees and thrown his hands up in praise. He was cured.

Taking his hands off the man's neck Jason stood up and looked around his new accommodation. A window with a grate overlooking another cell block. A stainless-steel toilet and washbasin. A desk and stool welded to the ground. A stack of six metal cubes in the corner. Jason walked over and looked at their contents. His cellmate had taken the top three. More clothes in one, packets of single serve margarine and jam in the next, along with the same red plastic cup, bowl and plate he had been given in the clear plastic bag at the reception area. 'Here's your prison show bag,' the guard had said, handing it to him. 'That was a joke mate,' the guard had added, noting Jason's blank expression. Jason had nodded. He had wanted the guard to understand he now knew it had been a joke.

In the third cube was a pile of books. Excited, Jason picked them up. Three westerns and a horror. Nothing he would have read on the outside, but he supposed he would have to start getting used to new things. A pleasant smile came over Jason's face as he sat down at the stool and opened the first book. He wondered what they would bring him for lunch, and if they would give him a new cellmate.

Epilogue

Five years later

The guard half opened the cell door, enough to stick his head in and make sure Jason hadn't escaped during the night. Or hung himself.

'Morning Jason,' he said.

'Good morning Mr Phillipson,' Jason replied. The guard closed the door and made his way to the next cell in the segregation wing. Jason didn't understand why they didn't just install security cameras in the ageing prison.

After being found with his dead cellmate, Jason was transferred to segregation. He wasn't allowed to have contact with any other inmates, but that was how he liked it. If the other inmates were anything like the first one he had met, Jason didn't want to spend time with them anyway.

Sitting up on his single bed, Jason yawned, then went to turn on his light. The irony had long occurred to him that here in prison he owned more possessions that he ever had in his life. Since his accommodation was stable, and permanent, he wasn't burdened by stressful thoughts of having to leave at a moment's notice one day and taking all his things with him. He had a clock radio, a kettle, a fan, a sandwich maker. For the first time in his life he owned a television. He had been hesitant to watch it at first, but after a time, he came to like the documentaries on the educational channels. And the film channels were frequently entertaining; they had actually played Judge Dredd twice since he'd arrived now. Sometimes he even watched the music video channel, but he mainly stuck to radio stations when he wanted to listen to music.

The shelves next to his desk were filled with arts and craft supplies. Jason had decorated almost his entire cell with his many sketches. He asked the guards to laminate them for him when they were finished and then fixed them to the wall with toothpaste. He also had a few paintings hanging up. Jason had never painted before coming to prison, but he had become quite fond of it. He had painted all kinds of things. Animals, landscapes, trees and sunsets. Every couple months when they did the routine searches of the cells, the guards would comment on how good all his art was. Some of his paintings were on sale in the art gallery attached to Long Bay Correctional Centre, a part of the rehabilitation program, but Jason kept all of his favourites in his cell. He didn't need the money. The guards never spent much time searching Jason's cell anymore, having learnt long ago that he never had any contraband. He would have liked a pair of scissors. Cutting the matchsticks he used to build various things from picture frames to model cars was tedious using a broken razor. But rules were rules.

Jason looked at his clear digital watch. 7:35 AM. He still had over an hour. He went to his desk and turned on his laptop. He'd been surprised to discover he was allowed to have a laptop if he was studying. He'd finished the master's degree in information studies last year, part-time over four years instead of full-time over two. Life was much less stressful when you only had part-time studies. This year he had started a new bachelor's degree: modern history. He was enjoying it, but it wasn't going to lead anywhere of course. His file would have been stamped 'never to be released' even before his cellmate's murder. But he enjoyed it and they couldn't stop him from studying. He also had a textbook to learn how to speak Latin, which he perused at his leisure. The prison was obligated to help enrol him in the courses he wanted to do – all inmates, whether they would be released on not, were entitled to rehabilitation – and thanks to the money the police had let him keep, he had ample funds to purchase his own education textbooks. He frequently purchased reading books as well, but he never kept those in his cell. Once he had read them he donated them to the prison library. If he wanted to read them again he could borrow them. In the meantime it was nice to let the other people here have access to them. Jason didn't want to be greedy, and besides, he loved the prison library.

The new degree wasn't going to lead to any employment opportunities, but the old one had. Once he had shown interest in information studies, the degree to be a librarian, the prison education officer had offered him the job of looking after the prison library. Jason loved his job. He hadn't minded the first job he had been given in prison, sweeping and mopping the corridors. The guards had let him out for an hour a day to clean, and Jason took pride in keeping the area spotless. He particularly liked how the job didn't involve interaction with other people. Other inmates would yell out to him from their cells, but Jason wasn't supposed to talk to them, and he didn't want to anyway.

His new job was much the same in that regard. They let him out every weekday an hour after they brought him his breakfast. Escorted to and then locked in the library, Jason placed all the books in the returns box back on the shelves before he cleaned the place. The education officer would leave him various other duties. Contacting and cataloguing new books. Binding together material for the inmates doing the basic literacy and computer skills courses. Jason felt like he was being helpful. He was making a difference. A small one, but a difference all the same. It was the best job he'd had by far. The only part he disliked was when he found books that were damaged. Some useless prick in the prison was fond of ripping pages out of books, generally the last few at the end of the story. Jason often thought about what he'd do if he somehow managed to catch the bastard in action. Cut out his eyes probably. *Hard to rip out pages when you can't find where the books are, isn't it you scum sucking parasite?* But for the most part, his new life was serene in comparison to his old one.

When the guards came to take him back to his cell Jason would take a book or two with him. Jason had read nearly every book in the library now, but he did enjoy re-reading his favourites. There were a lot of his old favourites, almost all the works of Robert Heinlein and John Wyndham for starters, but he'd found some new friends he never thought he would have made. John Flanagan was always good for an adventure, and Robert G. Barrett guaranteed a laugh. Your favourite books were the best company to have, regardless of where you were. They'd take him back to his cell where he would have his lunch. Jason heard other inmates complaining about the meals, but he didn't think they were bad. Some of them were better than the simple meals he used to cook for himself. Jason had always thought, since childhood, that if you were eating something there wasn't much to complain about. All food is good food. And here he got three meals a day, all delivered. Life was so much less stressful when you didn't have to worry about cooking, or running late for work, or getting to class – his educational materials, like his meals, were brought to him. He didn't even have to worry about making time for the gym. After lunch the guards came and got him for his one hour in the segregational wing's tiny gym room. The gym equipment was ancient, but it still worked just fine.

Jason wouldn't have gone as far as to say he enjoyed being in prison. He missed his late-night walks. He missed his favourite park. But he did enjoy the structure, order and convenience of prison a lot more than he had enjoyed trying to survive on the outside.

Sitting at his laptop Jason was busy working on the latest short story he was writing. He printed off copies in the library for other inmates to read, and was told they were mostly well received. He had been so engrossed in it – a story about a soldier going to war, and all the training and armour in the world not being able to save him – that he had completely lost track of the time. Thankfully the guards had come and got him to tell him he had a visit. They always came and got him. It was so convenient.

Jason smiled. He had known he was getting a visit today. It was the fourth time she had visited. She came on the last Saturday of every month. She had offered to come more often, but he didn't want to burden her. The amount of time it took travelling to the prison and then waiting for processing at visits turned their two-hour visit into an all-day event for her, and he knew she was young and should spend more of her time having fun and less visiting a prison.

She had started writing a couple years into his sentence. Jason had been overwhelmed with joy to get her first letter. He'd gotten some fan, and hate mail before, but nothing so personal. She talked about how hard life was having lost both her parents. Jason could empathise with that, even if their circumstances were so different. Jason's parents had been degenerate scum. Hers had been good people that were taken from her. One by cancer when she was eleven, the other by a madman two years later. She talked about the challenges of growing up in foster care. Jason could really empathise with that. 'The front of the neck is the weakest point in the human body, next time you catch people stealing your stuff strike there first,' he had written to her, trying to be helpful. She had declined to utilise this pearl of wisdom. She thanked him for rescuing her.

Even if the police were on their way there was no way of telling what Silverman would have done if he was cornered with her. She told him she looked forward to coming to visit him when she turned eighteen. Her foster parents refused to accompany her to prison, not thinking it appropriate for her to be visiting him, and the prison wouldn't let a minor in on their own.

But she was eighteen now. Eighteen and four months. Out of foster care, living with two other girls who were also in their first year at the University of Sydney. Psychology. If nothing else, it certainly gave them more to talk about. Jason had a good memory of his psychology studies and was happy to give her some advice about hers. She continued to come every month. As her degree progressed she'd be able to accurately describe what she already knew. Jason probably belonged where he was. He had anxiety and stress disorders, his style of thinking was clearly conflicted, there were schizoid elements and he was obviously on the autistic spectrum. But that didn't change how she felt about him. While she knew he was a danger to society, she also knew he was no danger to her.

Traversing the series of hallways and locked doors with his guard escort, Jason was finally led into the one-on-one visiting room. She stood. Smiled. Jason smiled back. He looked at her the same way a boy might look at his brand-new baby sister. He took Sonia in his arms. Held her. Closed his eyes. For the first time, Jason felt like he had a family.